To save her cozy Florida diner, Gia Morelli must choke down a heaping helping of murder . . .

New York native Gia Morelli is just getting used to life in Florida when she gets word that the town government wants to shut down her pride and joy: the charming little diner known as the All-Day Breakfast Café. A forgotten zoning regulation means that the café was opened illegally, and hardboiled council president Marcia Steers refuses to budge. Gia is considering hanging up her apron and going back to New York, but before she gives up on her dream, she discovers something shocking in the local swamp: Marcia Steers, dead in the water. There's a secret buried in the books at town hall, and someone killed to keep it hidden. To save her café and bring a killer to justice, Gia and her friends will have to figure out a killer's recipe for murder . . .

SCONE COLD KILLER

An All-Day Breakfast Café Mystery

Lena Gregory

LYRICAL PRESS
Kensington Publishing Corp.
www.kensingtonbooks.com

First Electronic Edition: January 2018
eISBN-13: 978-1-5161-0462-8
eISBN-10: 1-5161-0462-5

First Print Edition: January 2018
ISBN-13: 978-1-5161-0465-9
ISBN-10: 1-5161-0465-X

Printed in the United States of America

Elaina, thank you so much for all your support, encouragement, and help. I love you, and I'm so proud of the young woman you've become!

Acknowledgments

This book would not have been possible without the support and encouragement of my husband, Greg. We've built a wonderful life together, and I can't wait to see where our journey will lead next. I'd like to say a big thank you to my children, Elaina, Nicky, and Logan, and to my son-in-law, Steve, for their understanding and help while I spent long nights at the computer. My husband and children are truly the loves of my life.

I also have to thank my best friend, Renee, for all her support, long conversations, and reading many rough drafts. I still wouldn't know how to use Word without her help. I'd like to thank my sister, Debby, and my dad, Tony, who are probably my biggest fans and have read every word I've ever written. To my agent, Dawn Dowdle, thank you for believing in me and for being there in the middle of the night every time I have a question. Words cannot express my gratitude to Martin Biro for giving me this opportunity and for his wonderful advice and assistance in polishing this manuscript.

Chapter 1

"I'm just surprised you got out of New York without killing that son of a—"

"Savannah!" The harsh sentiment hurled with all of Savanah's sweet, easy-going, southern-girl charm caught Gia Morelli off-guard, and she stared at her best friend.

"What?" Feigning innocence, Savannah propped a long, hot pink nail beneath Gia's chin and shoved her mouth closed. "It's September in Florida, honey. You keep that open too long, you're bound to get a mouthful of lovebugs."

"What's a lov—" Gia waved her off. "Never mind. It doesn't matter."

"All that matters is that you're here now." Savannah hefted Gia's overnight bag from the back seat of the cab she'd taken from the airport while Gia paid the driver. As the cab pulled away, Savannah slung her free arm around Gia's waist. The four inch heels on her sandals only brought her to Gia's chin. "I'm just glad it's over."

If that wasn't the understatement of the year...

Gia wrapped her arm around Savannah's shoulders and squeezed. "Me too."

The two of them stood together on the sidewalk, staring up at the glossy new sign above the shop—Gia's shop—door. *All-Day Breakfast Café.* A Grand Opening banner hung limp in the humidity beneath it.

Gia's gut cramped. The hot Florida sun threatened to melt the makeup right off her face. The long skirt, light sweater, and knee-high leather boots that had left her slightly chilly in the brisk, early-morning, fall air in New York a few hours ago, were practically suffocating her now. She wiped her forehead, ignoring the flutter in her stomach and the fact that her nerves, rather than the stifling heat, were probably making her sweat.

"Enough of that. Come on. Let me show you what I've done with the place since you were here last." Savannah's growing excitement was contagious. The knot of tension loosened a little.

"I was just making sure everything was ready when the taxi pulled up." She grinned and started forward. "I thought you weren't coming in until tonight?"

Gia shrugged, not yet ready to explain her need to escape sooner. She forced a smile. "Last-minute change of plans."

"Well, I'm glad you're here to stay this time." Savannah weaved her fingers through Gia's and squeezed her hand. "But you should have called me. I'd have picked you up at the airport."

Gia glanced at her, trying to hide the pain and fear she knew her friend would see anyway. "Thanks, Savannah. I know you would have, but I needed to do it myself."

A brief flicker of pity softened Savannah's expression, but then a smile emerged. She tugged on Gia's hand, then released her and started toward the front door. "Well, you're home now. And wait until you see the finishing touches I've made to the shop. You're going to love them."

Gia took another moment to admire the historical, two-story building that housed the shop. *Her* shop. The pale yellow paint with white trim had been a great color choice. Standing proudly on one corner, it fit nicely with the other shops along Main Street in the small, artsy, tourist town of Boggy Creek. Nestled a bit south of Central Florida's Ocala National Forest, the town was known for its festivals, art and craft shows, and seasonal fairs. Her breakfast café would be the perfect addition. She hoped.

Shaking off another attack of nerves, she caught up to Savannah where she'd waited on the walkway.

"I can't believe you're finally here to stay this time," Savannah said.

"Me neither." The past year, since she'd found out about her husband's— *ex*-husband's—illicit and illegal activities, had flown by in a blur of confusion and betrayal. Savannah had been her rock, the one person who'd steadied her and helped her move toward a future. "Flying down for a day or two at a time wasn't easy."

"No, it wasn't, but you did it," Savannah reminded her, then gestured toward the café. "And just look what you've got to show for it."

Pride surged. "You're right."

"Do you like the sign?" A small wooden sign with hand-painted lettering hung in the front window framed by blue and white gingham curtains, proclaiming the café, *Closed.* "I picked it up at the fair last weekend."

"I love it." She turned to her friend. "Thank you, Savannah. For everything. I never would have been able to get the shop set up or the house or anything without your help."

Savannah shrugged it off, as she always did. "You're very welcome. But the truth is, you're a strong woman, and you would have managed, even without my help." She grinned. "I just made it a little easier. Now, come on. Enough dwelling on the past. It's time to take your first step toward the future."

"You're right." Taking a deep breath, Gia scrubbed the tears from her cheeks and headed up the walkway to the door. She had a lot to accomplish if she was going to open the next day. And she was definitely going to open the next day, no matter what.

Savannah held the door open.

Gia paused. Despite the intense heat, a chill raced through her, raising goose bumps. She glanced over her shoulder. People walked along the sidewalk, a few kids on bicycles headed toward the park at the end of Main Street, and cars crept through the crowded town. No one seemed to be paying any attention to her, and yet...

The sensation had become all too familiar since word of her husband's scam had been made public. But that was in New York. And she was no longer in New York.

"Are you sure you want to open tomorrow?" Leaning against the open door as if she had all day, Savannah waited, eyes closed, face tilted up toward the warm sun.

"I'm sure. It's time to move on." Leaving the past behind her, Gia strode through the doorway and tried to see the shop as a customer would for the first time. She'd been hoping to create the cozy feel of home. With Savannah's help, she'd nailed it.

Savannah let the door fall closed. "We could take a trip down south, maybe head to the Keys for a week or so. Lie on the beach, paddleboard, enjoy the night life..."

"As appealing as that sounds, I need to jump right in. It'll be easier for me if I'm busy."

Savannah shrugged, accepting Gia's answer, even if she couldn't understand it. She spread her arms wide and turned in a circle. "So, what do you think?"

Before Gia had left a few weeks ago, she'd ordered the tables and chairs. Now, round tables of varying sizes dotted the room, covered in navy blue cloths. Light-colored, wood chairs with homemade cushions, surrounded them. Savannah had always been amazing at anything craft related. A skill Gia didn't share, but admired immensely. "Did you make these?" "I did. I got the fabric months ago at a craft fair." She untied a cushion from one of the chairs and turned it over. "See, there's a zipper in the back of each one, so you can take them off and throw them in the wash. There are stacks of them in the storage closet in the back by your office."

"My office?"

"Yup. Come on back."

Gia followed her through the shop, her footsteps echoing off the distressed bamboo flooring.

Since she'd been there last, Savannah had added some beautiful finishing touches, including paintings of local scenery—at least, Gia assumed it was local. It seemed like it, but she hadn't had time to see much on her visits. Most, well, pretty much *all,* of her time had been spent setting up the shop. She hadn't even seen her new house yet, though Savannah had sent tons of pictures, and it looked beautiful.

Savannah pushed open a swinging door at the back of the dining room, but instead of turning left and heading into the kitchen, she let the door swing shut behind Gia and opened a door on the right.

Gia stepped into the small office space. A desk and chair took up most of the room. Not just any desk, but Savannah's desk. The same desk she'd crammed into the closet of a bedroom they'd shared when the two of them had been roommates in New York. For years she'd skirted around that desk, stubbing her toes more often than not on her way past. But Savannah would never get rid of it, said her Pa had made it, and it had sentimental value. "That's your desk."

Savannah smiled. "I'm not using it right now, anyway, so I took it out of the spare bedroom and put it in here. Just for now, mind you. You can give it back once you get on your feet and get your own."

Gia swallowed back tears and surveyed the rest of the small room. A battered file cabinet sat in one corner behind the desk, and a set of wooden bookshelves lined one wall. "Oh, my gosh, Savannah. I don't know what to say."

"I figured you'd need quiet space now and then to place orders and stuff."

"It's perfect." Gia turned in a circle as she tried to recall the layout of the back rooms. "Wasn't this part of the storage closet?"

"Yup. I had my brother, Joey, extend the closet to the back wall, so you didn't even lose that much storage space. I figured you'd want your office to be right by the door, though, so you can still hear what's going on in the kitchen and the café if you leave the door open."

"It's amazing, thank you." She threw her arms around her friend's neck. "You've done so much for me, Savannah."

"That's what friends are for." Savannah hugged her, then stepped back. "I'm just glad you're out of there now. I was worried sick every time you went back."

"I know. I'm sorry."

"Don't be silly. It wasn't your fault." She lowered her gaze, but Gia didn't miss the flash of anger in her eyes. "I'm just glad you're here and ready to start over."

Gia just nodded. There was really nothing to say. Her divorce had been a bitter disaster, played out in the media for the whole world to see. Everywhere she'd gone, she'd been hounded by reporters—when she was lucky. On the worst days, her husband's victims had been pounding on her door and blowing up her phone.

The only respite she'd had through the entire ordeal had been the weekend escapes during which she'd managed to set up her shop. Thankfully, she'd been smart enough to keep working throughout her marriage, despite Bradley's insistence that she quit. Between that nest egg and the meager divorce settlement that was left after the lawyers and victims had been compensated, she'd been left with just enough to put a down payment on the beautiful building that housed the café and upstairs apartment and to buy a small house. She'd thought about living in the apartment for a while, and had stayed there on her brief visits, but she really wanted a place to go home to separate from the café. Of course, she wished she'd seen the house first, but beggars can't be choosers, and it was pretty much all she could afford anyway.

A loud crash from outside the back door startled her. She jumped and whirled toward the sound. A tremor shook her. Sweat sprang out on her forehead and trickled down the side of her face.

Something squeezed her shoulder.

Gia practically jumped out of her skin.

Savannah jerked her hand back and frowned. "Are you all right?"

How could she explain the panic attacks she'd suffered this past year? How could she reveal the paranoia, the prickling sensation at the back of her neck that would come over her at random moments, the absolute conviction that someone was watching her? How could she tell Savannah about the death threats she'd received without making her worry even more? Easy, she couldn't. "I'm sorry. I'm fine. You just startled me." She forced a laugh. "What was that noise, anyway?"

Savannah's eyes narrowed, and she stared at Gia for a moment longer, then, thankfully, she let the matter drop. "Sounded like the dumpster in the parking lot out back."

Desperate to escape the claustrophobia threatening to suffocate her, as well as Savannah's far too observant gaze, Gia shoved open the back door. The instant she emerged from the air-conditioned shop, the humidity slammed into her chest. Her breath shot from her lungs as if she'd gotten punched.

Savannah's laughter helped shake the last of the paranoia that had gripped her. "Don't worry. You'll get used to it."

"I'm not so sure."

"Trust me. It won't take long before you're looking for a jacket when the temperature falls below seventy."

"Somehow, I doubt—" She stopped short, not sure what exactly she was looking at. A man, clad in dirty, threadbare jeans, hung from the dumpster.

"Harley? Is that you, Harley?" Savannah strode toward the dumpster, then stopped and propped her hands on her hips. "You get down from there right now. What has Trevor told you about taking stuff out of dumpsters?"

The man pulled his upper body out and swung himself down to the concrete. His cheeks flushed, though whether from the intense heat or embarrassment, Gia had no clue. He lowered his gaze to the ground and smoothed a hand over his scruffy, more-gray-than-blond beard. "Sorry, ma'am."

Savannah's tone softened. "Don't be sorry. You didn't do anything wrong, but you're going to get sick if you eat stuff out of dumpsters." She reached as if to put a hand on his arm.

He lurched back.

"It's okay, Harley. But if you're hungry, just ask. You know that."

He nodded, glanced longingly at the dumpster once more, then headed off across the parking lot, slowed by a bad limp.

"Harley?" Gia called after him.

He stopped and turned but didn't make eye contact.

"I'm opening tomorrow, and if you come in, I'll treat you to breakfast on the house."

He nodded and started away again.

Savannah leaned close, pitching her voice low. "He won't come inside."

She didn't know his story, but something about him touched her. Perhaps the lost look hovering just below the surface in his bright blue eyes. She yelled after him. "I'll leave a bag out back, right beside the door."

He waved over his shoulder but kept walking.

Gia stared after him, as he shuffled across the remainder of the parking lot, his gait steady but stilted, and disappeared into a bunch of trees bordering the lakefront park. "What's up with him?"

"Don't worry about Harley. He's harmless. Everyone around here..." She gestured toward the row of shops behind them. "Well, they sort of take care of him."

"He's homeless?"

Savannah shook her head. "I don't really know, but he won't even go inside a building, so I assume so."

"Where does he live?"

"Wherever he can find somewhere to hang out."

"What about when it rains?" Weird how she'd walked past dozens of homeless people every day back home, without ever really seeing them as individuals, but this one man touched her in a way they hadn't. She wished she could go back and take notice, see each of them as a unique person with their own story, their own tragedy.

"The park has picnic areas and other sheltered spaces without walls. Technically, he's not allowed to be there, but no one chases him away. Now, come on."

"Huh? Come on where?" She shook off her concern. She'd leave something for him to eat when she closed tomorrow. Hopefully, he'd take it. "Where are we going?"

"To see your new house, silly. I'm so happy you got here in daylight." A small thrill coursed through her. Her very own house.

"And I assume you'll want to come back to the café afterward...."

Gia nodded as she held the door for Savannah to reenter the shop, then hurried through after her. "I want to make sure everything is perfect for tomorrow. I'll probably do a lot of the prep tonight."

"So we should swing by the shelter on the way to the house."

"Shelter?" The glass-domed cake dishes lining the counter distracted her from whatever Savannah was going on about. They'd be perfect to display quiche and breakfast pies, a variety of muffins, and scones. A row of stools allowed for counter seating, which would give her room for an extra ten or twelve customers. She started counting the stools.

"Yeah. Can you believe they just shut down a pet store last week? The animal shelter is overloaded with puppies."

Her concentration faltered, and she lost count. "Puppies?"

"Yeah." Savannah grinned.

"You're getting a puppy?"

"No, you are."

"Why in the world would I do that?" The thought of a pet was appealing. She'd never had one before, not even as a kid, and the company would be nice, but she'd probably choose something less...intense. Like a fish, or maybe a parakeet.

"For protection."

Hmm... She hadn't thought of that. Her ex had left some very angry former clients in his wake, some of whom had pounded on her apartment door and others who had gone into the deli where she worked looking for her on more than one occasion. But surely they wouldn't find her over a thousand miles away. And, hopefully, whoever had sent the death threats wouldn't follow through on his promise to hunt her down. Okay...a dog might not be a totally bad idea. "I doubt any of Bradley's..." The name left a sour taste in her mouth. "Victims would follow me to Florida."

"Well, you never know. And you'll be living out at the edge of the forest alone, so you'll get a dog, because it'll make me feel better." She grabbed her bright orange canvas bag from the counter, fished out her car keys, and opened the front door. "Besides, a dog will warn you if there're any bears around."

Wait. What! "Bears?"

"Coming?" she tossed over her shoulder with an innocent smile as she walked out.

"Hey," Gia called, running after her. "You're kidding about the bears, right?"

Chapter 2

Gia took a deep breath to steady her nerves and flipped the sign on the front door to *Open*. She smoothed her fingers over the handcrafted, wooden sign and reminded herself she could do this. Inspired by diners in New York City that served breakfast 24/7, she'd chosen to open a breakfast café. After all, she'd worked the breakfast shift in a busy New York deli for years, and she was an excellent cook—breakfast, anyway—lunch and dinner not so much. But she was also a hard worker. And she was going to make this happen.

She turned back to the two employees she'd hired last time she was there. Willow, a young woman with a nose ring and an eager smile, and Maybelle, a middle-aged woman who looked like she was still half asleep. "You guys ready?"

Willow grinned. "Yes, ma'am."

Maybelle nodded and yawned, stretching her arms over her head, then turned and headed for the kitchen.

Gia tried to ignore a small tug of apprehension. Maybelle had assured her she'd been working breakfast for years. She was probably just tired. It was only five o'clock on a Sunday morning; she couldn't really blame the woman.

There was nothing she could do now, anyway. Maybelle would work in the kitchen, Willow would take the orders and ring up the customers, and Gia would bounce back and forth where needed. All the prep work was already done, since Gia had spent most of the night doing it, only grabbing a few hours of sleep on the beat-up couch in the upstairs apartment. As soon as she got on her feet, she'd hire more employees, but for now, she'd have to make do.

The front door opened, and Gia whirled toward the sound. *Ugh... I have to stop being so jumpy.*

A huge smile lit Savannah's face as she strode through the door. "I can't believe this is it."

"Me neither," Gia said.

"How are you doing?"

Gia laughed. "I'm a nervous wreck."

"Come on, now. You worked the breakfast shift in that deli since you were a teenager. This is pretty much the same thing."

Banging out orders as quickly as possible was one thing. Creating an atmosphere where people could relax and enjoy a meal was something else entirely, but she wasn't about to get into that argument, again.

The door opened again, and an old man walked in, yanked the fisherman's cap from his head, and nodded toward Gia. "Morning, ma'am."

"Good morning." Gia plastered on her best smile. She loved greeting customers, and it would come more naturally with time, but at that moment, she was still battling her nerves. She approached the man and held out a hand. "I'm Gia Morelli. It's nice to meet you."

"Earl Dennison, ma'am." He shifted his cap and took her hand. "Pleasure to meet you."

"Would you like to sit at the counter or a table?"

"Counter's fine."

The spring in his step belied his coarse, leathery skin and thick gray hair, making it near impossible for Gia to guess his age. She placed a menu in front of him. "Can I get you some coffee?"

"Sure thing." He slid the menu aside.

Willow started toward him, but Gia waved her off, and she returned to wiping down the already spotless counter by the register.

Gia would take care of her first customer. Her first customer! She couldn't even believe this was really happening. She resisted the urge to pinch herself and make sure it was real.

Savannah busied herself taking the quiche and breakfast pies from the oven and arranging them in the glass cake dishes. The savory aroma of peppers, onions, and eggs filled the room.

Gia placed a mug of coffee in front of Earl. "Milk or sugar?"

"Nothing, thanks."

"Can I get you anything else?" She gestured toward the menu, then grabbed an order pad and pen.

"Yup. Don't need a menu, though. I eat the same breakfast every day." When he smiled, his eyes twinkled with mischief, and Gia took an instant liking to him.

She'd have to remember to keep his order slip so she'd get it right if he came back. She wrote *Earl* across the top of the page. "What'll it be?"

"Bacon, sausage, three scrambled eggs, grits..."

Uh oh.

"Two biscuits and a side of gravy."

Okay, the gravy she was prepared for, thanks to Savannah who soaked biscuits in gravy for breakfast all the time, but grits? "Uh..."

He laughed and patted his flat stomach. "That's why I eat my breakfast out. My Heddie always pitched a hissy fit when I ate all that at home, said I'm gonna clog my arteries, or some such nonsense. My arteries have been just fine for close to eighty years now, and I've been eatin' the same thing for near on seventy-five of those years."

"Well, you certainly don't look like you eat that amount of food for breakfast every morning." She smiled. That was certainly true. Though slightly stooped, he was rail-thin. "The thing is, I don't have grits this morning. I'll have them tomorrow, though."

"No grits?"

She had only a vague idea of what they even were.

"Hmm..." He frowned.

"I do have some amazing home fries," she rushed on.

He stared at her and scratched his chin beneath the gray goatee. "How do you not have grits?"

Savannah walked past with a quiche just then and stopped short. She offered an apologetic smile, turned, and headed back toward the kitchen.

Somehow, Gia had a feeling Earl wouldn't be the only one looking for grits that day. "Would you be willing to give the home fries a try? On the house, of course."

"Huh... Okay, why not? I'll give them a try. But you'll have grits tomorrow?"

"You bet I will."

She hurried toward the back to give Maybelle the order and find out why no one had told her she should have grits. When she pushed through the swinging door, she stopped short.

Savannah stood by the sink, her long, blond hair tied back in a bun, apron covering the dress she'd worn for work, washing the couple of dishes Gia had left earlier.

Maybelle sat on a stool in the middle of the kitchen.

"What's going on?"

Maybelle shifted as if to get more comfortable. "Nothing. Just waiting for some orders, so I can start cooking."

Savannah rolled her eyes and turned back to the dishes.

Okaaay... She had no clue what was going on, but whatever it was would have to wait until later. "Well, here's your first order."

Maybelle took her time getting up, then took the slip from Gia and pinned it up over the grill. Although she moved as slow as a snail, she seemed to know what she was doing as she started everything on the grill. Of course, the bacon and sausage had already been cooked—because Gia had done it herself earlier that morning—and now sat in warming trays on one side of the grill, so all she had to do was heat them up while the eggs cooked.

Gia walked over to Savannah. The kitchen was too small to have a conversation you didn't want overheard, so she simply kept her back to Maybelle and drew her eyebrows together.

Savannah's gaze darted past Gia's shoulder, and she gave one discreet shake of her head.

Gia gave up. She'd have to find out what had gone on later. "So, what's the deal with grits?"

Savannah's cheeks reddened. "Sorry. I didn't realize you wouldn't know about them."

"We lived together for five years, and I never once saw you eat grits."

"That's because I don't like them."

Hmmm... Well, what could she say to that?

"Yeah, I was wondering where the grits were?" Maybelle piped in. "Everyone eats grits for breakfast."

Gia turned on her. "Well, why didn't you ask?"

"Not my job to plan the menu."

A dull throbbing started at Gia's temples. "Okay. Is that order ready?"

"Not yet."

The home fries—thinly sliced potatoes with diced onions and crumbled bacon—and the light, fluffy biscuits Gia had baked from scratch the evening before, were also kept in covered warming trays, so all Maybelle really had to do was scramble and cook a few eggs, then plop everything on a plate.

Even still, it took Maybelle at least five minutes longer than it should have to get the order together. If things kept up the way they were going, it was going to be a long day.

She grabbed the plate from Maybelle, shoved through the swinging door—probably a little harder than necessary—and returned to the dining room. She slid the plate in front of Earl, then crossed her fingers behind her back. Hopefully, he'd like the home fries as much as grits. "Enjoy."

Ignoring the urge to stand over him until he took his first bite, she turned her attention to the other customers who'd entered while she was in back. Willow had already seated two tables, given another elderly gentleman a seat at the counter, and was smiling and chatting while she took an order. Her easy-going style seemed to make the customers feel relaxed and at home. Exactly the atmosphere Gia had been hoping for.

At least, one of her new employees was working out. Savannah was generally very laid back. Her casual attitude had made it difficult for her in New York. The rigorous pace, fierce competition, and cut-throat attitudes were more than she'd wanted to deal with, and she'd given up her dreams of becoming a Broadway star to return home to Florida. If she was already rolling her eyes about Maybelle, chances were, Maybelle was on her way out.

Gia grabbed two menus from the counter and approached a young couple who'd just entered. "Welcome to the All-Day Breakfast Café. Just the two of you today?"

"Yes, thank you." The woman's perky smile gave Gia a boost of confidence. Maybe the day would get better, after all.

"Follow me." She tried to sneak a peek at Earl from the corner of her eye while she seated them. She couldn't see his face, but he was lifting his arm at regular intervals, so she figured he was eating. That was a good sign. She hoped.

After assuring the couple Willow would be right over, Gia returned to the counter and grabbed an order pad to take the elderly gentleman's order. Only one seat separated him and Earl, but even face to face, she couldn't tell from Earl's expression if he was happy. Although, the generous pile of home fries definitely looked smaller than it had been.

She shifted her attention to the other man, who sat a good head taller than Earl. "Good morning, sir. Can I take your order?"

"I'll just have coffee for now, if that's all right. I'm waiting for my son to join me."

"Of course." She poured a mugful and slid it in front of him. "I'm sorry, I didn't get your name. I'm Gia."

"Hello there, Gia. I'm Judd."

"It's nice to meet you, Judd."

His cell phone rang, and he excused himself to answer it.

She glanced at Earl. The suspense was killing her. "So, how are the home fries?"

"Well..." He pursed his lips and tilted his head. "They ain't grits."

"Excuse me?" Judd interrupted before she could answer.

"Yes, sir?"

"My son is almost here, running a little late with his new baby and all, but he told me to go ahead and order, so if it's okay..."

"Yes, of course." She lifted the pad and pen from the counter. "How old is his baby?"

The man sat up taller on the stool. "Two weeks today. My first grandson."

"Congratulations." His pride warmed her heart. "So what can I get for you this morning?"

"My son will have the western omelet with home fries."

Gia jotted down the order, grateful he hadn't asked for grits. "And for you?"

"I'll have two eggs, over-easy, with bacon and grits."

Ugh... She caught herself just before she cringed.

Earl smirked, then lowered his head and kept eating. His shoulders shaking gave away his laughter.

"I'm sorry, Judd. I don't have grits today. I'll have them tomorrow, though. Would you like to try some home fries instead?"

"Oh. Uh... I don't know..."

"They're delicious," Earl offered around a mouthful of food. "Best I've ever tasted."

"Yeah?" Judd returned his attention to Gia. "Well, if they're good enough for Earl, then what the heck. I'll give them a try."

Earl winked at Gia and went back to eating.

A smile tugged at her. "Great. You won't be sorry." She scanned the dining room as she headed toward the kitchen. One man had a plate in front of him. His companion gestured for him to go ahead and start eating.

Gia frowned at Willow.

She shook her head and continued her conversation with a middle-aged woman she seemed to know.

Gia quickened her stride. She shoved through the kitchen door.

Maybelle stood in front of the grill. Seven order slips hung from the post above the grill. Gia added the one in her hand. "What's going on?"

Maybelle flipped two eggs, then stood waiting for them to cook. She slid them onto a plate, added bacon and home fries, then dropped two pieces of bread into the toaster. While they toasted, she propped a hand on her hip and turned to Gia. "Just working on this order."

"One order?"

"Yeah, one order. What do you expect?"

"I thought you said you've been working breakfast for years?" She scanned the order slips, then yanked the pancake batter from the refrigerator. "Sure have. Between my husband and five teenage sons, I feel like I'm running a restaurant every morning."

"But have you ever actually worked in a restaurant?"

"Not exactly, but what's the difference? Breakfast is breakfast, no matter where you cook it."

Gia dropped ladles of pancake batter onto the hot grill, then set the bowl aside, drizzled some bacon grease onto the grill, and cracked a dozen eggs onto the sizzling oil. "If you fill the orders one at a time, it'll take all day. Why don't you get that order out to Willow, and I'll help you get the rest done."

"Sorry, hon. Servin' the food ain't my job." She slid the plate onto the counter in the cut-out between the kitchen and the dining room and rang the bell, then leaned against the counter and folded her arms.

Willow grabbed the plate and ran toward the front.

"Where's Savannah?"

"Said she had to go to work."

Oh, right. Savannah rarely worked Sunday's and she'd forgotten she had to work today. She must have lost track of time. "Okay, can you start making the toast?"

Maybelle looked at the first order slip. She sauntered over to the row of toasters, dropped two slices of bread into one, then leaned over, rested her elbows on the counter, and waited while it toasted.

Gia's blood began to boil. She tried to control her rising temper. With orders piling up, there was no time to deal with Maybelle now. She'd have to talk to her later. She flipped an egg with a little too much force, broke the yolk, and had to start over.

When the toast popped up, Maybelle buttered it, put it on a plate, cut it, then dropped two more slices of bread into the toaster.

"Maybelle, why do you think I have five toasters?"

"No idea."

Gia piled food onto the plates, tossed them onto the counter, and rang the bell. She clenched her teeth to keep from blurting out anything she might regret later. "So you can make more than two slices at a time."

"Hmm…" She nodded but made no move to put more bread in before the next two pieces popped up.

"You know what, Maybelle? Why don't you go help Willow, and I'll do this?"

Maybelle walked out, leaving Gia to continue filling orders.

She muttered to herself for the next hour while she cooked, occasionally taking a quick peek through the cut-out into the dining room. At least staying so busy kept her from seething about Maybelle. A little anyway. As soon as there was a lull, though, that woman was so out of there.

She slid two more plates onto the counter and rang the bell, then peered into the dining room.

Willow seemed to have everything under control, moving from table to table, making sure everyone was happy and had what they needed.

Scanning the shop, Gia allowed herself one moment of pride. She'd done it. She'd actually done it. Despite a few mishaps, people seemed to be genuinely enjoying themselves. Of course, she wished she could be out in the thick of things, greeting customers, getting feedback on what they liked and didn't like, but obviously, she'd be working the kitchen for a while. At least, until she could hire and train someone else.

She cringed. Training. Maybe she needed to shoulder some of the blame for the situation with Maybelle. She'd hired the woman on the spur of the moment without checking her references… Come to think of it, she hadn't even looked at her application to see if she'd listed references. She'd just been grateful to find someone who said she had experience in the kitchen.

Now that things had slowed down a little, and the worst of the rush seemed to be over, maybe she should bring Maybelle back and train her a little.

Willow would be fine alone for a little while longer, and Gia could always keep an eye on the dining room through the cut-out and run out and help if needed. She'd put together a couple of breakfast pies, and if the shop was still slow when she was done, she'd bring Maybelle back and offer to train her. If she didn't work out after that, well, at least Gia could say she'd done everything she could.

She took out four pie tins and sprayed them with cooking spray. The meat lover pies seemed to be going best, so she'd make two of those, one western and one veggie lovers. She lined the bottoms and sides of the pans with home fries, then set them aside.

The routine of cooking soothed her, and she began to relax. She scrambled a bowl of eggs, then dropped in pre-cooked crumbled bacon and sausage, diced ham and sautéed onions, mixed it and poured the mixture into one of the tins. She repeated the process and filled a second tin. The next egg mixture contained diced ham, peppers and onions, and the last held spinach, zucchini, tomatoes, peppers, and onions. Once all the potato lined pans were filled with an egg mixture, she sprinkled a generous serving of shredded cheddar cheese over the tops and slid all four pans into the oven.

With that done, she put the eggs and cheese back into the refrigerator, washed the dishes, and put them away. The aroma of the pies cooking filled the kitchen, and she inhaled deeply. Her stomach growled. She'd never gotten a chance to eat anything, and she was starved, but first she had to talk to Maybelle.

Even with stopping to fill an occasional order, the whole process had taken no more than half an hour. Having avoided the coming confrontation as long as possible, she untied the apron she'd donned after splashing bacon grease on her new shirt and tossed it aside, then strode through the swinging door to the dining room.

Maybelle leaned her folded arms on the counter and chatted with a woman who kept nodding and glancing at her watch.

"Excuse me, Maybelle." Gia nodded to the woman who was trying to eat her breakfast.

She offered a grateful smile and returned to her omelet, keeping her gaze glued to her plate, probably afraid Maybelle would start yapping again if she even glanced up.

"I'm sorry to interrupt, but I need you in the kitchen."

Maybelle only turned and walked away.

Gia trailed after her, all intentions of working to train her better flying right out the window. The woman was rude, obnoxious, and lazy. She'd just fire her and be done with it.

Another customer entered.

Since Willow was in the middle of taking an order, Gia turned around and went to seat him. A couple of minutes to cool off might be just what she needed.

"Good morning." She forced a smile.

"Ma'am."

The unmistakable New York accent caught her off guard, and she faltered. "Uh...I mean, um..." She shook her head. She was going to have to get a grip on herself. She couldn't break out in a cold sweat every time someone from New York walked into her shop. A lot of New Yorkers vacationed in Florida every year, many of them owning homes in both places. "Sorry, I was distracted for a moment. A lot on my mind." And the tall, muscular stranger from New York just catapulted to the top of the list.

He narrowed his eyes. "No problem."

"Will anyone be joining you today?"

"Nope. Just me." After studying her another moment, he smiled, crinkling the corners of his eyes—the darkest green eyes she'd ever seen, their irises surrounded by an even darker ring and framed by thick, black lashes any woman would envy.

"Would you like to sit at the counter, or would you like a table?"

"The counter is fine, thank you."

She led him to the counter and handed him a menu. "Coffee?"

"Yes, please. Long flight." He raked a hand through his stylishly disheveled dark hair. "Well, actually, that's not exactly accurate. The flight wasn't that long, the delay beforehand was."

She laughed. "From New York?"

He shot her a charmingly crooked grin. "How'd you guess?"

"Hmm... I can't imagine what gave it away." Some of her tension eased. "So, what brings you to Florida?"

"A little business." He leaned closer and lowered his voice to a husky whisper. "Hopefully, a little pleasure."

"Why Boggy Creek?" she blurted.

"Seems nice. Have you been here long?"

"Actually, I'm still in the process of getting settled."

"Gia?" Willow caught her lower lip between her teeth and rolled her eyes toward the kitchen.

Oh, right. She'd left Maybelle back there alone with the breakfast pies cooking. Yikes. What was she thinking? "If you'll excuse me, I have to get back to the kitchen. Willow will be right over to take your order."

"Sure. It was nice to meet you, uh..."

"Gia." She extended her hand. "Gia Morelli."

He took her proffered hand. "Caleb Williams."

"Pleasure to meet you, Caleb."

He held her gaze and her hand a moment longer than necessary. "I assure you, the pleasure was all mine."

Chapter 3

Gia tied up the last garbage bag. "Well, today could have gone better," she muttered to herself, as she'd been doing pretty much all night. "Of course, it could have gone worse, too. Probably." She laughed. What else could she do? There was no sense in brooding over everything that had gone wrong. It wouldn't change anything. Hopefully, things would go smoother tomorrow. Once she fired Maybelle, anyway, since she'd lacked the energy to deal with it today. Convincing herself she should at least give Maybelle one more chance had allowed her to put off the unpleasant task. She sighed and dropped the garbage bag by the others beside the back door. She probably should have just gotten it over with. Then she wouldn't have to brood over it all night.

She walked through the shop one last time to double check everything was locked up, then grabbed her purse and keys from her office. She was looking forward to a long, hot bath, a cup of tea, and a good book. She'd bought one at the airport in New York but hadn't been able to clear her mind enough to read on the plane. With one more sigh for good measure, she slung her purse over her shoulder, hooked the key ring over her finger, then lifted the garbage bags and shoved the door open with her hip. After waiting to make sure the lock clicked into place when the door shut, she headed toward her car.

Darkness had already begun to fall, and the thought of going home to her empty house brought a small surge of anxiety. She loved the house, but maybe Savannah was right. Maybe she did need a dog, or at least something for company. She should probably have thought about that before she'd talked Savannah out of stopping at the shelter. No matter. Knowing Savannah, which she did, she wouldn't let it drop, and they'd be at the shelter before the end of the week anyway. Her mood lightened. Besides, the house would be a lot warmer and more welcoming once she managed to unpack everything.

A foul stench hit her. She slowed and wrinkled her nose as she neared the dumpster. If she didn't have her hands full of garbage, she'd have pinched her nose closed to block the odor. As it was, all she could do was keep taking shallow breaths through her mouth. It didn't help. She still gagged. Who'd have thought garbage could smell so rotten, even if it had baked in the hot Florida sun all day? She was going to have to call the company and have the dumpster emptied more often if the stench persisted.

She slowed, squinting to see in the waning light.

Something hung from the top of the dumpster. It seemed to be caught between the rim and the partially open lid. From where she stood, it looked like an arm. But that couldn't be right, could it? Unless...

Her gaze shot to the bag she'd left beside the back door for Harley, still sitting untouched, as far as she could tell, exactly where she'd left it before she'd started cleaning up.

She stopped and let the garbage fall to the ground. "Harley?"

She fumbled the phone from her purse, lit the flashlight, and aimed it at the dumpster. Yup. Definitely an arm. "Harley, is that you?"

She moved closer. Had something happened to him? A lump clogged her throat as she inched closer. The light played over the pale hand and forearm hanging over the dumpster's edge. Then it fell on the fingers... and the perfectly manicured nails. Not Harley, for sure.

The light glinted off a ring, black onyx surrounded by diamond chips. Not just any ring. "Bradley?"

Fear choked her. It couldn't be. What would he be doing there? Bradley hated Florida. Hated the way the humidity wreaked havoc on his perfectly slicked hair and his impeccably pressed suit. Besides, Bradley wouldn't be caught dead in a dumpst...

Oh! Oh, no!

She had to get out of there. Her gaze darted everywhere at once. Obviously, Bradley hadn't crawled in there like the rat he was and died on his own. Any one of the shadows crowding the back lot could easily conceal his killer. But still, she stood frozen, unable to move, breath caught painfully in her lungs.

Okay, think. Think, think, think. She had to get a grip on herself. She was only assuming he was dead, though the small cloud of flies buzzing around the dumpster might indicate her assumption was correct.

Her breath whooshed out, breaking the grip fear held, and she spun back toward the shop. She had to get help. Something banged against her hip, and she screamed. Her purse. It was only her purse. She lurched toward the shop, fumbling her keys as she tried to find the one that would open the back door. Sweat soaked her hands, and her phone shot out onto the concrete, then landed with a loud crack.

She looked over her shoulder, her hands shaking too badly to get the key into the lock.

Bradley's arm still hung out of the dumpster, right where it was a minute ago. A vision of him crawling out and coming after her made her cry out. She had to calm down. On the off chance he was still alive, she had to get help. No matter how she felt about him, she'd never let another human being die if she could help it. Not even Bradley.

She took a deep breath, worked to hold her hand steady, and shoved the key into the lock, then got the back door open, snatched her phone from the ground, and reached through the doorway to hit the light switch. The driving need to be out of that parking lot consumed her, but no way was she walking into a dark room.

With the lights on and the door locked behind her, she tried to steady her breathing. Tears blurred her vision. Cursing at the shattered screen, Gia dialed 911, then pressed the phone against her ear and listened to it ring.

"911. What is your emergency?"

"My husband..." She couldn't force the words out past the lump blocking her throat.

"Excuse me, ma'am?"

She swallowed hard and tried again. "Yes. Uh...my ex-husband. He's dead. At least, I think he's dead. He's in the dumpster."

Silence stretched over the line. Had the woman hung up?

"Are you there?"

"Yes, ma'am. I'm dispatching help. Where are you located?"

How could she be so calm? Didn't she understand there was a dead body out back?

"The All-Day Breakfast Café." She recited the address, disconnected, leaned her cheek against the cool metal refrigerator door, and waited for help.

To say things with Bradley had ended badly would be the understatement of the year, but still, finding him, if it even was him, dead, if he even was dead, in a dumpster, *her* dumpster, was more then she could take. She turned so her back was against the door, then slid down and sat, pulling her knees against her chest.

Who would have done something like that? Okay, stupid question. A long line of people wished Bradley Remington dead. But who would have the nerve to follow through? It made no sense.

Shock and fear overwhelmed her, and a sob tore free. She'd loved Bradley once upon a time, with all her heart. Had the pain he'd caused her, caused so many people, made her so cold she couldn't grieve for him, couldn't be heartbroken at his fate? Was she so broken, so emotionally distant after feeling so much hurt, anger, even fear over the past year, she had nothing left? Or was she simply numb, her feelings dulled by the shock of finding him?

If it was him.

She forced the anguish aside. There would be time to examine her feelings later. No matter what Bradley had done, he certainly didn't deserve to end up where he was.

Banging from the front of the shop jerked her back to reality. She stumbled to her feet and ran toward the dining room. By the time she realized it could be the killer, the officer's uniform was already visible through the front door.

When she reached the door, she stopped short and looked down at her hands. The phone was still clutched tightly, but the keys were gone. Where had she left them? She held up a finger through the door, mimicked turning a key, and pointed to the lock.

The officer's jaw clenched. He did not seem amused.

She turned and fled toward the back of the shop, found the keys on the floor by the back door, and grabbed them.

The officer stared into the door, hand resting on his gun, and spoke into a radio clipped to his shoulder.

She held up the keys, then unlocked the door and pulled it open. "I'm sorry, Officer. I forgot the keys in the back."

Ignoring her apology, he took her keys out of the lock and kicked down the doorstop, leaving the door propped open as he looked around the shop. "Are you Gia Morelli?"

"Yes."

"I'm Officer Leo Dumont. You called 911?"

"Yes. M-m-my ex-husband. I found him in a dumpster out back."

She started toward the back of the shop, intent on showing him where Bradley was, but he stopped her. "We already have officers out back. Why don't you just tell me what happened?"

A second cop entered the shop, and the officer handed him her keys. Some sort of silent communication she couldn't interpret passed between them; then the second officer started talking into his radio as he turned and walked outside.

"I was closing up for the day."

He glanced at his watch. "Kind of late, isn't it?"

She shrugged. "It was my first day, and it..." All the day's mishaps suddenly seemed sort of trivial in light of the situation. "Well, things didn't go as well as I'd hoped."

His expression finally softened a little. "Apparently not."

She offered a small smile. "Anyway, when it started getting late, I sent everyone home and finished cleaning up myself. No sense making everyone stay."

Of course, if Maybelle had done her job, Gia could have started cleaning up while the café was still open.

"How did you find the body?"

The second officer returned and nodded to his partner.

"Umm... I'd just finished up and was getting ready to go home. My car was parked out back, so I was going to drop the garbage in the dumpster on my way to the car."

"Mmm...hmm..." He wrote something down on a pad similar to the one she used for taking orders.

His partner still stood beside the open door.

"It was getting dark, and shadows blocked the dumpster, so I didn't notice anything at first, but as I got closer, I saw a hand sticking out. I thought Harley had gone back in there, because he was there this morning, but then I saw the hand and knew it wasn't Harley, so I came back in and called the police." She clenched her teeth to stem the rambling flow of words.

He frowned at her. "And what makes you think it's your ex-husband?"

What *had* made her so certain it was Bradley? The ring, but anything else? Because surely he wasn't the only man in the world to wear that ring. "His ring. And the perfect manicure, of course."

He lifted a brow. "Of course."

What did he mean by that?

"I'm going to have to ask you to stay here for a little while until the detectives get here."

She had no doubt it was a command, not a request, but in the spirit of seeming cooperative, she answered anyway. "That's fine. Can I make some coffee?"

"Not yet."

That was probably for the best. As jittery as she already was, caffeine was the last thing she needed.

"I'm sorry, I didn't get your name." He might have said it, but her mind had been so clouded at the time, she couldn't remember.

"Officer Dumont."

"It's nice to meet you. I'm Gia Morelli..." Heat crept up her cheeks. "But I guess you already knew that."

"Yes, ma'am."

"Do you know if it's Bradley?"

"The body hasn't been identified yet." His gaze shifted toward his partner, a subtle shift, but enough for Gia to suspect they knew exactly who was in the dumpster. "When was the last time you saw your ex, Ms. Morelli?"

A clear image of Bradley being led out of the courtroom in handcuffs flashed into her mind. He'd stared directly at her, anger etched into every line of his hard expression.

"Ms. Morelli?"

"I'm sorry. I...uh... The last time I saw him was back in New York about a month ago." It would be foolish to try to stall. It wasn't like they wouldn't figure out who he was on their own anyway. Heck, they probably already knew. But she'd been so determined to leave her past behind her. Admitting the truth now seemed...an awful lot like reliving the nightmare. She sighed. "When they were leading him out of the courtroom after he was convicted."

If Officer Dumont was surprised, it didn't show in his expression. "Have you had any contact with him since then?"

"No. He's out on bail. He was due in court for sentencing sometime, but I'm not sure when." Even though she'd been present for the conviction, once the judge had proclaimed him "guilty" all rational thought had fled.

Dumont stared at her a moment longer than necessary. "He's still out on bail while awaiting sentencing?"

"He has a great lawyer." She shrugged off the uncomfortable feeling searching for a hold on her. "And he had already filed an appeal."

One of the main witnesses against him had recanted her testimony, risking perjury charges, then disappeared. Officer Dumont could figure that one out on his own. All he had to do was google Bradley Remington's name and all the sordid details would pop right up. She was tired and had no intention of rehashing the past year of her life.

Her mind flashed back to the stranger from New York. Caleb, he'd said his name was. She thought of mentioning him to Officer Dumont but dismissed the idea before she could blurt out his name. Millions of people lived in New York. Of course, they didn't all happen to be in her café on the very day her ex-husband was found in her dumpster, and yet...

She shook off the far-fetched idea. If he had killed Bradley, why would he come into the café and risk being seen? Besides, she knew all too well how it felt to be dragged into an investigation you had no knowledge of, and she could never do that to another person.

Two officers emerged from the back of the shop. Officer Dumont's partner must have opened the back door.

Gia braced herself for the stench and inhaled tentatively. Thankfully, it didn't reach the dining room.

Another officer strode through the room and leaned close to Officer Dumont.

She had no idea how many officers were out back, but she assumed there were probably quite a few. Murders didn't often happen in Boggy Creek, at least, according to the statistics Savannah had spewed when she'd been trying to talk Gia into moving to the small town.

Great. She'd barely been there a day, and already the murder quota for the year had been met. She flopped onto a chair at the table closest to the open front door, as far away from the back parking lot as she could get. She had a feeling it was going to be a long night.

Chapter 4

Gia slouched in the chair and traced circles with her finger on the dark blue tablecloth. Around and around, while she waited for the detectives Officer Dumont promised were coming to show up. He still hadn't let her make coffee. He also hadn't let her call anyone, though who she'd call was beyond her. Savannah, probably. But why wake her in the middle of the night? Not like there was anything she could do to help.

"Ms. Morelli?" A man's voice startled her.

She jerked upright and stared up into big eyes the color of melted chocolate. Her stomach growled, and she pressed a hand against it. Heat flared in her cheeks. "Uh, sorry. I haven't eaten in a while."

"We'll let you get something in a few minutes," he promised.

Gee, thanks. She bit her tongue to keep anything sarcastic from flying out. Whoever this guy was, although he only wore jeans, a black T-shirt, and work boots, his confident bearing and hard expression screamed importance. She got the impression she shouldn't mess with him.

"I'm Detective Quinn." He extended a calloused hand.

It's about time. "Nice to meet you."

"Pleasure's all mine." All southern gentleman, in a dangerous predator sort of way. He pulled out the chair on the other side of the table and studied her as he sat. "I know you've already spoken to Officer Dumont, but would you mind walking me through what happened tonight."

It was definitely not a question. "I went to put the garbage out and found my ex in the dumpster." She thought about elaborating, but what more was there to say, really?

"And what made you think it was your ex?"

"As I told Officer Dumont, I thought I recognized his ring, and Bradley had manicures regularly." More often than she did, actually, but in her own defense, it was hard to keep her nails perfectly manicured while working in a deli. "He always said, 'the first thing you do when you meet someone is reach out a hand. Hands say a lot about a person.'" And his just screamed pompous ass. Hmm… Maybe he was right about that after all.

She looked at her own hands, a little rough, despite the lotion she used every night, nails neatly polished in a deep maroon but kept at a comfortable length. What did they tell the detective about her?

"When was the last time you saw Mr. Remington?"

Seriously? Did these guys read from a script? "Last month."

He pursed his lips. "He didn't come into the café today?"

"No." Of course, she'd been stuck in the kitchen a good part of the day. Firing Maybelle just shot to the top of her to-do list. "At least, not that I know of. I was in the back cooking most of the day."

He nodded, fished a small notepad out of his shirt pocket, and flipped through a few pages.

The need to know who was in the dumpster hammered her. She couldn't wait any longer. "Do you know if it's Bradley?" she blurted.

He considered her a moment, and she didn't think he was going to answer. "Yes. He's been positively identified."

The news came as a physical blow. Her chest tightened, squeezing her lungs, making it almost impossible to get enough air.

"Do you know of any next of kin?"

"No." Gia tried to force the words out but only managed to whisper, "None." Bradley never spoke about his family. Even when she'd asked, he'd simply said he didn't have any family. Maybe she should have realized then that he kept secrets, but she'd figured whatever had happened was too painful for him to talk about, and she'd respected his privacy.

"Are you all right?"

Still trying to gain control of her breathing, she only nodded.

He returned to flipping through his notebook.

Not that she hadn't expected it to be him. In her heart, she'd known from the moment she recognized his ring. And it didn't come as that much of a surprise, enough people certainly wanted him dead. But *knowing* the man she'd loved enough to marry at one time now lay dead in a dumpster behind her café brought a surreal quality she couldn't even begin to examine just then. She had to get out of there, had to go home. But where was home? She longed for her apartment in New York, needed the familiarity, the comfort going home would bring. Would it be safe to return now that Bradley was—

"Here ya go, Hunt." Officer Dumont handed Detective Quinn a plastic bag with a white paper inside.

"Thanks, Leo."

He nodded and left.

Quinn turned the bag over and over, not even shifting his gaze from her long enough to look at whatever was in the bag.

Her curiosity piqued, but she wouldn't give him the satisfaction of asking what it was. She held his stare, unwilling to drop her gaze for an instant. When he was done sizing her up, there was no way he'd be left with the impression she was weak. Or guilty of anything.

"Are you sure your husband wasn't in the café today?"

Don't look away. Don't look away. "I already told you, not that I know of, but I was back in the kitchen a lot of the day."

"Because this was found in his pocket." He laid the bag down and slid it toward her without looking at it.

Great, now she had to make a choice. Maintain eye contact, or lower her gaze to look at the bag. It seemed weird not to look at what he was showing her, so she glanced down, fully intent on resuming eye contact an instant after she checked out what was so important.

But the receipt encased in the bag gripped her and wouldn't let go. *All-Day Breakfast Café,* right there in bold print on top of a receipt for a vegetable omelet and coffee. Bradley had always loved her vegetable omelets. Had he been in the café? Had he known it was hers? He had to have. Why else would he have been there? A tear smacked the table.

Detective Quinn handed her a tissue.

She had no idea where it came from, but she thanked him and wiped her nose, then used her hands to swipe the tears from her cheeks. "I'm sorry. I…" She shook her head. "I didn't know he came in."

He pursed his lips and nodded.

"Gia!" Savannah rushed through the open door and straight to her side. "Are you all right?"

"Savannah? What are you doing here?"

A furious blush rode Officer Dumont's cheeks as he whirled away and busied himself with something.

Detective Quinn shot a scowl at his back.

Savannah wrapped an arm around Gia's shoulders and hugged her close, then pinned Detective Quinn with a frown. "What's going on, Hunt?"

"Just chatting with Ms. Morelli, here." A smirk played at the corner of his mouth. "I take it you two know each other?"

"You know dang well we know each other."

"Just following procedure, ma'am."

"Don't you, ma'am me."

A full-out grin shot across his face, and he held his hands up in surrender.

"All right, all right. Sorry, cuz."

"Yeah, well you'd better be, or I'll tell Aunt June you're acting up again. And have no doubt, Aunt June'll still take a switch to ya, no matter how big y'all are."

"Ain't that the truth." His deep, rich laughter transformed him. In an instant, Detective Quinn went from a hardened bad ass, to a not-so-scary-but-still-kinda-scary bad ass. "I'm sorry, Savannah. I wanted to get a chance to question Ms. Morelli before you stormed in like a pit bull and interfered with my investigation."

Savannah let out a surprisingly unladylike snort and dropped onto the chair next to Gia's.

Ignoring her, the detective leaned forward and rested his elbows on the table. "Look, Ms. Morelli—"

"Gia," Savannah interrupted, sliding forward to perch on the edge of her seat. "This is my friend Gia Morelli." She turned to Gia. "And this is my cousin, Hunter Quinn, but everyone calls him Hunt." Apparently manners took precedence over a murder investigation. At least, in Savannah's mind. Who knew?

Hunter stared at her a moment longer, then turned his attention back to Gia without acknowledging his cousin. "Pleasure to meet you, Gia."

"Nice to meet you, too."

With a self-satisfied smirk, Savannah leaned back and folded her arms across her chest.

Hunt just shook his head. Apparently, he was used to Savannah's behavior. "How long have you been in Florida, Gia?"

"I just arrived yesterday."

"Not a very pleasant welcome."

"No. It's not."

"Do you know anyone who would have any reason to kill your ex-husband?"

A snort slipped out, and she slapped a hand over her mouth.

"Take your pick. The list is long," Savannah answered for her. She leaned forward on the table and lowered her voice. "You can't possibly think Gia killed him and hauled him into that dumpster. Seriously? If she didn't kill him before she left New York, why bother now?"

"Savannah!" She had a sneaking suspicion Savannah wasn't helping matters.

But Hunt only shrugged and sat back. "She didn't have to do it herself. She could have hired someone. What better time to have him offed than after she was gone?"

"Oh, please. You have got to be kidding me. First of all, if she was going to have someone kill him after she was gone, why do it here? It would have made more sense to have someone kill him back in New York. Besides, between buying the café, flying back and forth on weekends to set it up, and buying a house, she doesn't even have any money left, barely enough to buy that stupid clunker of a car parked out back. You'd better—" Savannah shifted back in her seat, sitting up straighter, her gaze riveted on an older man who'd just walked in.

Hunt glanced over his shoulder, then stood. "Captain Hayes."

"Hunt." He nodded toward Savannah. "Savannah. How are you?"

"I'm doing well, thank you."

After introductions were made, which Hunt handled properly with no snide remarks from Savannah, who seemed to have sobered since the older man entered, they all returned to their seats, with Captain Hayes taking the last seat at the table.

Any friendliness Hunt had begun to show fled with the addition of his captain. "Ms. Morelli and I were just discussing the possibility of a hired assassin."

All eyes fell on her.

"Um... I don't know. I imagine someone could have hired a killer."

"Do you have any idea what Bradley Remington was doing in Florida?"

"I can't even imagine. He hated Florida, hated the heat and the humidity and the bugs." He'd indulged her once, taking her to Florida for a long weekend, and he'd done nothing but complain the entire time. She'd been ready to choke him by the time they got home. Speaking of choking... "Do you know what happened to him?"

Captain Hayes stared hard at her. "He was killed."

Heat flared in her cheeks. "I meant, do you know how?"

"He was shot in the head, Ms. Morelli." Hayes narrowed his eyes and studied her closely. "You don't seem surprised."

Hunt winced and shot Savannah a look Gia couldn't decipher, but he remained silent.

What could she say? Bradley's behavior had ceased to surprise her long ago. The fact he was killed didn't change that. Considering the sheer number of people he'd cheated, the biggest surprise was he hadn't been killed sooner.

Hunt flipped through page after page of his notebook, finally settling on something that caught his attention. "After Savannah told me about your situation last Thanksgiving..."

Savannah's chair creaked beside her.

"I sort of kept tabs on what was going on. Your ex was awaiting trial?" Hunt continued.

"No, he was sentenced already. He was awaiting an appeal."

"Oh, right. He was an investor?"

"Yes."

"Stealing money from his clients."

She shifted, uncomfortable under the Captain's steady stare and Hunt's interrogation. It wasn't like she'd done anything wrong. She hadn't even known what he was doing. He didn't discuss his work with her. Ever. Said it was boring. "Yes."

He nodded, contemplated his pad a little longer, then closed it and stood abruptly. "All right, Ms. Morelli, I'll be in touch if I have any more questions."

Gia looked back and forth between Hunt and Captain Hayes.

"Yes, ma'am. Thank you for your cooperation." Captain Hayes shook her hand and started to turn away.

Now what? Was she just supposed to go home and forget anything happened? Her stomach growled again. "Is it okay if I make coffee now?"

"Sure thing," Captain Hayes answered. "Not like your ex was poisoned."

Gia swallowed her anger—knowing full well it would burn a hole in her gut all night—and watched him strut toward the back of the café.

"Ignore him, Gia." Savannah followed her to the row of coffee pots behind the counter, then slid onto a stool while Gia started a fresh pot. "He's not worth getting your knickers in a twist over."

Gia just shook her head. "Would you like a cup?"

"Sure, thanks."

After starting all the coffee pots, Gia busied herself lining up mugs and setting out milk, creamers, and sugar on the counter. When she was done, and the coffee still wasn't ready, she filled a platter with muffins and set it beside the mugs.

"You okay?" She'd managed to wait longer than Gia had expected.

"I'm fine."

"Anything you want to talk about?"

"Like what? How I murdered Bradley and disposed of him in a dumpster?" She couldn't help the note of anger in her voice. Not that any of this was Savannah's fault—if anything, she'd saved her from a worse interrogation by showing up when she did—but Gia had been so sure she'd left Bradley and all his problems behind, and now here she was, saddled with them all over again.

"Shh..." Savannah looked over her shoulder at the police officers still lingering around the shop, then leaned across the counter. "Keep your voice down. You can't say things like that, joking or not. Especially not with Hayes lurking around."

Gia wiped the crumbs from her hands onto a dish towel and tossed it into a bin beneath the counter, then clasped her hands together and rested her elbows on the counter while she waited for the coffee. "I'm sorry. I just can't believe any of this happened." Her voice hitched, and she struggled for control. "I thought it was finally over. All I wanted to do was move on, open my café and be successful, enjoy my little house. I don't understand what I did to deserve all of this."

There it was. The sentiment seemed selfish and cold, especially because Bradley was lying dead out back, but what could she say? Most likely, he'd brought that on himself. She wouldn't lie to Savannah, nor to herself. It wasn't fair. In life, Bradley had taken almost everything from her, including her dignity, and now in death it seemed he might finish the job. While she could never hate him, or wish anything bad on him, she had finally accepted the need to have him out of her life.

"All you did was trust the wrong person." Savannah laid a warm hand over Gia's. "Coffee's ready, and your hands are like ice. Why don't you get a cup? Have you eaten anything today?"

Gia stood. "Not really. With Maybelle proving pretty much useless, I was in back all day. Oh, I meant to ask you, what was up with you and Maybelle this morning? It seemed like something was going on when I walked into the kitchen."

Savannah waved it off. "No big deal. She's just lazy..." She grinned. "And she didn't like hearing it."

"Maybe she'll get better." She didn't really think so, but the thought of hiring someone new didn't really appeal considering the added stress she'd just been dealt.

Savannah rolled her eyes but refrained from any sarcastic comments.

The chocolate chocolate-chip muffin had been calling to her all day, but her stomach roiled at the thought of food, so she settled for a cup of coffee instead. She set two pots out on trivets on the counter for the officers and left the others warming. "Can you let Hunt know the coffee's ready if anyone wants some? And there are muffins."

"Sure." Savannah crossed the shop and talked to Hunt, then returned. "Come on. As soon as you finish your coffee, I'll drive you home. I can pick you up in the morning and drive you back."

Gia had left her cell phone on the table. She'd have to find a store and replace it, or at least see if they could fix the screen. "What time is it?" Savannah took her cell phone out of her purse and hit the button. "Almost midnight."

Hunt poured himself a mug of coffee, then lifted it toward her. "Thanks."

"You're welcome." She sipped her coffee. "Thanks anyway, Savannah, but there's not much sense making the twenty-minute drive home only to come back in a few hours. I'll just crash in the apartment upstairs again." At this rate, she'd never get to sleep in her own house.

"Nah, it'll only take ten, maybe fifteen minutes to get there at this time of night with no one on the roads."

"That's all right. I'm going to have to go find grits somewhere between now and five o'clock too."

Savannah laughed. "This isn't New York, honey."

"Great, now I'm going to have to start another morning without grits." Hopefully, Earl wouldn't come back in until after she could get to the store. Of course, she couldn't leave the shop to go anywhere with Maybelle running the kitchen. A dull throb started at her temples.

Hunt chose a blueberry muffin and plopped it on a napkin. "I wouldn't worry too much about getting back in the morning. You won't be able to open anyway."

Captain Hayes moved up beside him, turned over a mug, and lifted a coffee pot.

Savannah sat up straighter on her stool.

"What do you mean, I won't be able to open?" Gia asked.

Hayes tilted his head and stared at her as if she were daft. "We're in the middle of a murder investigation."

"So?" All right, so that came out a little snippy. Or maybe even a lot snippy. But she couldn't help it. She was at the end of her rope.

He raised a brow. "So, we won't be finished in time for you to open."

"When will I be able to open again?"

The pot still hovered over the captain's mug. "That, Ms. Morelli, depends entirely on what we find, but I'd suggest you don't leave town."

So much for going home.

Chapter 5

"Thanks for driving me home, Savannah."

"No problem. Just give a call if you need anything. I'll come get you and drive you back as soon as they say you can take your car out of the lot." Gia pushed the door open and started to climb out.

Savannah grabbed her hand. "Are you sure you'll be all right?"

"I'll be fine. All I want right now is a hot bath and my warm bed." And to find out what the heck Bradley had been doing in Florida, but she'd keep that to herself for the moment. She squeezed Savannah's hand before turning away.

Who'd have thought she'd be freezing in Florida? But the chill that had gripped her earlier wouldn't let go. Just like during winter in New York, the cold permeated all the way to her bones.

She ran up the walkway, thankful for Savannah's headlights lighting her path. She'd left lights burning on the front porch and above the garage, but the little puddles of light they emitted didn't do much to fight back the intense darkness. Funny, when she'd been there with Savannah during the day—was it only yesterday?—she hadn't noticed the lack of streetlights in the development.

Of course, she'd been fixated on her house at the time, hadn't been able to tear her gaze from the Spanish style ranch she couldn't believe was really hers. The cream-colored stucco and scalloped terra cotta tile roof she'd fallen in love with in the pictures Savannah had sent was even more beautiful in person.

She fit the key into the lock, opened the door, and flipped on the foyer light, then waved to Savannah before closing the door and turning the deadbolt. The light shining into the front windows disappeared as

Savannah pulled out of the driveway, leaving the living room bathed mostly in darkness. She stood with her back against the front door, keys still dangling from her hand.

Silence descended.

What in the world was a girl from New York City doing in the middle of the forest?

A click startled her.

The soft hum of the refrigerator followed, and she sagged against the door. She needed to get a grip. The police would find out who killed Bradley. Probably. Once they did, she could decide if she should go home and try to put her life back together, or stay in Florida and try to make a new life for herself. If her first day was any indication, maybe Florida wasn't right for her.

She shoved away from the door and flipped on the light switch in the living room, then skirted a mountain of boxes as she made her way to the kitchen. Savannah had overseen the movers, making sure the bigger furniture was in place, but they'd left piles of boxes everywhere. She'd have to move all of them into the two spare bedrooms until she could sort through them.

After switching on the kitchen light, she simply stood in the doorway, staring at the boxes marked *Kitchen* scattered throughout the room. No way was she starting a search for her teapot tonight. It would have to wait for tomorrow.

As would the phone calls she needed to make to New York to try to find out what had been important enough to make Bradley leave town while out on bail and travel over a thousand miles to the small town of Boggy Creek. Of course, she could leave that to the police, but if Captain Hayes's attitude was any indication, they might not try too hard to figure it out. For now, though... She'd had all she could take. Somehow she had to shut her mind down for a few hours at least. She couldn't do anything before morning anyway.

Leaving all the lights on, she dropped her purse and keys on the counter and headed for the bathroom. Thankfully, only four boxes had been marked *Bathroom,* and they all sat in one corner. She started the tub, then dug through the boxes in search of bubble bath and towels. Maybe luck was finally with her, since she found them in the first two boxes. She poured some eucalyptus bubble bath into the tub. She'd never tried it before, but the bottle said stress relief, so it certainly couldn't hurt.

The minty fragrance filled the bathroom, and she inhaled deeply. Hmm... Maybe the bottle was right. She pulled the door shut behind her to keep the steam in, then grabbed pajamas from the suitcase on her bed. They were the same ones she'd slept in last night, but who cared? It was better than searching through boxes for something clean.

A loud crash shattered the silence.

Gia dropped her pajamas. Where was her cell phone? She patted her pockets but came up empty. Her purse. She'd thrown it in her purse before she'd left the shop. And her purse was in the kitchen. Even though the house was small, the kitchen seemed a million miles away. She looked around for something she could use as a makeshift weapon and saw her cordless phone sitting on its base on the nightstand.

Oh, thank you, Savannah!

She grabbed it and punched in 911, then waited in the silence.

Silence. Except for the sound of the bath water running, complete silence enveloped her. Having lived her whole life smack in the middle of New York City, silence was a new concept. One she wasn't sure she liked.

"911. What is your emergency?"

She jumped, startled by the voice in her ear. What was she doing? This was ridiculous. She couldn't call 911 every time she heard a noise.

"Hello?"

She was living on the outskirts of a forest. Certainly there were animals that made noise. What had Savannah said? Bears? Bears were big. They probably made a lot of noise. She swallowed the lump clogging her throat and hit the button to end the call.

That was it. Since she couldn't open the shop anyway, first thing on tomorrow's to-do list was go to the shelter and pick out a dog. A big dog. She clutched the phone and started down the hallway. She'd just double check everything was locked, then go take her bath.

She could tell from the kitchen doorway the deadbolt on the back door was turned, but she crossed the room and checked it anyway. Maybe she'd dig out the teapot after all. Not like she had to get up early for anything. A warm bath, a pot of tea, and her new book. Sounded like the perfect night.

Three heavy thuds stopped her short. The phone slid out of her sweat-soaked hand and hit the tile floor with a crack. She scrambled to pick it back up.

The thuds came again. "Police! Open the door."

Oh, boy. As she ran toward the front door, blue and red light bathed the living room. She might have noticed that sooner if she hadn't left every light in the house blazing. She peeked out the window beside the door—she was going to have to get curtains up—and found Detective Quinn standing on her front porch, his expression hard.

She flung open the front door. "What happened now?"

He frowned. "We got a 911 call from this address. Is something wrong?"

Heat flared in her cheeks. "I...um..." She swallowed hard.

He waited.

Her heart still hammered painfully. "You scared me half to death. Why didn't you just ring the bell?"

"There isn't one."

She peeked around the doorjamb, and sure enough, no doorbell. She ignored his smirk. "Oh, fine. I heard a noise and called the police, then realized how foolish I was acting and hung up."

He raked a hand through his hair, then propped it on his hip. "For future reference, when you call 911 and hang up, the call has to be investigated anyway."

"Sorry you had to come all the way out here." Wait a minute. Detectives didn't answer 911 calls. At least, in New York they didn't. Here, who knew? Besides, she'd only called a few minutes ago. "How did you get here so fast?"

"I was in the neighborhood."

She tamped down her annoyance. He obviously wasn't going to answer her question, and there was no sense standing in the doorway all night. Bugs were getting in. She stepped back and ushered him in, then closed the door behind him. "Do you always hang out all the way out here in the middle of the night?"

"Only when dead bodies turn up in dumpsters behind shops belonging to residents."

Touché. She led him past the stacks of boxes to the kitchen. Thankfully, the table and chairs had been set up. "Have a seat. Umm...

She looked around at the mess of boxes. "If you give me a minute, I think I can probably find the coffee pot here somewhere."

He waved her off and gestured to the seat across from him. "Sit down. We have to talk."

Great. What now?

"Ms. Morelli—"

"Gia."

A semi-smile finally softened his expression. "Gia. Your garage window's been broken from the outside. Do you know how that happened?"

Fear returned with a vengeance. "No. Savannah had the movers put boxes and stuff in the garage, so I haven't even bothered going in there."

He nodded and wrote something down in his notebook, then leaned back in the chair, tapped the pen against his full lips, and studied her. "It seems you might be a bit wealthier than you let on this afternoon."

Her insides went numb. "What are you talking about?"

Though still draped casually on her kitchen chair, the intensity in his eyes didn't lessen. If anything, suspicion darkened them even more. "When we were discussing the possibility of a paid hit on your husband—"

"Ex."

"Ex-husband," he conceded. "Savannah implied you had no money left, but you never actually got a chance to answer the question before we were interrupted. So, assuming Savannah might not be fully aware of your financial situation, I'm going to give you a chance to answer for yourself."

"Look, Detective, I don't know what you're talking about, but I can assure you, I am far from wealthy." Truth be told, she was swimming in debt. Her divorce agreement and nest egg had allowed her to open the café and buy the house, but it hadn't been enough to cover flying back and forth on weekends to set things up, nor had it covered her actual moving expenses, which had added up much more quickly than she'd anticipated.

He leaned forward, clasped his hands, and rested his elbows on the table. "You may not have been wealthy before your *ex* was killed, but since you're his only heir..."

"Wait." Heir? Bradley had left her on his life insurance policy? That couldn't be right. Why would he have done that? Their divorce had been in no way friendly. "You must be mistaken."

"Nope."

"First of all, Bradley never would have left me as the beneficiary on his life insurance. His lawyer made it very clear he was taking me off." Not that she cared. All she wanted at the time was to be done with Bradley Remington for good. She hadn't asked for a single thing in the divorce settlement. Instead, she'd simply taken what they offered and walked away. "And second, Bradley had nothing left to leave me or anyone else. All of his assets were frozen when he went to trial."

Hunt pursed his lips and sat back. "I spoke with his lawyer a little while ago. All he said was that you were his only heir. He didn't say what you'd inherit, just that you would. And he didn't seem to care much that his client had been found dead in a dumpster."

"I doubt he cared at all, that snake, unless it hurt him in some way." But she added Bradley's lawyer to the mental list of phone calls she'd make first thing in the morning. Maybe he could shed some light on what was going on.

The front door opened, and footsteps came toward them. Since Hunt didn't seem concerned, she assumed the newcomers were with him.

Officer Dumont stuck his head in the doorway. "That's all we found, Hunt. We'll take a quick look around the house, though."

"Thanks." He nodded and returned his attention to Gia. "Look, Gia, I don't know what's going on here yet, but if you'll cooperate with me, I'll figure it out."

"Thank you, Detective—"

"Hunt." He reached across the table and patted her hand. His gaze captured hers and held it.

She looked away. "Thank you, Hunt. It's not that I'm trying to be uncooperative, it's just, well... Apparently Bradley was living an entire life I knew nothing about. I was just happy to get out of it and move on." For a while she'd been a nervous wreck she would end up in jail with him. Or worse. No one seemed to believe she'd been blind to his activities.

"Hunt? Could you come here?" Officer Dumont's call saved her from having to answer any further questions. At least, for the moment. Unfortunately, she had a sneaking suspicion he wasn't going to let go so easily.

Gia followed Hunt toward the back of the house. Water soaked the hallway. And the bedroom. And the bathroom. At least, one of the officers had turned off the faucet. The scent of eucalyptus wafted to her. It did nothing to relieve her stress.

Leo had the decency to turn his back and cover the laughter dancing in his eyes with a coughing fit before he left the room.

Hunt simply laughed out loud, a deep, sexy laugh that grated on Gia's last frazzled nerve.

"I'm so glad you're enjoying yourself."

He shook his head, still chuckling. "Where are your towels?"

She pointed to the two waterlogged boxes sitting in the flood where she'd left them after getting her bath stuff ready.

He looked at her and grinned. *Grinned!* "Girl, you are having one heck-uv-a bad day."

Gia's mouth dropped open. How dare he—

"Now, come on. Let's get this mess cleaned up." He sloshed into the bathroom without looking back, though his shoulders still shook suspiciously. He picked up the first box, careful to keep the bottom intact, and plopped it on the counter with a wet thud. Then, with the front of his shirt and pants soaked, he bent to retrieve the second box. When he straightened, shampoos, conditioners, and an assortment of lotions, poured out the bottom and crashed to the floor with a splash, despite his best efforts to hold everything in.

Tears pricked the backs of Gia's eyes. *How could this day possibly have gone any worse?*

"Oops." Hunt shot her an apologetic look, but humor still lit his eyes. After a quick survey of the mess, he said, "Look at the bright side. At least, there was nothing breakable in the box."

A laugh bubbled out. She couldn't help it. Tears streamed down her cheeks. More laughter poured from her, hysterical laughter she couldn't control. Laughing? Crying? Who knew? A little of both. A stitch cramped her side, and she pressed a hand against it, and still the laughter came.

Leo poked his head in the doorway. "Y'all okay in here?"

Hunt studied her. "I think she might have lost it."

Wiping the tears from her face, Gia tried to regain some semblance of control.

Leo stared at her, and said, "Can't say I blame her."

Chapter 6

Gia rolled over and pulled the covers over her head. Every muscle in her body screamed in protest. By the time she'd gotten the bathroom cleaned up, the sun had already started to peek through the ridiculously tall pine trees in her backyard. But she hadn't stopped there. Instead, she'd moved on to the kitchen, emptying box after box until she couldn't stand up any longer. Then, finally, she'd stumbled to bed and passed out.

With a groan, she pulled the covers back, swung her legs over the side of the bed, and sat up. No sense lying there thinking about the mess she'd left scattered across the kitchen, or the mess her life had become. Not like either of those messes was going to clean itself up.

She disconnected the phone from the charger and scrolled through her contacts. The mess in the kitchen would wait, the rest of the mess, not so much. But who to call. Who would Bradley have told he was going to skip bail and go to Florida? And of the people he might have shared his intentions with, who would even give her the time of day?

She stopped at Jim Harte's number. Bradley's best friend. The last time she'd seen him, he'd stalked right past her without even so much as a "drop dead." But he would probably know something. She hit the number and pressed the phone against her ear before she could lose her nerve. Her hand shook while she counted the rings.

It took three before Jim's voice finally came over the line. "Yeah?"

She yanked the phone away from her ear. Her finger hovered over the disconnect button.

"Hello? Gia? Is that you?"

She clenched her teeth and put the phone back to her ear. Dang caller ID. "Yes, Jim. It's me."

"What do you want?"

Okay, so much for pleasantries. "I need to know what Bradley was doing in Florida."

Static hummed on the line.

"Jim?"

He heaved in a deep breath but remained silent. She was about ready to hang up when he finally spoke. "Did he find you?"

Technically he had, she supposed, since he did go into the café for breakfast. "Yes."

"Did you give him what he needed?"

If he knew she had no idea what he was talking about, he'd probably hang up and she'd lose her opportunity to find out what was going on. "He didn't get a chance to tell me what he needed." *True enough.*

"Look, Gia, is there something I can do for you? I'm a busy man."

Yeah right. The guy spent his days in the gym and his nights blowing his trust fund making the nightclub rounds. "I need to know what Bradley was doing in Florida."

"What do you mean was? He left?"

Not exactly. "I'm sorry, Jim. Bradley was killed."

His breathing turned ragged and harsh. "What?"

"He was murdered and left in the dumpster behind my café. Please, Jim, is there anything you can tell me about what he was doing here?"

"Ah, man…"

He seemed more resigned than surprised, almost as if he'd expected the news. Obviously, Jim knew more than she did. No surprise there.

She waited, giving him a moment to collect himself. She'd never cared much for Jim, but he and Bradley were as close as brothers. Gia had no doubt Jim had been involved in whatever schemes Bradley had cooked up, but Bradley had never ratted him out. Even though he'd allowed her to be dragged through the mud with him, he'd kept Jim out of everything.

"I can't tell you anything."

"Can't? Or won't?"

"Same difference. But whatever he was doing there, it obviously got him killed. If Bradley is dead, someone will probably contact you and ask you to hand over the information he left with you. Do yourself a favor, Gia; hand everything over and then stay out of it, before you end up in a dumpster somewhere too."

"But I—"

He disconnected before she could finish her protest.

"Don't know what he left me," she finished over the dead line. She replayed his words. An innocent warning from a paranoid man? Or something more sinister? Because the more his words played over and over in her mind, the more they sounded like a threat.

She resisted the urge to hurl the phone across the room and searched through her contacts again. She hit Rabinowitz's number, asked his receptionist to patch her through, and waited. His voice mail picked up and she left a message: "This is Gia Morelli. It's urgent that I get in touch with you. Please, call me back." She rattled off her number and disconnected. Fat chance she'd ever hear from him.

She sighed and returned to her contact list. Bree Mathers. Gia had been friends with Bree at one time, and Bree and Bradley had always been close. Too close, though he'd sworn up and down they were only friends. Until it came out at the trial that they'd been involved for years.

Her finger lingered over her name, but she couldn't bring herself to press the button. Whatever Bradley was involved in, she wasn't desperate enough to call Bree to find out. Soon, maybe, but not just yet. There had to be a better way.

She padded to the bathroom, grateful she'd put everything away the night before. At least one small segment of her life held some sort of order. As she leaned over and turned on the shower, she rubbed a knot in her lower back. With any luck at all, which seemed highly unlikely lately, the hot water should ease the worst of the aches and pains. A couple of Ibuprofen should take care of the rest.

Leaving the water running, she started to open the medicine cabinet, but stopped when she caught her reflection in the mirror. Dark circles ringed her eyes, dulling the usually bright blue irises. She ran her fingers over her cheek bones. She'd always been thin, but her cheeks had taken on a hollow look she'd never noticed before. Even her dark brown hair, usually full of body thanks to its natural curls, hung in limp strands. With a sigh, she turned away, then quickly stripped off her pajamas and stepped under the hot spray.

Bradley had taken so much from her. She'd been forced to give up a job she'd enjoyed, customers she'd known for years. One by one her friends had abandoned her, some believing she'd known what Bradley was involved in, others unable to deal with the fallout. Not that she blamed them. The constant barrage of questions from reporters, the irate victims, the death threats…

She wet her hair, then shifted it over her shoulder and moaned when the hot spray pulsed against the tension in her neck. She had to stop thinking about the past. This was her opportunity to move beyond all of that. Thanks to Savannah, the one friend who'd stuck by her side through everything.

Maybe she should ignore her initial urge to run back home. What was left for her there anyway? Even with Bradley gone, perhaps she should stay in Florida and start a new life, somewhere people didn't stare at her with anger blazing in their eyes...or pity.

Giving up on any hope of relaxation, she hurried through her shower, then dried off, wrapped a towel around her hair, and slid into her silk robe. She'd make coffee, then get dressed and start sorting through boxes. At least then the day wouldn't be a total waste. Leaving the bathroom door open to get rid of the steam, she headed toward the kitchen.

Suddenly, a man's voice drifted down the hallway.

She stopped dead in her tracks. She couldn't make out what he was saying, just the deep timbre of his voice, followed by...a woman's laughter? Had she left something on? Impossible. She hadn't unpacked anything yet, and as far as she knew, the cable hadn't even been turned on.

She cinched the belt on her robe tighter and crept down the hallway. She had no idea what she'd do when she got to the kitchen, where the voices seemed to be coming from, but no way was she dialing 911 again unless she knew she was in danger. The last thing she needed was Detective Tall, Dark, and Dangerous banging on her door.

"Well, you still should have called me." There was no mistaking Savannah's voice, or the not-so-veiled reprimand it held.

Gia smiled. Someone was on Savannah's bad side. She almost felt sorry for whoever it was; then she walked through the kitchen doorway and stopped short.

"I did call you." Detective Quinn leaned against her kitchen counter, arms folded across his chest, smug expression firmly in place.

Savannah propped her hands on her hips and snorted.

Gia tamped down the small spark of pity that started to flare. He'd obviously done something to earn Savannah's wrath. Let him deal with the consequences. He probably deserved them.

"Well, you should have called me last—" Her eyes widened when she spotted Gia, and she cut her rant short.

Too bad. She would have enjoyed watching Savannah take him down a peg.

"Are you all right?" Savannah hurried toward Gia. "Hunt told me what happened. This morning, of course, since no one bothered to call me last night."

Uh oh. It wasn't quite as much fun being on the receiving end of Savannah's tirade, so she cut her off before she could even get started.

"I'm sorry, Savannah. I didn't want to bother you, and I was fine. Really. I was so exhausted, and I just wanted to get some rest."

"I know, honey. I'm sorry things didn't start out so well, but I think you'll love Florida once things settle down." She caught her bottom lip between her teeth, a sure sign she was worried about something.

"I'm sure I will." Gia smiled. No sense bringing up the notion of moving back to New York just then. Savannah had worked too hard to help her get where she was for her to bail as soon as things got a little rough. She'd made it through worse. Besides, moving to Florida hadn't caused her problems. Truth be told, her problems had followed her from New York. Well...problem, anyway. Bradley Remington had been nothing but one big problem for the past year.

"I thought you might need this." Savannah held up a large coffee cup, then looked around the kitchen and frowned. "I didn't expect you to have so much unpacked."

"I know. After the police left, I couldn't sleep. I thought maybe if I could get the house organized, I'd feel better. More in control." She looked around the cluttered kitchen. Instead of organization, she'd ended up with a mish mash of kitchen stuff all over the place.

"Oh, sweetie." Savannah handed her the coffee and rubbed a hand up and down Gia's arm. "Things'll work out. They always do."

As much as she wanted to believe that, it just didn't ring true. Hoping Savannah would drop the subject, Gia took a sip of the lukewarm coffee to avoid answering. She peered over the rim at Detective Quinn.

His good-natured smirk had been replaced by a frown. His shoulders rounded slightly.

Okay, something was going on. First Savannah acting all motherly, and then Hunt seemed to be shouldering some heavy burden. "Is something wrong?"

Savannah's gaze darted to her cousin.

Gia's patience had worn thin. "Okay, whatever it is, spill it."

"Uh..." Savannah never had been good at dealing with bad news. Her sunny disposition and upbeat personality weren't compatible with stress, so she chose to ignore sadness more often than not. "Well..." She winced.

"Why don't you sit down?" Hunt lifted a blender from the table, then looked around for somewhere to put it before finally wedging it between a stack of plates and a half-filled box on the counter. He pulled out a chair and gestured for her to sit.

"What happened?"

Ignoring Gia's question, Hunt pulled out a chair for Savannah.

She sat next to Gia and took her hand. "It'll be all right."

"What will?" Gia barely resisted the urge to pull her hand away, knowing it would hurt Savannah but desperately needing to distance herself to deal with any more bad news.

"We found this in your mailbox." Hunt picked up a clear plastic bag from the counter and handed it to her.

The sheet of white printer paper and the blocky black lettering brought an immediate wave of panic, but she tamped it down. She didn't need to read the all-too-familiar words to know what they said. *Hand it over or you and everyone close to you will die.* She'd been dealing with the same death threats for months. She handed the bag back to him.

"You don't seem surprised," Hunt said.

What could she say? She didn't trust Detective Quinn, but she did trust Savannah, and she seemed to trust him. Still, there was no way she was sharing the intimate and nasty details of her divorce with a stranger, no matter who he was. Or how much Savannah trusted him.

"I take it this isn't the first threat you've received."

She couldn't think with him hovering over her. "No."

Savannah squeezed her hand. "Why didn't you say anything to me?"

"I'm sorry, Savannah. I didn't want to burden you with all of this. Besides, I reported it to the police in New York, and they didn't seem too concerned."

Hunt inserted himself between Savannah and Gia, then leaned over, propping one hand on the table and one on the back of Gia's chair. "Did anyone break into your apartment in New York?"

"Not exactly..." *Well, sort of.* "But there were other incidents."

"Like?" Damp tendrils of thick, dark hair curled over his collar. The woodsy scent of his aftershave enveloped her, fogging her brain. Boy, this guy was not going to let this go, and he needed to back up.

She launched herself from the chair, and he jerked back. When the chair crashed to the floor, Gia jumped, then pressed a hand against her chest.

Hunt righted the chair without ever taking his gaze from hers.

She backed up until she hit the counter, then stopped and folded her arms. Maybe if she just answered him, he'd leave her alone. Then again, if he knew the truth, he might not let Savannah anywhere near her. That would probably be safest for Savannah anyway. Defeated, she sighed. "People showing up at my apartment at all hours, pounding on the door, screaming obscenities. I had to change my home phone number three times before I finally gave up and just had it disconnected. Some of them even showed up at my job." She lowered her gaze. If his powers of observation matched his tenacity, there's no way he'd miss the hurt in her eyes. "And then came the letters."

"Like this one?"

She nodded, careful to keep her gaze averted. "Exactly like that one. My boss let me go when one of them showed up in my locker at work, said he couldn't compromise the safety of his workers by keeping me." *No matter how much he liked me or how long I'd been there.*

Hunt took his notepad from his pocket and sat at the table, then started frantically scribbling notes.

Without him right in her face, the dark intensity of his gaze boring through her, some of the tension seeped from her rigid muscles.

"Was that the last letter you received?"

"Huh?"

"The letter left in your locker, was that the last one you received?"

"Um…no. I wasn't supposed to leave New York until late Saturday night. I had a million errands to run on Friday, so I was out all day. When I went to get ready for bed that night"—at least, ready to slip into the sleeping bag that had served as her bed once she'd shipped all of the furniture to Florida—"there was a note just like that one taped to my bathroom mirror."

Hunt stopped writing and glanced up at her.

"I called the police." She left out the heart-wrenching fear that had all but consumed her while she'd waited for them to arrive. Tears leaked out and rolled down her cheeks. She couldn't help it. That had been her breaking moment, the instant she'd known she couldn't take any more, had to get out of there and start over. The moment she'd fled. "They couldn't find any sign of forced entry, at either the apartment or the deli, yet someone had managed to get into both places without leaving as much as a single clue. So, technically, I guess no one broke in, but someone did get in. Somehow."

Savannah leaned against the counter beside her and wrapped an arm around Gia's waist.

As much as she wanted to lean on her friend, she stood straighter. Everyone she'd known in New York had abandoned her, but Savannah had stood by her side, refusing to give up on their friendship, refusing to give up on her. And now she was in danger just because she was close to Gia. Her tears flowed heavier. "As soon as the detectives left, I threw the rest of my stuff in a bag and went straight to the airport. I sat there the rest of the night. Thankfully, there was an open seat on the first flight out that morning, so I took it."

"Come sit down, honey." Savannah took her elbow and tried to lead her toward the table.

Gia yanked her arm away. "Don't you get it, Savannah? You're in danger now. Because of me. You have to get out of here. Stay far away from me." Tears shimmered in Savannah's eyes. "I'm your friend, Gia. I'm not leaving you."

"You have to. I couldn't take it if anything happened to you. You are my best friend. I'm so sorry. I thought if I left New York, everyone I cared about would be safe. I never in a million years thought someone would follow me here," she finished on a sob.

A strong arm encircled her shoulders, and Hunt held out a paper towel. "Calm down."

"Calm down?" She whirled on him. "How can I calm down when my whole life is in shambles?"

He stepped back. "We'll figure this out. I'll talk to the detectives in New York and see what, if anything, they know about the suspect, but it would help if we knew what he was after."

Gia shook her head, grabbed the paper towel he still held, and dropped onto her chair. After wiping her face, she gulped her cool coffee, the bitter taste turning her stomach. "That's just it, I have no idea what he could possibly want. I already told you, there is no money."

"As far as you know."

"What do you mean?"

He sat down next to her. "You said you didn't know what Remington was involved in—"

"I already told you—"

He held up his hands. "I know, I know. I'm just saying, if you didn't know what he was involved in, which I completely believe, maybe he stashed money away that you don't know about."

Everything inside her stilled. She hadn't thought of that. "Is that possible? I mean, with all the investigating they did, I guess I just assumed they found everything he had."

Apparently satisfied her meltdown was over, Hunt leaned back in the chair. "Anything is possible. Did your ex leave any papers lying around?"

"Yes, boxes and boxes full."

"Where are they now?"

She looked around the cluttered kitchen. She hadn't taken the time to sort through anything while in New York. She'd just wanted to be out of there, so she'd packed up everything and shipped it all down to Florida. She figured she could sort it out when she got there. "Somewhere in this mess. I put all his belongings in a storage unit when I packed up the apartment, but all our papers were together in his home office, so I just shoved everything into boxes. But the detectives went through everything and took whatever paperwork was related to his...scheme, so I doubt there's anything to find."

Savannah laid a hand on Gia's. "Your hands are ice cold."

She squeezed Savannah's hand, then pulled hers away and dropped it into her lap. She had to distance herself from her if she was going to keep her safe, no matter how much she needed a friend just then.

"Do me a favor, Savannah?" Hunt tucked his notepad into his pocket.

"Sure, what do you need?"

"I need a few minutes alone with Gia."

She frowned at him.

"Please."

After a moment of some sort of silent communication Gia didn't understand, Savannah slid her chair back and headed for the door.

"Don't leave the house," Hunt called after her.

She waved over her shoulder as she walked out.

Great. Just throw me to the wolf. Some friend...

Chapter 7

With Savannah gone, the room seemed even colder, and Gia clasped her hands together and slid them between her knees for warmth.

"You know, Savannah and I have always been close. She was closer to me than she was with any of her five brothers, since we didn't bicker the way they did," Hunt started.

"I know. I remember her mentioning her cousin a few times, but I didn't realize you were that cousin. She said you gave her a really hard time when she wanted to move to New York."

When he grinned, a small dimple creased his cheek, erasing some of the hard edges his expression usually held. "Yeah, I guess you could say I wasn't too happy about it."

She tilted her head and lifted a brow.

His laughter filled the kitchen. "All right, all right. But Savannah was the only girl in a big family full of boys, and we might have been a little over protective. But in my defense, Savannah was…delicate. I don't know what she's told you about her past…"

"To be honest, not much." Surprisingly little considering they'd lived together for five years.

"Well, that's her story to tell, but I will say, Savannah was sensitive, and kind, and…naïve. I wanted to keep her here, where I could look out for her." He leaned forward, folding his arms and resting them on the table. His genuine affection for his cousin softened his features.

"That's understandable."

"But Savannah is also stubborn and determined. She was dead set on trying to make it on Broadway before she settled down and started a family."

Gia did know that much. Savannah had set a five-year limit. If she couldn't reach her goals within five years, she'd return home and move on. "She's also smart, and she knows what she wants and she sets goals and strives to achieve them. That's a good thing."

"Sometimes," he conceded. "But when she first moved up there, she was staying in an apartment with a bunch of dancers. They all worked other jobs in addition to their shows, and some partied, a lot, so they came and went at all hours of the night. She was always nervous something would happen and no one would notice she was missing, so I used to make her text me when she got home at night, just so I could make sure she was safe."

"She never told me that."

He shoved a hand through his hair. "Then one night, she didn't text me. Do you have any idea how frantic I was?"

She shook her head. She could only imagine the panic he must have felt more than a thousand miles away and unable to even look for her.

"By the time she called me the next morning, her brothers and I already had a flight booked."

Gia laughed. Somehow, that didn't surprise her.

"After she apologized up and down, she told me she was no longer living in that place. She had moved in with another woman who worked in a deli. That night, she'd gotten in late and had been exhausted. She fell asleep on the couch before she'd remembered to text me."

Savannah and Gia used to do that a lot, curl up in blankets on the couch with a bucket of popcorn between them and an old movie, and they often fell asleep before it ended.

"She said you waited up for her at night, even though you had to be up at four o'clock every morning for work." He studied her for a long moment, but she couldn't read anything in his expression, so she just waited. "She stopped texting me every night then, because she felt safe. You made her feel safe. That's what family does. They take care of each other."

Tears rolled down her cheeks, and she used the crumpled paper towel to wipe them away.

"I don't know if you even realize how much you did for her, or if you know how much it meant to her. Because of you, she was able to do what she wanted to do. You are family, Gia. Savannah is not going to back off." He huffed out a breath and sat back. "So the only way to keep her safe is to find out what's going on and end it. Now. But to do that, you have to cooperate with me. You have to trust me."

She'd never given much thought to how scary it must have been for Savannah, going somewhere new, where she didn't know anyone. At least, when Gia had agreed to move to Florida, she already knew Savannah, already had a friend. Her respect for her friend's courage and determination increased, but she still didn't know if she could let down her guard enough to trust Hunt, or anyone else for that matter. But she would try. For Savannah. Unable to speak without the tear-fest starting again, she simply nodded.

"Good. Now, go get dressed. You are making it almost impossible for me to concentrate." He wiggled his eyebrows suggestively.

Gia looked down at her robe, the silk fabric clinging to her. How could she have forgotten she wasn't dressed? Her cheeks flamed hot as she pulled the robe closed tighter.

Hunt only laughed as he slid his chair back and stood. "Savannah said she's taking you to the shelter this morning to pick out a dog. Let me know when you're ready, and Leo will follow you both over there while I see what I can find out from the detectives in New York."

* * * *

After throwing on a pair of jeans and a long-sleeve T-shirt, since her shorts were still buried in a box somewhere, Gia pulled her hair into a knot at the back of her head and headed for the shelter with Savannah.

Savannah hadn't asked what Hunt wanted to talk to her about, so Gia hadn't mentioned anything about their conversation.

She checked the passenger side mirror, again. Yup. Leo was still back there, following right on their bumper.

"So, how do you like it out here?" Savannah asked.

Gia hadn't had much time to appreciate the scenery, but she took a moment to look around before answering. The Rolling Pines development she now called home, at least for the time being, consisted of almost a thousand one acre lots, only about half of which had been built on. That left a lot of undeveloped land.

Huge evergreen trees towered over shorter palm trees. Smaller, fan-shaped palm bushes and what looked to Gia like cactuses—though she was no expert on plants, having grown up in the heart of New York City—crowded the lots. Silence, but for the soft hum of their tires against the pavement, surrounded them.

"I'm not sure. It's gorgeous, for sure, but I have to admit, the quiet is a bit unnerving."

Savannah laughed. "Imagine how it felt for me moving to New York. Horns blaring at all hours of the day and night, people yelling, sirens, music, the constant, steady stream of traffic. I don't think I slept for the first few months I was there. Too much noise. But I got used to it."

Point made. "I'm sure I will too. I do love it. I just wish my past hadn't followed me."

"Don't worry. Hunt will figure it out. He's nothing if not persistent."

That I can believe.

"Here we are." She pointed toward a hand-painted sign nailed to a stake in the ground that read: *Give a pet a home.* Even though there wasn't a car around for miles, except for Leo, who knew exactly where they were going, Savannah hit the turn signal, then turned onto a narrow dirt road.

Sweat slicked Gia's hands. "Are you sure this is a good idea? I've never owned a pet before. Not even a fish."

"Well, a fish isn't going to scare off an intruder, so you'll have to settle for a dog." Laughter danced in Savannah's eyes.

"You're enjoying this a little too much," Gia muttered as they pulled into the gravel parking lot.

Savannah laughed out loud. "Oh, come on. I love looking at puppies. Sometimes I come out here and just play with them for a little while. I always feel so bad leaving them here."

"So, why don't you get a dog?"

"Because we already have four, and if I come home with another one, my dad just might throw me out to make room." She scrunched her nose. "Of course, if I could get him to throw Joey out instead…"

Ignoring her, Gia got out of the car and looked around at the sprawling white ranch. Four dogs? What on earth would anyone do with four dogs? The thought of one dog was making her heart race a little too fast for comfort.

Savannah came up beside her and hooked her arm through Gia's. "It's gonna be fine. I promise. You're going to pick out the perfect dog, and before you know it, he'll be your best friend."

"We'll see about that." The instant she stepped through the front door, the air conditioning raised goose bumps on her arms.

"Hi, Debby." Savannah greeted the woman behind the counter with a big smile.

"Hey there, Savannah. Did y'all come in to play with the puppies? We got a bunch of new ones in from that puppy mill they shut down last week."

"I brought my friend, Gia, in to pick out a puppy. She just moved into the area."

"Oh, yeah? Where to?"

"Rolling Pines."

"Beautiful up there. And some of my best customers." She turned to Gia. "How many pups you looking for?"

"Uh…" Was she serious?

Good thing Savannah was there to answer for her. "Just one for now."

For now?

"Come on back and take a look. See if anything tickles your fancy." She held open a swinging half-door for them, then gestured toward another door behind the counter.

The tinkle of a bell stopped Debby short as the front door swung open and a delivery man walked in.

"You go on ahead, Savannah. I'll be back as soon as I take care of this." She held the door for them. "Just make sure you sanitize your hands before handling any of the pups."

Handling? Fat chance. Sweat broke out on Gia's forehead. Maybe she wasn't cut out for dog ownership.

Gia stayed close to Savannah as she walked through the door and into the kennel.

Several rows of baby cribs filled the large space, more than half of them filled with bouncing, barking puppies.

A tiny ball of fluff, no bigger than a football, chirped as he jumped up and down against the crib bars.

"Aww! How cute is he!" Gia reached in, tentative at first, but then the little pup curled against her hand, and she scooped him up and petted his tiny head with her finger.

Savannah's eyes widened. "You can't possibly be serious."

"What?" Gia feigned innocence.

"He's adorable, but what in the world is he going to do if someone breaks in?"

"Weell…"

"If you decide you want a second dog, he's perfect. For now, look for something bigger."

Gia played with him a few more minutes, then returned him to his crib and wandered through the room, randomly petting dogs that poked their heads up to study her.

Savannah picked up pup after pup, squealing each time they squirmed around to lick her face. She was definitely a natural when it came to puppies.

Gia was sure she'd never be quite that comfortable in a roomful of barking, nipping puppies. Although, the idea of picking out her own puppy and taking him home with her had begun to appeal. The more she weaved between the cribs, looking into big hopeful eyes, the more she wanted. *Uh oh.* Winding up with more than one of these sweet creatures suddenly made perfect sense. Time to pick something out and get out of there before she ended up with a houseful.

A big pup flopped his head over the side rail of the crib next to her, startling her from thoughts better left untouched. A mane of black fur surrounded his head, and his paws looked too big for his body. The fat ball of fur looked more like a bear than a dog.

She slid her fingers into his soft mane. "How about this one?"

Savannah ran over and checked a card at the bottom of the crib. "A Tibetan Mastiff." She caught his face between her hands and rubbed his ears with her fingers. "Oh, he's adorable."

"How big do you think he'll get?"

"I don't know, but we can check. There's a computer in the corner." She headed toward the far corner, where an ancient desktop sat atop a scarred wooden desk.

Gia started to follow, still carrying the dog, but he squirmed and twisted, then launched himself from her arms and landed on the floor. After a moment of scrambling for purchase on the slick tile, he darted for the door.

"Oh, no you don't." Debby blocked his path before he could get free. She scooped him up and carried him back to the pen with an ease Gia envied, then plopped him back into the crib.

"Sorry." Maybe she needed something a little smaller.

Debby laughed. "Don't worry about it. They escape all the time. That's why we have the half-door. Keeps 'em from going too far. Lawd knows I ain't chasing these things all over creation."

"So, do you know how big he'll get?"

They started toward Savannah. "That boy'll reach a hundred fifty pounds easy."

"A hundred fifty pounds? That's more than I weigh." *Give or take.*

Savannah clicked *images,* and rows of Tibetan Mastiffs popped up. The first showed a full grown dog, mid-lunge, dagger-like fangs bared, a long line of drool hanging from his mouth.

"Oh!" Gia jumped back. That pudgy little fur ball would turn into a demon. "No. Oh, no, no. That is not going to work."

Debby laughed. "With plenty of love and proper training, he'll grow up into a sweetheart. That said, I don't think a Mastiff is what you're looking for. They can be stubborn and difficult to train, not the right combination for a first-timer."

The statement caught Gia off-guard. Was it that obvious she had no clue what she was doing? "How'd you know?"

She waved a hand. "Don't look so shocked. Nothing supernatural, I assure you. Savannah told me she was bringing a friend by last week, and she mentioned you've never owned a dog before. Now let's see if we can find you something a little less..."

"Yes. Definitely a little less."

"I'm sure we can find something in between the two you've picked out so far." Savannah winked, then headed off through the rows.

"Everything's between the two I picked out so far." She turned to Debby. "Do you have something that's good with kids?"

Savannah gasped and stared at her, eyes wide.

"Oh, knock it off. A girl can hope." She grinned. "Who knows? Dogs live more than ten years. Maybe in that time, I'll come across Mr. Right." Probably not, considering she'd most likely never trust another man, but a girl could fantasize. Besides she never thought she'd own a dog either. "Stranger things have happened."

Savannah snorted and went back to looking at puppies.

"What do you think of this fella?" Debby held out a furry black puppy with white and rust-colored markings.

Gia petted the side of his head, as she'd seen Savannah do, and the little guy tilted his head into her hand and peered up at her, a plea for love beaming from his big, brown eyes. "Oh, my. He's perfect."

Debby handed him over and went to the computer.

He nuzzled against Gia, then dropped his head against her like a baby. She petted the white fur on his belly, and he wrapped his paws around her wrist. "Oh, please tell me this boy doesn't grow up to be Cujo."

"Nope." Debby pointed at the screen.

The first picture showed a full grown black dog with a strip of white between his eyes and down his nose, rust fur ringing his eyes, rust and white paws, and a white belly, a bigger version of the cutie lying there hugging her arm. The dog in the picture lay on the floor, a toddler snuggled up against him, using his side for a pillow. "What kind of dog is he?"

"A Bernese Mountain Dog. I think you should be able to handle him, though I do suggest training."

"Oh, definitely. Do you know anywhere I can have him trained?"

"We offer classes here a few times a week. The information will be in the adoption packet along with everything else you'll need to know."

Hope flared. "You mean they come with an instruction manual of sorts?"

"Not exactly." Debby grinned. "Want to take him out back and play with him."

Savannah's squeal was all the answer Debby needed.

She opened the back door and led them into a fenced pen.

Gia reluctantly set the pup down.

He immediately took off, bouncing around the pen, running this way and that. He grabbed a squeaky toy and brought it to Gia.

As she started to squat down, a chill raced up her spine. She stood and scanned the woods surrounding the clearing. Nothing she could see, but then again, the underbrush was extremely thick, and large trees provided more than ample hiding places. Should she go out front and get Leo?

The puppy stopped frolicking and stood beside her, alert and wary, but not barking or threatened, just watchful. Of course, he was just a baby, but still. He was probably just reacting to her getting spooked, not any impending sense of danger.

She lifted him back into her arms and hugged him close, desperate to get in out of the heat and whatever else might be out there. "What do I have to do?"

"You want him?" Debby asked.

"Yay." Savannah clapped her hands together, then caught Gia's gaze and froze. She frowned and looked around before leading Debby inside.

The pup nuzzled Gia's neck, then licked her face.

With one final scan of the woods, she backed toward the door. Her imagination was probably just playing tricks on her. She wiped the sweat from her face. Either that, or it was heat stroke.

Chapter 8

"Now what?" Gia stood beside the car holding her wriggling new pup, on the verge of a full-blown panic attack.

Savannah patted the pup's head. "Now we go to the pet supply store."

"I don't even know what I need."

"Don't worry about it. I do."

Leo approached them, his grin stretching from ear to ear. "Will you look at him?"

Gia turned so he could pet her new pup. Hmm... He was going to need a name.

"He sure is a sweet little fella."

"He is, isn't he?" Should she say anything about the weird feeling she'd had out back? Most likely, her mind was just playing tricks on her. If Leo had seen anything out of the ordinary, surely he wouldn't be standing there playing with a puppy. She shook off her unease.

Leo's gaze darted around. He didn't seem alarmed, or even concerned, just cautious. "So, where are we headed? Pet supply, I'm assuming?"

Why was it everyone seemed to know what to do but her? She was going to have to get better at this pet parent thing. "And I have to call the vet for an appointment. Do you know a good one?"

"We've been using Doc Ames forever. He's the best. I'll give him a call for you when we get back to the house," Savannah offered, then opened the driver's door, got in, and turned on the car.

"Thanks." Gia waved to Leo, rounded the car, and slipped into the passenger side with her new bundle in her lap. The warm seat and stifling interior chased away some of the chill the incident in the yard had left her with. She started to buckle the seat belt, but burned her hand on the buckle. "Ouch."

"Gotta be careful when you first get in, especially if the car's been sitting in the hot sun."

Savannah adjusted the air conditioning vents, buckled her seat belt, and shifted into reverse, then paused. "Everything okay?"

Gia forced a smile. "Sure, why wouldn't it be?"

"I don't know. You seemed a little creeped out back there."

She didn't want to worry her friend, but at the same time, she did want her to be careful. "I get a weird sensation sometimes, like someone is watching me, but when I turn around, no one is there. I'm sure it's nothing, but—"

Without a word, Savannah shifted into park and got out.

"Hey, where are you—"

She slammed the door behind her and stalked toward Leo's car. After leaning into the window and talking to him for a minute, she returned to the car.

"What was that all about?"

"Leo's there for a reason. Obviously, Hunt thinks you might be in danger, or he wouldn't have someone keeping an eye on you. You have to tell him everything, or he can't protect you." Her voice held a bit of reproach, and Gia didn't bother to argue. Savannah was probably right.

She started down the narrow dirt driveway.

"So, what do you think I should name him?" Gia held his face between her hands and scratched beneath his ears.

Savannah glanced at the puppy before she hit the turn signal and pulled out onto the two-lane road. "He looks like a bear cub."

"Kind of."

"How about Grizzly?"

Gia studied the pup's features, his round body, his chunky paws, those huge brown eyes. "I don't know. He doesn't seem like a Grizzly to me. More like a teddy bear."

"So, how about Teddy?"

It still didn't seem quite right. She remembered how he'd stilled in the pen when she'd gotten nervous. He'd stood so straight, so proud. Protective. She could almost imagine him standing with his hands on his hips, his cape billowing in the wind behind him. Of course, since arriving in central Florida, she hadn't even witnessed enough of a breeze to ripple his cape, but still… "How about a superhero name?"

Savannah laughed. "The only superheroes I know are Batman and Superman, and I doubt you want to open your back door and yell either of those." She was quiet for a moment. "Oh, and Thor. And I only know Thor because Chris Hemsworth played him in those movies, and mmm… mmm did that boy look fine with long hair."

"Honey, that boy looks fine with anything."

"Ain't that the truth."

Gia laughed with her. It had been too long since she'd experienced the simple joy of being with a friend, laughing, being silly. Her recent short jaunts to Florida had been filled with nothing but work…and fear of both the unknown and the known. She shook off the darkness trying to encroach on her happiness. "Thor it is, then."

When Savannah didn't respond, Gia tore her gaze from her puppy and glanced over at her.

Savannah's gaze darted between the rear view and the side view mirrors, with an occasional glance at the road in front of her. Her eyes narrowed in concentration, her bottom lip held between her teeth, tight enough to draw a spot of blood.

Gia whirled around. The seatbelt tightened against her chest, jerking her to a halt. She sat back, then turned slowly to look over her shoulder. Thankfully, the seatbelt released her. "What's wrong?"

"See the white car coming up behind Leo?"

A white car barreled up the rural road, not slowing at all as it approached the back of the patrol car. "Yeah."

"Sit back, and hold on to the puppy."

Gia tightened her hold. Eyes glued to the mirror on her side, she watched the car continue until it was so close to Leo its hood disappeared behind the patrol car.

Leo held something in front of his mouth. Calling for backup? Maybe. They'd better arrive in a hurry.

She couldn't make out the driver of the white car at all, not even enough to tell if it was a man or a woman.

The car jerked suddenly to the left and whipped around Leo's car as if he was standing still.

Leo hit the lights and siren.

But the driver continued on the wrong side of the road as they rounded a curve. If he moved even an inch to the right, he'd side swipe them and push them off the road into the swampy underbrush.

Gia hoped the water wasn't too deep. And that there were no alligators lurking nearby.

Savannah kept the car straight, her hands rock steady on the wheel.

Gia's hands trembled violently as she hugged Thor closer and made soothing sounds.

When the car finally pulled even with theirs, Savannah's profile reflected back at them from the darkly tinted windows.

Savannah slammed on the brakes.

The other car rocketed past as Leo's brakes screeched behind them.

Savannah pulled toward the grassy shoulder, slid a little on a strip of loose gravel, then stopped abruptly.

The patrol car skidded to a stop beside them, narrowly avoiding their back bumper.

Thor whimpered in her arms, and she loosened her hold. "I'm sorry, boy. Are you okay?"

Savannah blew out a breath and lowered her forehead onto the steering wheel without releasing her white-knuckled death grip.

A knock on the driver's side window made both of them jump. Leo whipped open the door. "Are you all right?"

Gia nodded. "He's getting away. Why aren't you going after him?"

"My job is to protect you. Period. There are other officers up ahead who will hopefully be able to stop him. Are either of you hurt?"

"No. I don't think so." She examined Thor, but he seemed okay.

"I'm fine, just a little shaken." Savannah's usually tan, glowing face had paled. Lines creased her brow. "Is the pup okay?"

Thor looked back and forth between them. He appeared more confused than anything. "I think he's fine. But we have to bring him back."

"What?" Leo and Savannah said in unison.

"How can I keep him when he is in danger just by being close to me?" she screamed, half hysterical. "Everyone is. Everyone who comes near me." No matter what Hunt said about family, she couldn't continue to endanger the people she loved.

"All right. Calm down." Leo lifted his hands as if in surrender, but the look of sheer panic in his eyes gave him away. He'd obviously never dealt with a hysterical woman before.

"Calm down? Calm down? Seriously? That's the best you can do?"

He'd also never read the top ten list of things never to say to a hysterical woman.

"Uhh…" He glanced at Savannah, but she sat staring open-mouthed at Gia. He wasn't going to get any help there.

The crunch of tires against gravel saved him having to come up with anything better as an olive-green jeep pulled over behind them. Hunt climbed out and strode toward them.

Savannah dove from the car, practically knocking Leo out of the way, and ran to Hunt. She threw her arms around his waist.

Gia climbed out of the car and watched them, stifling the small surge of envy that started to flare. She'd never had siblings or even cousins. Her mother had died when she was young, and her father had tossed her out the day she graduated high school. She'd never had someone who cared enough to wait up until she got home. Never had someone who'd book a flight only hours after not hearing from her. Until Savannah.

Hunt hugged Savannah close, staring hard at Gia over her head.

Gia started toward them. Tears streamed down her cheeks, but she made no move to wipe them away. She owed both an apology, and afterward, she'd head back to New York where she belonged. These people didn't deserve what she'd brought on them. Neither did the innocent puppy in her arms.

When she almost reached them, she stopped.

Hunt opened one arm and gestured her toward him.

Crying softly, she slid into his embrace beside Savannah, cradling Thor between them.

"Are you okay?" he asked softly.

She nodded against his chest. "Just scared."

"All right." He set them both back and examined them. Apparently satisfied they weren't lying about being hurt, he propped his hands on his hips. "Who wants to tell me what happened?"

"It's my fault. I'm sorry. I didn't mean to cause all this trouble," Gia said.

He held up a hand to stem the nervous rush of words. "We have no way to know this had anything to do with you. It could just as easily have been a reckless driver. Someone who drank a little too much or took Daddy's car for a joyride."

She met his stare without flinching. "You don't believe that."

"No. But that doesn't mean it's not true."

"But it's also not likely."

He pursed his lips. "No. It's not likely."

"Did they catch him?" She already knew the answer. No way would Hunt be standing on the side of the road chatting with them if they had a suspect in custody.

"They already found the car abandoned in a bar parking lot a few miles up the road. A rental."

"Can you find out who rented it?"

"Maybe. If they were stupid enough to use their real ID."

Gia sighed. They all knew how likely that was. Not very. "So what now?"

"Now, Leo takes Savannah home, and I take you to the pet supply store."

"Hunt, I can't ask you to—"

"You didn't ask. I offered. Now, get what you need from Savannah's car, and I'll have a deputy pick it up and drive it home for her."

She wanted to argue on principle alone. Who did he think he was, flipping orders like she was one of his men? Then again, she was grateful for his help, and Savannah wouldn't agree to go home if it meant leaving Gia alone. So she'd do as he'd ordered. This time. But he'd better not get too used to it. "Will you be all right, Savannah?"

"I'll be fine." She smiled, but tears still swam in her blue eyes. "Nothing a hot bath and a cup of tea won't fix."

"It was a good thing you were driving." With public transportation in New York readily available at all hours, Gia had never had much need to drive. She'd learned to drive in high school and gotten her driver's license, but she didn't have a lot of experience. They probably would have wound up in the swampy ditch at the side of the road or wrapped around a tree if she'd been behind the wheel. She hugged Savannah. "Thank you."

"I'll meet up with you later." She petted Thor's head, then retrieved her bag from the car and handed Leo her keys. When she turned and saw Gia still watching her, she waved, before climbing into Leo's car.

Gia waved back, then spun on Hunt and pinned him with a glare meant to intimidate.

If the cocky smirk on his face was any indication, her death stare only amused him.

"Look, Detective Quinn, I understand what you said before, about family and all, and I appreciate the sentiment, but I can't keep doing this. I don't know about you, and I don't have the experience you have with family, but I don't put the people I love in danger." She turned and walked away from him, hugging Thor closer and scanning the empty stretch of road for any more threats. Let him think about that for a bit, because she was going to distance herself from Savannah, no matter what Detective Tall, Dark, and Sexy thought.

She leaned into the car and grabbed her bag and the envelope with Thor's paperwork. She had no choice but to go with him, unless she wanted to walk, which didn't appeal at all, but it was time to lay down some ground rules. She stood and slammed the door, then turned and ran straight into a rock-hard chest.

No trace of amusement lingered in Hunt's hard expression. "You look, Ms. Morelli, Savannah is already in danger. If this incident was related to your troubles, the perpetrator already knows about Savannah, and she may or may not be a target. You can't change that. What you can do, is work with me to end this as quickly as possible. That will solve everything, and you and Savannah will both be out of danger. All right?"

Fair enough. She didn't have to put all her trust in him, not like they were dating or anything, but she would cooperate as best she could. Problem was, she didn't know anything, and no one seemed to believe that, the good guys or the bad guys.

Jim's words played over in her head again. Gia might not know anything, but it certainly seemed Jim Harte knew more than he was letting on.

"I made a phone call this morning," she blurted before she could change her mind.

He needed to back up, but he didn't budge.

"I called Bradley's best friend. His name is Jim Harte. He told me now that Bradley was dead, someone would probably contact me for whatever he left with me. He said if I didn't hand it over, I'd probably end up dead in a dumpster too." She stopped short of accusing him of threatening her. She couldn't be sure he'd meant it to intimidate, though she was sure it wasn't meant as friendly advice.

"What did he leave with you?"

"That's just it, as far as I know, nothing."

"All right. I'll look into it. In the meantime…" He leaned closer, crowding her against the car, scorching heat radiating from him. Or maybe the heat came from the hot Florida sun. Hard to tell. "Leave the investigating to me. No more phone calls. I mean it, Gia. Okay?"

She nodded. She wouldn't initiate any more phone calls—probably—but she couldn't help it if the lawyer called her back.

"Good. Now, get in my car."

Oh, no. His order flinging days were about to come to an end.

His smile deepened the dimple in his cheek. "And another thing, I thought I told you to call me Hunt."

Her mounting anger dwindled. When had she become so high strung that she couldn't even take a little teasing? She narrowed her eyes. "You're not the boss of me."

His grin widened. "That's what you think."

She stuck her tongue out at him. Immature, maybe, but then again, so was her last comment, but it was the best she could come up with at the moment.

He laughed and tucked her hair behind her ear, letting his fingers linger just a moment longer than necessary. Then he pressed his hand against the small of her back and led her and Thor toward his jeep. "Now, let's go get this little guy what he needs."

Chapter 9

Hunt hefted another box from the garage onto the growing pile in Gia's living room. "There has to be something in his paperwork that might give us a clue about what's going on."

They'd been at it for hours. After getting everything she needed from the pet supply store, Hunt had carried it all into the house and even put together Thor's crate. Then he'd gotten down to business. Somewhere in the mess of papers she'd shipped down from New York, there had to be a clue as to what was going on, so Hunt had started digging through the garage, opening boxes, and piling everything that contained so much as one sheet of paper in the middle of her living room.

"Yeah, well, it would help if I knew what half of this was." She tossed a stack of papers aside, stood, and stretched her arms over her head. "I need a break, and Thor has to eat dinner and go out."

Hunt studied the boxes as if something would jump out and give him answers.

Nothing did.

"You're right. We need a break. Speaking of dinner, are you hungry?"

She pressed a hand against her empty stomach. It had been rumbling for the past hour, but she hadn't wanted to give up looking for answers to go get something to eat. "I'm starved. Unfortunately, I haven't gone to the supermarket yet, so our options are limited to a few boxes of trail mix I picked up at the airport on my way down. Unless you want to share Thor's dinner."

He laughed. "That's okay. I'm hungry, but not that hungry. Why don't you take care of Thor, and I'll see what I can do about dinner."

"Good luck with that." Being that she lived in such a rural area, finding someplace that delivered wasn't likely. Weird. In New York, she could have called any number of places and gotten delivery, or at worst, she could have walked a couple of blocks in either direction and hit ten places to grab a quick bite. She was going to have to get used to keeping her kitchen stocked.

"Don't worry about it. I'll work something out."

Thor pounced on the stack of papers Gia had set aside and started chewing one corner.

"No," she corrected gently.

He glanced at her, then continued chewing.

"No." She scooped him up and headed toward the kitchen, leaving Hunt to figure out what to do about dinner. She petted the spot behind his ears that made his eyes roll back in ecstasy. "You can't eat the papers until I know what's in them, silly."

But if it belonged to her loser ex, and didn't offer any explanation about what was going on, all bets were off. Thor could munch on the stack of papers until the living room was covered in confetti.

The memory of Bradley's arm hanging out of the dumpster came unbidden, and a pang of guilt shot through her. She'd never wanted to see Bradley dead. Not really, anyway. Despite what she'd yelled at him when the prosecutor had paraded his long line of mistresses through the courtroom. Gia had found out what an unfaithful creep he was along with the rest of the world. Until then, she'd stood by his side, had at least tried to believe his claims of innocence. *Yeah right.* Bradley had played her for a fool, had taken advantage of her love for him.

She shook off thoughts of Bradley and plopped the pudgy puppy on the kitchen floor. She was supposed to start over, not get sucked back into the past.

Thor trotted along beside her as she set out a bowl of water and one of food. "Here you go, boy."

She could get used to having him with her all the time. In the few hours he'd been with her, he'd never left her side, lying against her leg on the living room floor while she'd searched through boxes, chewing one of the numerous toys she'd bought. She'd caught herself talking out loud to him more than once and wondered if that was normal. Maybe she'd finally lost it. She didn't care, though. Normal or not, Thor seemed to enjoy the sound of her voice, and she enjoyed having him to talk to.

Thor finished eating, sniffed around the side of the bowl to make sure he hadn't missed anything, then squatted by the back door.

"No." She sprinted for the door and ripped it open just as a puddle started to form beneath him. "Ugh…too slow. No, Thor. That goes outside." As soon as he was done, he bolted out the back door.

Keeping an eye on him as he frolicked on the back deck, she grabbed a handful of paper towels and bleach and quickly cleaned up the mess. As soon as she walked out the door, Thor pounced.

"Come on, boy. Want to go for a walk?" She hooked the leash to his collar and led him down the deck stairs onto the patches of grass and dirt that served as her back lawn.

He scooted backward, trying to slip out of the collar, but as soon as she started walking, he trotted at her side.

"Good boy." She inhaled deeply, sucking in hot, thick air and the scent of the forest.

Her property sat at the far edge of the development, backing up to the Ocala National Forest. Primitive looking woods surrounded her land on three sides, with about half an acre in the center cleared for her house and yard. After spending her entire life living in an apartment, the enormity of the surrounding forest overwhelmed her.

She walked along the edges of the clearing. She'd have to find out from the Homeowner's Association if she was allowed to have a fence installed. Since she hadn't expected to get a dog, she hadn't noticed what the contract stated. Truth be told, she had no clue what was in the contract. She recalled a long set of dos and don'ts, but she had only skimmed through them in her rush to sign on the dotted line. She couldn't let Thor out, though, and risk him running off into the forest.

She turned and walked along the back of the property. A giant oak tree, it's thick, gnarled branches draped with Spanish moss, blocked her view of the house. It would be a beautiful spot for a nice wicker set, maybe a love seat and a few chairs right there in the shade of the tree. She started a mental to-do list. She'd write everything down when she went inside. At least, that's what she told herself. Of course, she was probably lying.

A sudden movement beneath the tree startled her.

She squinted against the setting sun, searching the shifting shadows for whatever had caught her attention.

A black animal about as big as a medium-sized dog rolled from behind the trunk and lurched to his feet, then sauntered toward the tree line. Before he made it halfway there, a second animal dropped from a low branch and pounced on him. The two rolled across the lawn, twined together in a chubby black mass of fur.

It took a moment to register that she was watching two bear cubs playing in the middle of her yard. When it finally did, she couldn't help but laugh at their antics.

Thor barked and lunged toward them.

The sudden move caught Gia off-guard. Thankfully, the leash tightened and brought him to a halt. With a whine, he glanced up at her. It seemed Thor was looking to make friends.

"Gia." The alarm in Hunt's voice pulled her attention from the animals. He pressed a finger to his lips and waved her toward the far edge of the property, away from the bears.

She responded immediately. Picking Thor up, she skirted the edge of the tree line, keeping the bears in sight.

They'd stopped playing and stood close together, eyeing her as she moved, but making no attempt to follow.

Hunt held something in his hand as he descended the two steps from the deck to the yard, then edged toward her, his attention split between keeping an eye on the bears and scanning the yard. He breathed a sigh of relief when he reached her but guided her quickly back onto the deck.

Once they entered the kitchen, he closed the French doors and rounded on her. "Have you had any experience with bears before?"

"Seriously? I lived my whole life smack in the middle of Manhattan. Unless you count a trip to the Bronx Zoo when I was in third grade, then no." Gia petted Thor, then put him on the floor and watched out the doors as the bears bounded off into the forest. "They are adorable, though."

He stared at her as if she had ten heads. "Yes, they are, but you have to be careful. Where there are cubs, there's a mama. And you do not want to piss her off."

"Oh." Her heart hammered hard against her ribs. "I hadn't thought of that."

"This is a beautiful place to live, but there's wildlife here, and if you're not careful, you can get hurt."

Gia's experience with animals was limited to the stray cats that made their home in the alley beside the deli where she'd worked, her friend's Chihuahua, which barked incessantly but hadn't ever actually hurt anyone, even with an occasional nip, and the rats she sometimes came across in the subway. "Define wildlife."

"Bears, alligators, snakes, some poisonous—"

"Poisonous?" Her chest tightened. Her breathing turned ragged, her lungs straining for air. She gripped the counter to keep from passing out. What had she gotten herself into?

"Gia?" Hunt wrapped an arm around her and led her toward the table. He pulled out a chair and motioned for her to sit, then opened the refrigerator and closed it again without taking anything out. Probably because there was nothing in there. "Are you all right?"

She nodded, not yet able to form words.

"This house sat empty for a long time. That's why you got such a good deal on it. For the most part, bears avoid humans. You probably caught them as off-guard as they caught you." The humor in his eyes softened the reprimand.

She nodded again, beginning to regain some of her composure. "Thanks."

"Sure. You okay now?" He lifted her chin, forcing her gaze to meet his.

"I think so. I'm just a little out of my element is all. I'll get used to it." *Maybe.*

"It's not like you're going to run into something every time you walk out the door. You just have to be aware of your surroundings."

"You mean like watching for muggers?"

His deep laughter touched something in her. He had that same carefree attitude Savannah always had. An easy-going way that was as foreign to Gia as the bear cubs frolicking in her yard. "Yes. Like watching for muggers."

She offered a weak smile. "That I can do."

"Good. And always carry this with you." He held out the small canister he'd been holding when he'd come outside to rescue her.

"What is it?"

"Bear spray."

"Bear..."

"Spray. Like pepper spray, but designed to stop bears."

She extended a hand tentatively toward the can.

"It's not going to bite you." He seemed to be getting a bit too much enjoyment from her discomfort...sheer terror...whatever.

"Fine." She took the can and propped it on the table. "Will it hurt the bears?"

"No. Only spray a short burst at a time, and only if you are in danger. It'll make the bear uncomfortable, but it won't do any lasting damage, and it should deter him long enough for you to get away."

She sighed. So far, living in Florida hadn't turned out to be the paradise she'd envisioned. Long, hot afternoons by the pool or at the beach, book in hand, piña colada at her side, seemed to be as much a fantasy in Florida as it would have been in New York in the dead of winter.

Hunt lifted a box from the table and put it on the floor in the corner of the kitchen. "On a brighter note..."

Thor immediately sniffed around the box, then settled down to chew on one corner.

"Thor, no." She tossed him one of the abundance of chew toys scattered around the house.

"Xavier's Barbecue is right down the road, and they deliver."

"What's Xavier's Barbecue?"

He stopped, holding the second box in his hands, and stared at her. "You mean to tell me, all the times you've been down here, Savannah's never taken you to Xavier's?"

"I haven't really been down that many times, and when I was, I didn't have a minute of spare time."

"Well, I hope you're hungry, because I am, and I didn't know what you liked, so I ordered some of everything." He continued clearing the table, while she grabbed dishes from a stack on the counter, then searched for silverware.

"Don't worry about that. They send paper plates and plastic utensils with the order. I ordered sweet tea too."

"Mmm... I'm definitely parched. I have to get to the supermarket and pick up some food. I never had to worry about that back home." She paused a minute. Would she ever come to think of Florida as home? Or was she doomed to a permanent vacation and a state of perpetual homesickness.

A knock on the door saved her from considering that any further.

Hunt went to answer with Thor weaving wildly between his feet.

She hadn't even been there a week, and so far it had been too eventful for her to get any sense of how she felt about Florida. Besides, even if it turned out Florida wasn't for her, she didn't have to go back to New York. She could always move on to somewhere new. Somewhere she and Thor could make a home. Because Thor was the one thing she was sure of.

The big puppy bounded back into the kitchen, followed by Hunt juggling three bags and a cup holder with two super-sized drinks.

"Oh, sorry." She ran and took the cup holder from him and set it on the table. "I didn't realize you were actually serious about ordering everything."

He set the bags down on the table.

If the scent wafting from the bags was any indication, barbecue was her new favorite food.

"There's chicken, ribs, crushed potatoes with herbs, coleslaw, corn bread..." He unpacked the bags as he rattled off everything he'd ordered.

Once she'd filled her plate, she bit into a piece of chicken. The savory barbecue flavor melted in her mouth. Florida life was looking up.

Hunt waited for her to swallow. "Well?"

"Amazing."

"Told you so." He bit into a rib.

The fact that she was enjoying Hunt's company surprised her. He was different from any of the men she knew back home. More…rugged. Down to earth. Easy-going. He took his time with everything he did, never seemed to rush. She couldn't help but wonder if that held true in every aspect of his life. Heat crept up her cheeks. She could get used to Hunt hanging around.

Hunt's cellphone rang, interrupting him midbite.

"Sorry, I have to take this." He wiped his hands on a napkin and answered. "Yeah."

She knew right away he wouldn't be finishing dinner.

"When?" He threw a couple of ribs onto a napkin and wrapped them up, then grabbed his tea. "I'm on my way."

"Everything okay?"

"Better put Thor in the crate and grab your plate if you want to eat on the way." He started closing containers of food and tossing them in the fridge.

She hurried to crate Thor. "What happened?"

"That was dispatch. Someone broke into the café."

Chapter 10

Gia sifted through the papers scattered across her office floor. As far as she could tell, the intruder had gone through her office and the area behind the register where she kept some paperwork, but nothing important.

"Can you tell if anything's missing?" Hunt stood with his hands on his hips and looked around at the scattered papers littering her office.

She shook her head. "I didn't have much here. Mostly bills and receipts from the work I did to open the shop, catalogues, employee files—"

"Wait." His gaze locked on hers. "What kind of employee files?"

"Well, I only have two employees, so there's not much here." She lifted a manila file folder from the floor and handed it to him. "Names, addresses, social sec—Oh, man."

He paged through the thin file and made a note on his pad. "I'll let them know their social security numbers have been compromised."

"All right, but tell them I'll pay for Identity Theft Protection for them, at least until we figure out what's going on here."

"Uh...we?"

"What?" She offered her best innocent look.

His eye roll indicated he didn't buy it. "You are not going to get involved in this. You are going to let the police handle it, right?"

"Um...sure. I just meant, until the police figure out what's going on."

"Mmm...hmm... Just stay as far away from this as you can. I already have one body in the morgue. I don't need another."

Well, when he put it that way...

He started toward the door. "We're about done here. Do you want a ride home?"

"Am I allowed to take my car out of the lot yet?"

"Yes, the crime scene techs are done back there."

A spark of excitement flared. "Does that mean I can open the café tomorrow?"

"Maybe the day after. Depends on when the glass can be replaced in the front door."

Oh, right. She'd forgotten about that. Whoever had broken in had gained access by tossing a cinder block through the front door. "I'll have to clean up all that glass too."

Hunt gripped her shoulders and helped her to her feet, then gently guided her toward the door. "You'll have plenty of time tomorrow. For now, why don't you go home and get some rest?"

"I guess."

He was right. She'd accomplish a lot more after a good night's sleep. She stepped over a small stack of files and headed for the door. Besides, she'd left Thor home alone, and he was probably nervous. Thinking of Thor brought a new worry. One she should have thought of before bringing him home, but she'd fallen so in love with the roly-poly pup she hadn't thought of much. "Do you know anyone who takes care of dogs? I can't leave Thor home alone in a crate all day once I open again."

"There's a doggie day care center three blocks over, right on the edge of the park. A lot of the officers use them."

"Thanks." She grabbed a pen and pad that had been tossed in the corner of her office and wrote *doggie day care* on the first line. If she didn't make a list of what she had to do, she'd never remember. Leaving the mess for later, she followed Hunt to the front of the café, where the crime scene unit was just finishing up.

Glass crunched beneath their feet and ground into the floor as they carried their equipment out.

Call insurance company went on the list next. Great, she'd been in Florida less than a week, and she already had to file two claims. One for the broken window at the house and one for the café. She'd be lucky if her rates didn't fly through the roof. She contemplated paying for the damage herself and scribbled *get estimates for glass* on her list, then tossed the pad onto the counter.

"Do you want a cup of coffee?" As late as it was, she'd need the caffeine to keep from falling asleep in the twenty minutes it would take her to drive home, especially after getting only a few hours of sleep the night before.

"Sure, thanks." Hunt continued talking to officers and techs.

Gia started the coffee pot, then headed for the small, private bathroom off her office. Maybe a little cold water on her face would wake her a little.

She flipped on the light and shut the door behind her, then turned on the cold water and scooped a few handfuls onto her face. Even at this hour of the night, humidity still weighed heavy in the hot air, and the cool water was refreshing. She wiped the water from her eyes, then reached behind her for the towel hanging from the rack on the opposite wall.

Movement in her peripheral vision caught her attention. She searched the shadows beneath the small corner cabinet that held towels and supplies. Something black moved again.

Gia brushed away the water dripping into her eyes. What the...

A giant, dark-colored spider with orange striped legs scuttled out from beneath the corner cabinet. It stopped next to the wall, halfway to the door.

She gasped and her chest constricted, like a giant vice squeezing her lungs. She tried to scream, but only a faint wheeze escaped.

The spider's leg twitched.

Gia leaned back onto the counter and yanked her feet up off the floor, desperately struggling for air to call for help. The overwhelming sense of arachnophobia she'd suffered since childhood held her paralyzed.

The spider started forward, tentatively, moving away from the wall. Toward the cabinet Gia now clung to.

The breath shot from her lungs, and she slid farther onto the counter, pulling her feet closer to her body. She sucked in as much air as she could manage and screamed. As desperate as she was to squeeze her eyes closed and block the image, she didn't dare. She kept her gaze firmly riveted on the furry creature, certain he knew exactly what he was doing as he stalked her. She tried to scoot back farther, but the corner of the medicine cabinet dug into her back, halting her retreat.

"Gia," Hunt yelled, then yanked open the door, gun in hand.

"Shoot it." All she managed was a hoarse whisper. With her hand and arm shaking wildly, she pointed at the spider and tried again, each repeat of the word getting louder. "Shoot it, shoot it, shoot it..."

He glanced at the spider and relaxed his stance.

Relaxed? What was wrong with him? Could he not see the monster threatening her?

Then he turned and moved between the other officers surrounding the doorway with their guns drawn. "It's all right. Just a spider."

Just a spider? Was he crazy? The thing had hair for crying out loud!

The spider twitched and started moving again. At least this time it was moving away from her, back toward the safety of the corner cabinet. Every instinct screamed at her to go after it, to step on it before it reached its hiding spot and disappeared. Step on it? Who was she kidding? That thing was bigger than her foot.

She'd never be able to walk back into the café knowing that thing was lurking somewhere in the shadows. Yet, she still sat frozen, unable to fight the grip fear held on her. Knowing her fear was irrational did nothing to calm her.

Hunt strode through the doorway and slapped one of the glass cake dish covers over the spider, then squatted down next to it and examined the foul creature as it tried to climb up the glass.

Some of the tension seeped from Gia's body, leaving her shaking, sweat and tears pouring down her face. Strands of hair clung to her face, tickling her when she moved, giving her the feeling of something crawling down her face and neck. She slapped at it, then yanked it behind her back.

"Are you all right?" Hunt took her arm and tried to help her down.

"No." She curled farther into the corner. "It's going to get out."

He glanced behind him at the trapped spider. "It's not going to get out."

"Are you sure? I'm pretty sure it can move that cover."

Hunt laughed.

Seriously?

She shot him a dirty look and tried to get a grip on herself.

"It's just a spider, Gia."

"Just a spider? Just a spider? Are you kidding me? That thing needs to be on a leash. Are those things running all over the place down here? Am I going to have to be afraid of running into one every time I walk into a dark room?" She sobbed, the thought too intimidating to contemplate. She couldn't do this. Maybe Florida wasn't for her. Maybe now that Bradley was dead, she could go back to New York and pick up the pieces of her shattered life. Maybe—

"Well, you see, that's the thing. That right there..." He pointed toward the offending creature. "That's a tarantula. And they are *not* indigenous to Florida."

She stilled. "What are you talking about?"

"We don't have tarantulas here. Unless someone was keeping one as a pet and it escaped, which we'll check into, but I don't expect that's the case."

"Pet?" What kind of madman would keep something like that as a pet? She wrapped her arms tighter around her legs, pulling her knees against her chest.

"Who else knows about your irrational fear of spiders?"

"Irrational? I'll have you know..." His words started to penetrate. "You think someone put it there?"

"Let's go into the other room and talk."

She eyed the spider.

"Don't worry. One of the officers will collect it as soon as we leave. I don't want anyone to lift the cover while you're still here."

That thought motivated her like nothing else could have. She launched herself off the counter and bolted for the door. When she reached the dining room, she dropped onto a chair, then pulled her feet up with her.

"Can I make you a cup of tea or something?" Hunt asked. "The last thing you need right now is caffeine."

She'd forgotten all about the coffee she'd put on. Hunt was right. She no longer needed caffeine. Thanks to her run-in with the mother of all spiders, she was wide awake. She might never sleep again. "No, thank you."

He slid out a chair and sat down across from her. He kept his feet on the floor.

Fool.

"So, who else knows how afraid you are of spiders?"

She shook her head. "I don't know. I'm pretty sure Savannah knows."

"Did Bradley know?"

"Well, yeah, but why would he do something like that?" she asked.

"Who knows?"

Okay, stupid question. Bradley had done a million things she considered irrational, but still… "Do you think he was trying to kill me? Is that thing poisonous?"

"Nah. Actually, tarantulas are pretty harmless. Even if he bit you, you wouldn't die. It might be uncomfortable, like a bee sting, but that's about it."

"Bit me? That thing could have scared me to death without ever coming close."

"Bradley knew you'd feel that way, and we know he was in the café to eat breakfast. I already questioned Willow, and she doesn't remember him, but I'll try again. See if she remembers seeing a man with a box or bag. He would have had to carry it in something."

She nodded, though she really couldn't see Bradley doing something like that. There'd been more than one time during their marriage that he'd come home to remove a spider from the apartment. Granted, he wasn't far from home at the time, but still. If he didn't understand her phobia, why would he have done that?

"Come on, let's get you home. Want me to drive you?"

"No, thanks. I'll be all right." She just wanted to go home and get in bed, wanted this day to be over. "But could you do me one favor?"

"What's that?"

She swallowed hard. No matter how much she didn't want to give in to the fear, reality was she was still shaking too badly to function. If she tried to drive like that, terrified a spider like the one in the bathroom would creep out from beneath a seat at any — she cut the thought off before she ended up begging Detective Tall, Dark, and Protective to drive her home.

"Check my car for spiders before I get in it?"

She had to give him credit. He didn't laugh, but the corner of his mouth twitched as if he wanted to.

"Sure. Come on." He placed a hand on the small of her back and started to guide her toward the back door.

She stopped in her tracks before they reached the back room. "Is it gone yet?"

"I'm not sure." Hunt pushed open the door.

Gia stood staring. Her car sat only a few feet from the dumpster where Bradley had been found. No way she wanted to go out there. She couldn't go out there. "Would you mind bringing my car around, and I'll meet you out front?"

"Come on." This time he didn't laugh. His dark eyes bored into her; then he placed a gentle hand on her back and led her back toward the front of the shop. He stopped and spoke quietly to an officer, then handed him her keys before leading her through the broken glass and out the front door. "Oh, I almost forgot. I spoke to Don Reynolds again today, and he said he'd be contacting you soon."

"Who's Don Reynolds?"

He paused, but she couldn't read his expression in the dark.

"Remington's attorney."

"What are you talking about? His attorney's name is Horace Rabinowitz." She should know. She'd spent over a year listening to that weasel defend her ex, all the while raking in a small fortune in legal fees. Everyone knew it was impossible for Bradley to have pulled off his scheme without the guidance of an attorney. Just saying his name out loud left a bad taste on her tongue.

Hunt pulled out his notepad, shined his flashlight on it, and flipped through a few pages. "The man I spoke to was named Don Reynolds. He said he was Remington's attorney, but maybe he was with the same firm or something." He stuffed the notebook back into his shirt pocket. "I'll look into it tomorrow."

Maybe that's why Rabinowitz hadn't called her back. Maybe he was no longer Bradley's attorney. If Hunt didn't find out anything from Mr. Reynolds, she'd have to call Rabinowitz back and see if he'd tell her what was going on, although she seriously doubted he'd be anything more than a dead end, but it couldn't hurt to try.

After walking her to her car and checking for spiders, Hunt followed her home and repeated the process in the house, searching every corner but coming up empty. Then he waited while she took Thor out.

She walked him to the door with Thor weaving between her feet and jumping up on her. Apparently, the few hours he'd spent in the crate while she was at the café were enough to rev him up again.

Hunt stopped behind the front door. "Are you going to be okay?"

She nodded. "I am, thank you."

Thor bounced up and down.

"Good luck with that." Hunt waited for her to grab Thor's collar before opening the door. "Lock the door behind me, and get some sleep."

"Thank you, Hunt." She shifted awkwardly, not sure what else to say. That she appreciated him tolerating her phobia and humoring her?

"Any time, ma'am." He grinned, then pulled the door shut behind him, saving her from having to say anything.

"Come on, boy. It's bedtime." She put Thor back into his crate in the kitchen with a pile of toys, then, dismissing the desire to fall onto the couch amid the papers she'd left scattered there, trudged toward the bedroom.

She got into her pajamas in record time, then dropped into bed. She should have brought her notebook and pen with her. She'd forgotten to write down *contact Bradley's attorney* on her to-do list.

She'd call Rabinowitz again in the morning and see if she could get anything out of him. She also had to find out who Don Reynolds was. Could Bradley have had a lawyer she didn't know about? Everyone had assumed Rabinowitz was in on his scheme, him being such a sleaze and all, but maybe he hadn't been involved. Maybe Bradley had another attorney to handle his illegal activities, but if that was the case, then why would he have handled his estate?

Too exhausted to think straight, she struggled to turn her mind off. She rolled over and turned off the bedside lamp, then laid still, cocooned in darkness…and silence. Pitch black. Silent as a vacuum. Anything could be crawling toward her.

She lurched up and flipped the light back on.

Okay. This is definitely not going to work.

She went to the kitchen and let Thor out of his crate, then dragged the crate down the hallway and—with a little creative maneuvering—through the bedroom doorway and placed it at the foot of her bed, then ushered Thor back inside and closed the latch.

There. That was better. She got back into bed, turned off the light and closed her eyes. If her eyes weren't open, she couldn't tell how dark it was. Okay, that was a lie. She could absolutely tell how dark it was. Manhattan was full of lights, probably millions of which shined into her apartment window along with the sounds of the city at night.

She sat up and turned on the light. Her TV wasn't set up yet, but she had her cell phone. She flipped on all the lights—despite the fact that Hunt had checked every inch of the house before he left—trudged back to the kitchen where she'd left her bag and grabbed her cell phone. After she plugged it into the charger on her nightstand, she searched her cable app for something to listen to while she fell asleep. She settled on a channel that showed old movies, then turned off the light and settled down again.

Letting her eyes drift shut, she dozed off amid the scream of sirens, explosions, and flickers of light pulsing against her closed lids as *Lethal Weapon* blared from her phone. Much better.

Chapter 11

After a fitful few hours of trying to sleep, Gia gave up and rolled out of bed. She tried to reach Rabinowitz but had to settle for leaving another voice mail. She held the phone in her hand, contemplating the cracked screen. At this point, she was no closer to figuring out what was going on than she'd been when she found Bradley's body. Actually, things were worse. Now people she cared about were in danger. She swallowed her pride and hit Bree's number.

"H-hello?"

"Hello, Bree. It's Gia Morelli."

"Um…hi, Gia." She sniffled.

"I wanted to talk to you about something."

"Okay, but first, I just want to tell you I'm sorry."

"Sorry?"

"For…well…everything that went on with Bradley." Bree sobbed. "I'm so sorry, Gia. You were my friend, and I can't begin to tell you how sorry I am for getting involved with him. I'll never forgive myself for that."

What could she say to that? It's okay? It wasn't okay. They were friends, and Bree had betrayed her by sleeping with her husband. That was far from okay. "What's done is done, Bree."

That was the best she could do. If Bree needed more to absolve her sins, she'd have to look elsewhere.

She cried softly for a minute, then sniffed. "What were you calling for?"

"Bradley's dead."

She gasped and let out a strangled cry.

"I'm living in Florida now, and he was found dead in a dumpster behind my café. The police seem to think he was trying to contact me for something, but no one knows what. I was hoping you could shed some light on what he might have been looking for." She waited, giving Bree time to compose herself.

"I'm sorry, Gia. I… I haven't seen or heard from Bradley in a long time."

"You were in the courtroom when he was sentenced." Gia had seen her sitting in the back of the courtroom as far from Gia as she could get.

"Yes, but not to support him. He stopped talking to me long before he was arrested."

No wonder she was so apologetic. Apparently, Bradley had dumped her. Although she felt bad for Bree, she'd be lying if she didn't admit to some small sense of satisfaction.

"I'm sorry I can't help you, Gia. Maybe I'll see you around some time?"

"Sure." Probably not. "Thanks."

Bree disconnected without saying good-bye.

Another dead end. Gia just couldn't seem to catch a break. Someone had to know what was going on, if only she could figure out who. She fed Thor and played with him in the backyard for a couple of hours, then put him in his crate. "I'll be back in a little while, boy."

On her way into the café, she stopped at the doggie daycare center and registered Thor. If she was going back to work tomorrow, she had to put him somewhere he'd be happy. No way was he spending most of his day in a cage. He could have done that at the shelter.

Then she stopped at a salad bar and got lunch to go. By the time she reached the café, she was starved. She parked out front, in no hurry to return to the back lot, then sat looking at the café. Her pride and joy. The one thing she'd worked so hard for. Tainted by her past.

The fear of going back in there after seeing that giant spider held her captive. She thought about calling Savannah to go in with her, but she had no doubt Savannah would leave work to help her, and she didn't want to put her friend in that position.

Her stomach growled, motivating her to stop procrastinating. Leaving the car and the air conditioning running, she slid her seat back, opened her salad, and ate it in the car. She told herself it would be easier to start cleaning up the mess as soon as she got in, but she knew it was a lie.

Once she was done eating, she rolled up the bag, got out of the car, and tossed it into the nearest garbage pail. Then she stood looking at her café. It was now or never. If she couldn't even walk in the front door, she may as well get on the next flight back to New York.

She took a deep breath, braced herself, and strode toward the door. Nothing would take what she'd worked so hard for. Not Bradley, not whoever was stalking her, not her own fear. Nothing.

Her hand shook as she slid the key into the lock.

"Excuse me?" A man's voice startled her.

She whirled on him and dropped the keys. "Oh, jeez, you scared me half to death."

Twin patches of red popped up on his cheeks. "I'm so sorry. I didn't mean to startle you."

"That's okay."

He bent and retrieved her keys, then handed them to her and held out a hand. "I'm Trevor Barnes."

She accepted his handshake. "Gia Morelli."

"I know. I-I mean, I know who you are, but not in a creepy, weird, stalkery kind of way, just in a, I've heard your name and figured it was you kind of way. I mean…uh…"

Gia couldn't help but smile. He had to be in his early thirties, but his awkwardness made him seem younger. Not only his demeanor, but his lanky build as well, tall and thin with long arms and legs. He kind of reminded her of Thor, who hadn't grown into his too big paws yet.

Trevor's short brown hair hung a little long in the front across his eyes, and he brushed it back as he spoke. "I'm sorry. Let me try again. I'm Trevor, and I own the ice cream shop just down the road. It's nice to meet you."

"It's nice to meet you, too, Trevor."

"Anyway, I won't keep you. I just wanted to introduce myself and let you know I'm sorry about the break-in. I called the police as soon as I noticed the flashlight beam, but I don't know how long the intruder was in there before I happened by."

"Wait. You called the police? Thank you. I assumed the alarm summoned them."

He shook his head. "There was no alarm going. I stopped at a friend's house after work, and I was on my way home when I noticed the light, like a flashlight beam. I might not have thought much of it, but then I noticed the broken door."

"Well, thank you very much for calling the police, and for noticing."

He stood a little straighter. "You're very welcome. We look out for each other around here."

"That's comforting to know."

"Was there a lot of damage?" He gestured toward the plywood now covering the front door.

"Nah, not really. Just the door, and someone will be here today to fix it."

"That's good. I hope they didn't take too much."

"Actually, I don't think they took anything." She unlocked the door. "It was a pleasure meeting you. If you're around tomorrow morning, come in for breakfast. My treat as a thank-you."

He blushed an even deeper shade of red. "Thank you. I'd like that. You're opening tomorrow? I...uh..." He pulled his T-shirt collar down a bit as if it was choking him. "I heard, you know, about the trouble... Anyway, I wasn't sure you'd be open for a while."

"The police finished their investigation of the café, and I would have opened today, if not for the damage."

"Oh, forgive my manners. Please, let me help you get this cleaned up." He started forward.

"Actually, I'm waiting for the insurance guy to come check it out. He'll be here in a little while. I can't clean up until he comes."

"Oh, right. Of course." He started to back away. "Well, if you want, I could come back later. You know, after he leaves, and I could help clean up."

"You're welcome to stop by any time. Thank you."

His smile brightened his already brilliant blue eyes even more. "Thank you. I'd like that." He started away, then turned back. "Welcome to the neighborhood."

After thanking him again, she turned back to the shop and braced herself. The thought of calling Trevor back to go into the café with her flickered through her mind, but she quickly dismissed it. She pulled open the door and strode through.

Glass crunched beneath her feet. Shadows hung over the foyer where the plywood covered the door, and she quickly flipped on the lights. Better. She scanned every inch of the floor she could see, trying to peek into as many of the nooks and crannies as possible. She moved through the shop tentative at first, terrified at any moment one of those creatures would come rushing out from his hiding spot and give her a heart attack. Or worse.

She stopped walking halfway to the counter and stood in the middle of the dining room. Her heart's erratic beating made her lightheaded. Her hands shook violently as she lifted her hair from the back of her neck, letting the air conditioning someone had left running cool the sweat soaking the back of her neck.

The front door opened, and she whirled toward it.

"Hey, there." Earl picked his way carefully through the glass. "You okay? Look like you seen a ghost."

She couldn't even imagine how pale she must look, especially in a state where you could easily keep a year-round tan. "Hi, Earl. It's great to see you. I'm fine, thank you. Just a little...overwhelmed."

He looked around. "I can see that."

"I'm sorry I can't offer you breakfast. I'll be open for breakfast tomorrow, though. I can make coffee now if you'd like."

"No, thank you. Don't go through any trouble. I was down the street and saw you come in, so I figured I'd stop and say hello." He shifted from one foot to the other, looking around the café. Was he avoiding eye contact?

"Is everything all right, Earl? Do you want to sit? I have tea in the fridge."

He held up his hands. "No, no, thank you. I just wanted to let you know I'm sorry for your trouble, and I'll still be comin' in for breakfast once you get open. I...uh..." He finally met her gaze. "Rumor has it, you killed your ex and stuffed him in the dumpster out back...."

She gasped.

"But, well, I just wanted to make sure you know I don't believe gossip."

Tears threatened, but she held them back. "Thank you, Earl. I appreciate that more than you know."

"Well, then. I guess I'll see you tomorrow morning. Bright and early." He nodded and tipped his fisherman's cap, then grinned. "And don't forget the grits."

"Don't worry, I won't." Gia watched him go, then stood in the middle of her shattered dreams. She had no doubt Earl's words had been meant as a warning. Boggy Creek was a small, close-knit community. If she'd been labeled a killer, her business had probably died with her ex.

What a mess. At least Earl's visit had released the panic that had been gripping her. She might not be able to clean up the glass yet, but there was plenty of other stuff to do. After searching thoroughly, mop in hand, for anything creepy in the supply closet, she grabbed a garbage bag and set to work. If she was to open tomorrow, she'd have to get everything cleaned up and prep for breakfast. Hunt had promised he'd have someone to replace the glass for her as soon as the insurance guy left with his pictures.

She collected the coffee cups that had been left lying around while the police had conducted their investigation and threw them into the garbage bag, then washed the coffee pots and started a fresh pot. She went through the food she had left in stock. Stale muffins went in the garbage, as did the leftover bagels and rolls. The refrigerated food was fine, but she had to toss the breakfast pies she'd made Sunday night in preparation for Monday morning's breakfast crowd. They would have been fine in the refrigerator overnight, but a few days had left them looking dried out and unappealing. She'd make some more later. She'd have to fry fresh bacon as well. Oh, and she had to go to the store for grits. She'd have to remember to look up a recipe later.

She tied up the garbage bags and set them by the back door. The thought of going out to the dumpster didn't appeal. She'd just toss the bags in her trunk when she was leaving and throw them out at home. Of course, she couldn't do that every day.

She yanked a rag from the bin beneath the register with a little more force than necessary and slammed her funny bone on the edge of the counter behind her. "Ouch."

She threw the rag onto the counter and massaged her elbow. What was she doing? Why even bother opening? So she could fail even more miserably than she already had?

The door opened, and a man walked in.

She glanced at the driftwood clock on the wall above the cutout to the kitchen. Too early for the insurance adjuster. At the rate men were coming in this morning, maybe she'd forget about getting the glass replaced and just put in a revolving door. Hopefully, the steady stream kept up tomorrow morning when she opened. "Hi. Can I help you?"

"Mornin', ma'am." He crossed the shop and held out a hand. "Mark Cooper."

She shook his hand. "It's nice to meet you, Mr. Cooper. I'm Gia Morelli."

"Call me Mark." He took a quick look around the shop. "Are you the owner?"

"Yes. What can I help you with?"

"Actually, I want to help you."

She quirked a brow.

"Are you open for business yet?"

"Well, I was…" She gestured toward the mess by the front door. "But as you can see, I've had a bit of a setback." No need to mention the body found in the dumpster if he hadn't already heard the story. "I plan on opening tomorrow morning, though."

"That's perfect, then. I'm new in the area, and I'm looking for a job."

"Do you have any experience?" She'd already called Willow to let her know the shop would be opening again tomorrow if she wanted to return to work. Thankfully, she was excited to come back. Maybelle, on the other hand, had insisted she couldn't possibly work for a killer. That rush to judgment was the thanks Gia got for deciding to give the woman another chance. At least she'd saved Gia the trouble of firing her.

"I worked the breakfast shift in a busy diner right off the turnpike in Jersey for like, oh, I don't know… I guess about three or four years."

Hope flared. Maybe things were starting to look up.

"As a cook?"

"Yup."

"How long have you been in Florida?"

He wore jeans and a tunic style top. A shark's tooth hung from a leather cord, peeking from his open collar. Brown hair, highlighted with streaks of blond, skimmed his shoulders. He'd rock the surfer dude look, if not for the pale skin and dark circles under his eyes.

"Not long. I'm looking for a place to rent too. Someone mentioned an empty apartment above the café. If you're looking to rent it out..." He spread his hands wide and smiled.

The idea of having someone who knew what he was doing take over the kitchen did appeal, but she'd learned her lesson with Maybelle. The last thing she needed was another employee she'd have to get rid of, or at least hope quit, especially if she agreed to rent him the apartment.

"I'll tell you what," Mark started. "I'm not doing anything for the rest of the day anyway, and you must have a lot of prep work to do if you're opening in the morning. How about if I give you a hand, no charge, for the next few hours. I'll help you prep, and if you're happy with my work, you'll give me a chance. If not, then I'll be on my way and you're not out anything."

How could she argue with that? She smiled and shook his hand, the soft, smooth hand of a banker or a lawyer, not a cook who washed his hands all day long. Still... "You've got yourself a deal, Mr. Cooper."

"Mark."

"Mark. Thank you."

"Just point me toward the kitchen." He rubbed his hands together.

She only hoped his skill matched his eagerness to work as she walked with him toward the kitchen.

"I assume you'll need at least a few pounds of bacon precooked."

"Yes." Though she couldn't be sure how many customers she'd get, she had to be prepared. "And I want to make up some breakfast pies for the display dishes out front."

He nodded as she showed him around the kitchen and the supply closet, pointing out everything he was likely to need.

When she finished the tour, she stuck the breakfast pie recipe above the grill for him. "You can start with the bacon, because you'll need it for the pies."

"What about home fries and grits? You'll have to soak the grits tonight if they're going to be ready for the morning. If you want, I can start those while the bacon's cooking. I can't very well stand here and watch bacon fry when I could be getting something else done." He unwrapped a leather cord from around his wrist and tied his hair back, then washed his hands. "You know how to make grits?" And how to multitask? Okay, she could possibly be in love. He might just be the perfect man.

"Of course. What would a southern breakfast be without them?" Right. Where was this guy Sunday morning when she'd opened? "Unfortunately, I don't have any grits right now, and I can't run out because I'm waiting for the insurance adjuster."

"Don't worry about it. I'll run out and pick some up, then I'll come back and get started."

"You're sure you don't mind?"

"Are you kidding me? A job and possibly a place to stay are riding on me getting everything just right. Of course, I don't mind. I'll be right back." *Uh oh.* She hadn't agreed to rent him the apartment, just to hire him.

"Do you need anything else while I'm out?"

"Um…" She needed a cook anyway, and if he was as good as he seemed to be, he'd be perfect for the job. But having him live upstairs? "Sure. I could actually use a few things, and you'll save me a trip to the store."

She scribbled a short list, then dug money out of her bag and handed them to him.

"Be back in a jiff."

She'd just wait and see what happened when he came back. If he came back. Who knew? The way her luck was going lately, he'd probably skip town with the twenties she'd given him to pick up the supplies.

By the time the insurance adjuster arrived, she was already thrilled with her new employee. He'd returned with everything she'd needed, fried up the bacon, started cutting vegetables for the omelets and pies, and had the grits soaking. What more could she ask for?

When the insurance adjuster left, she approached Mark. "Everything looks great, Mark. Thank you."

"Ahh…but you haven't even tasted my signature dish yet?"

"Oh?"

"Homemade hash and eggs." He held out a paper plate with a spoonful of hash and a bit of scrambled egg over the top and handed her a fork. "Give it a try."

She put the plate on the counter, cut off a piece of egg and hash, and took a small bite. She'd never tasted hash so good. "Oh, mmm… This is delicious."

"Does that mean I'm hired?"

"Absolutely."

"Awesome."

She took another bite. "The hash is amazing. What's your secret?" "I mix mashed potatoes with the corned beef instead of diced, then fry it until the edges are brown and crispy." He grinned. "Makes all the difference in the world." "It certainly does," she agreed. "We start at five tomorrow morning." "Well, that shouldn't be too hard. Especially if I only have to walk down the stairs to get to work." "Um…" Oh, what the heck? It couldn't hurt to have someone in the apartment. No sense letting it sit empty when she could be getting an income, especially when she had no clue if any customers would even show up the next day. At least his rent would cover a portion of the mortgage payment. Besides, someone staying upstairs might deter any more break-ins. She smiled and extended a hand. "Then you shouldn't have any trouble making it on time."

Chapter 12

Gia eyed the growing pile of garbage against the back door. Taking home one bag made sense, sort of, but dragging several bags, most containing food remnants, through the café and tossing them in her trunk was insanity. It was going to have to go in the dumpster. "Would you do me a favor, Mark?"

"Sure. What do you need?"

"Could you please put the garbage out?" So she was a chicken. She'd get over it. Eventually. Probably.

He studied her for a moment, an intensity in his eyes she hadn't noticed before, then smiled. "Of course."

Had she imagined the brief moment where she felt as if he was staring through her? Did he know about the body they'd found out there? "That will be part of your job each day, to keep up with getting the garbage out back."

"No problem." He opened the back door a crack and gathered the bags in both hands.

"Oh, and I will add today's work to your pay check. You did a great job, thank you."

His cheeks flushed. "Thank you. I appreciate that."

Careful to keep her gaze averted when he opened the back door, Gia headed toward the front of the café. She'd still have to put the last of the food away, but that wouldn't take long. She may as well show her new tenant to his apartment and get out of there. Thor had already been alone for half an hour longer than she'd intended.

She grabbed her key ring from her bag just as Mark emerged from the back. She resisted the urge to ask if everything went okay. Wouldn't want him to think she was completely off her rocker. "Ready?"

"Yup."

She locked the café, rounded the side of the building, unlocked the door and held it open for Mark to precede her, then followed him up the steep stairway. "It's not much."

"That's okay. I don't need much."

They emerged in the small living room, the sight of the threadbare couch she'd spent too many nights on bringing an instant kink to her neck. "There's not much furniture, but you're welcome to use what's here if you want. If not, I can have someone put it out back before you move in."

"That's okay, thank you. I'll use what's here for now. Once I get my stuff moved in, I'll haul this out back for you." He walked through the kitchen and bathroom and poked his head into the tiny bedroom. Though the apartment was not roomy, it was immaculately clean. "It's perfect. I'll take it."

"Great." They agreed on an amount, and he promised to bring the first month's rent and the security deposit the following morning when he arrived for work. "Do I need to sign a lease or anything?"

She really had no idea how it worked, so she'd have to add talking to someone about it to her growing to-do list. If she didn't start writing more of the list down, she'd never remember any of it. Of course, she couldn't remember where she'd put the list she had started to write. "I'll find out, but for now, you're welcome to stay until I do."

Maybe it was better not to have a lease. Then, if he didn't work out, she could just ask him to leave.

"Sounds great. Thank you."

"Sure." She unhooked a key from her ring and handed it to him. "That's the key to the apartment door."

"What about the café? Won't I need a key to open?"

The apartment held nothing of value. At worst, she could just change the locks. No way was she handing the café key over to a stranger. She and Savannah were the only two people who held keys, and Gia intended to keep it that way. "I don't have a spare key to the shop, but I'll be there to open."

"No worries." He smiled. "You'll learn to trust me. Just give it time."

She smiled back but didn't acknowledge the comment. Whether or not she'd ever learn to trust anyone other than Savannah was questionable. "I'm going to go down and finish up, but you're welcome to look around if you want. Just lock up when you leave. I'll see you tomorrow."

"Bright and early. Thank you, again, for everything."

"You're very welcome." She left him standing in the apartment and headed back to the café. Everything had already been cleaned up, so all she had to do was put away the food they'd finished last. She set aside one breakfast pie to bring home for her dinner, then wrapped the rest and put them in the refrigerator.

Remembering her promise to Harley, she cut a large piece of pie, slid it into a foam tray, then put it in a paper bag with plastic utensils and napkins. She wrote Harley's name across the bag with a thick black marker, filled a large foam cup with sweet tea and set it on the counter beside the bag. Then she stared at the back door. If she was going to fulfill her promise, she'd have to open the back door. Okay. She could do this.

She unlocked the door, grabbed Harley's dinner, and started to push the door open. If she just cracked it a bit, she could shove the food out there without ever looking in the direction of the dumpster. But she'd left Harley's bag on the ground last time, and it didn't sit well with her. And he hadn't taken it.

She stared at the storage closet. She'd already been in and out of it several times that day, but Mark had been there. Somehow, it seemed a bit less intimidating when she wasn't alone. She reached in and turned on the light, then scanned the room from the doorway. When her gaze fell on the folded card table they'd used as a makeshift desk shoved into the farthest corner of the walk-in closet, she cringed. Of course, it was as far into the suddenly enormous closet as it could get.

Resigned, she strode straight to it without looking at anything else, dragged it out of its corner, and high tailed it out of there. She extended the table's legs and, without so much as a glance in the direction of the dumpster, she opened the back door, held it open with her foot, and maneuvered the table through. She quickly added a folding chair, then set the food and tea in the center of the table and let the door fall shut with a loud crack. Done. She could only hope Harley remembered she'd said she'd leave him dinner. She grabbed the bag holding her dinner and headed for the door. Time to go home to her puppy. Things were definitely looking up.

* * * *

True to his promise, Earl stood outside on the sidewalk gazing at the last remnants of the sunrise when Gia opened for business at six the next morning.

"Good morning, Earl." She held the door for him and led him to what she hoped would become his usual seat at the counter. She'd put his order slip up for Mark to start as soon as she'd seen him waiting outside, so she poured him a cup of coffee. "I'm glad you came back this morning."

When she set the coffee mug down in front of him, he patted her hand. "Of course, dear. I form my opinions about people from their actions not idle gossip. And I don't see a mean bone in your body."

"You're such a sweetheart. Thank you."

"Any time, dear, any time."

Bradley's murder and the subsequent investigation were the last things she wanted to talk about, so she changed the subject. "So, how's Heddie?"

Earl stared into his mug without answering.

Had she gotten his wife's name wrong? She was sure he'd said Heddie, and she'd concentrated on remembering small details about Earl, hoping he'd become a regular customer. She'd developed a knack for picking out regulars when she'd worked at the deli, those who would come in every morning, linger, and have a conversation, even if only about the weather.

Earl cleared his throat, and when he finally spoke, his voice had turned huskier. "My Heddie... She's been gone near on five years now."

"Oh, Earl, I'm so sorry. I didn't realize..."

"I know. It's okay, dear. Heddie spent most of our marriage complaining about how I ate. Only breakfast, mind you. I don't eat lunch, and I eat a healthy dinner. That was my concession when she got upset over my breakfast." His smile held only sadness. "When we were first married, Heddie used to enjoy a nice big breakfast with me. Then, when we had our first child, she stopped. Said she wanted to live to see her baby grow up. By the time he and our other children grew up, she wanted to live to see her grandbabies."

He paused and ran a finger around the rim of his mug.

Gia leaned her elbows on the counter and waited, giving him time to collect himself.

"Funny, don't ya think, that a heart attack took her." He shook his head, staring hard into his mug. "Anyway, when she first passed, I tried to eat breakfast at home, but I couldn't enjoy it. I would envision her...hear her voice in my head. It just seemed so unfair that I was still here. You know?"

Gia nodded.

"So, I returned to my normal routine of going out each morning. It felt better that way. More normal."

"Did Heddie get to see her grandchildren?"

Earl sat up straighter, and this time his smile was genuine. "Why, yes she did. Thirteen grandbabies. Quite a legacy that woman left behind."

"You have thirteen grandchildren?"

"It's fifteen now. Two more additions in the past five years."

"How many kids do you have?"

"Six. My Heddie raised five, hard-headed, feisty boys, bless her heart, before she finally got her baby girl."

Six kids? Wow. She couldn't even imagine having six kids. Savannah came from a big family too. She couldn't help but wonder if Hunt expected to have a lot of kids. She wanted kids, even though Bradley hadn't, but six? Shocked by the direction her thoughts had wandered, Gia jerked back.

"Now. Enough talk about that." His eyes gleamed with mischief. Had he read her mind? "Y'all got grits this morning?"

"You bet I do." Thanks to Mark. But no need to divulge that. A girl had to have some secrets.

"And if you don't mind, you could throw a bit of those home fries on the side. They weren't half bad." He winked and sipped his coffee.

Her heart soared. "You got it. I'll be right back."

Since she'd put the order slip up as soon as she'd seen Earl waiting outside, Mark should have had it done by now. No plates sat on the cutout counter between the kitchen and dining room. She peeked into the kitchen. Mark was nowhere to be found. Nothing was cooking, and the order slip still hung in its place above the grill. "Mark?"

Silence.

"Mark?" she called a little louder. Maybe she was destined to do all the cooking. If this was a repeat of Maybelle, he was so out of there.

"I'm right here." He emerged from the storage closet with a pen and order pad in hand. "Everything else is done, so I started going through your supplies to see what we'll need to order this week."

She just stared at him.

"I...uh... I'm sorry. I just though—"

"Where is the breakfast order I put up?"

"Oh, right, sorry," he continued, his words flying out as he walked. He tossed the pad onto a counter. "I saw you two talking, and it seemed pretty intense, and I didn't want the gentleman's food to get cold, so I put it in the oven to keep it warm."

Eggs and milk had been written in neat print. He'd started another word, but she couldn't figure out what it could be.

He grabbed a pot holder, yanked a covered dish from the oven, and handed it to her, pot holder and all, then followed her toward the dining room. "Sorry. I hope that was all right. I left the order slip up, because I didn't know where to put it. You obviously had it stashed somewhere, since you had it up before he even came in."

"It's fine. I'm sorry. I'm just a little…" A little what? She'd already been open more than half an hour, and so far, Earl was her only customer. "Could you please grab a side of home fries, too?"

He eyed the thin man sitting at the end of the counter for a second, then turned and walked away.

She set the food in front of Earl. "Enjoy."

She moved away but kept an eye on him in her peripheral vision until he tasted the grits. She'd tasted them earlier and wasn't a huge fan. Gritty, salty, and loaded with butter. Though Mark had assured her they were delicious with milk and brown sugar, she still had her doubts. Maybe it was an acquired taste.

Earl stuffed a forkful into his mouth and sighed. "Now that's breakfast."

Willow rushed in, then stopped short and glanced at the clock. "Uh… Good morning."

"Morning."

She gestured around the empty dining room. "Sooo…"

"Yeah. Not much happening this morning."

"You know what? People probably didn't realize you were open again. Maybe you could run a breakfast special over the weekend. Advertise it on a chalk board out front or something."

"That's a great idea, Willow." She perked up a little. She had a sneaking suspicion she had no customers because people thought more like Maybelle, but she'd give it a try. She'd known it would be hard to make a name for herself in the small town, but she hadn't expected it to be quite this hard. Maybe Willow was right. She'd get a sign and set it up out front advertising the weekend's specials. And maybe Mark's signature hash and eggs. Thanks to Mark giving her the rent and security for the apartment that morning, she'd be able to pay him and Willow for about two weeks. If she couldn't increase business by then, she'd have to let one of them go.

The front door opened and Hunt walked in, laying his hand on a woman's back as he ushered her in. A very pretty woman with short, blond hair and a killer smile.

Hunt kissed Gia's cheek. "Hi there. How's it going?"

"Okay, I guess." Not that he'd indicated any interest in Gia, but she'd kind of thought maybe he hung around more than necessary because he liked her. Now she realized he was just a nice guy who took his job seriously. And that's all she was. A job. And Savannah's friend. Family almost. Great. Maybe he viewed her like a cousin. She sighed. "Been better."

He rubbed his hand up and down her arm. A very friendly gesture. "Don't worry. Things'll pick up again."

She nodded.

He indicated the woman standing next to him. "Gia, this is Sonny."

Of course. "Hi, Sonny. It's nice to meet you." She shook her hand without even squeezing too hard. Okay, maybe a little hard. "Would you like a table?" With the way her day was going so far, she'd be lucky if she got through it without another body turning up. She wouldn't be heading out to the dumpster any time soon, just in case.

Chapter 13

Savannah came in a few minutes later, saving Gia from any more conversation with Sonny and her big blue eyes, framed by thick lashes. And a happy disposition to top it all off.

"Hey." Savannah waved a hello to Hunt and Sonny, then hugged Gia and sat at the counter. "What's going on? You look a little cranky."

Leave it to Savannah to cut right to the chase.

"Nah. Just a little slower than I'd hoped."

"How many customers have you had so far?"

"What's here now and Earl."

"I'm sorry."

"Yeah. Me too."

"It'll pick up. You'll see. Just give it time."

Her hopes started to lift when the door opened again, but fell flat when Maybelle walked in with a tall, stocky man at her side.

"What does she want?" Gia couldn't help it. Something about that woman rubbed her the wrong way.

Savannah turned. When she spotted Maybelle, her posture stiffened. "Well, bless her heart."

When Earl had said bless her heart about Heddie, the sentiment had been so sincere and heart-felt. When Savannah used the same expression, it sounded more like…well…something else entirely.

Savannah plastered on a fake smile, stood, and squared her shoulders. "Hello, Maybelle. What can I help you with?"

She ignored Savannah and spoke directly to Gia. "Just come to pick up my pay for yesterday."

She had to be kidding. The woman had barely done a thing.

Maybelle gestured toward the hulk of a man standing next to her, his jaw clenched. "Hank didn't want me meetin' up with no killer by myself."

Gia had had just about enough of this woman. "Look, M—"

"Come now, Maybelle." Savannah's southern accent thickened, sweetening the bitterness of her words. "You know you have to work before you can get paid, and you were about as useful as a steering wheel on a mule."

"Don't make no difference. I worked, and I deserve to get paid."

"Worked?" Savannah simply tilted her head and fluttered her lashes.

Hank looked down at the woman Gia assumed was his wife. "What's she talkin' about?"

"Nothin'."

Hunt came up beside Savannah and slung an arm around her shoulder. "Problem here?"

Hank puffed up his chest.

"No. It's fine. Everything is fine." Gia opened the register. This was getting out of hand. She'd just pay the woman for the day and be done with her before the situation escalated any further. She quickly counted out the pay they'd agreed on and handed it to Maybelle. "Just do me a favor, and don't come back."

"Is that a threat?" Maybelle asked.

"Threat? What are you talking—"

"I don't take kindly to someone threatening my wife." Hank took a step toward Gia.

Hunt stepped in front of her.

Savannah slid between them and placed a hand on Hank's thick chest. "That'll be enough now, Hank. You know Gia didn't mean no harm. But Maybelle, well, she didn't exactly do the right thing the other day."

He stared at his wife. "That true?"

She pointed at Gia. "That woman's a slave driver. And Savannah here, she just goes right along with her and her highfalutin ways."

"Look, I paid you for the day. Now let's all just move on." Gia wasn't about to let Savannah or Hunt fight her battles. But she had no fight left in her. Especially not for Maybelle. She simply wasn't worth the aggravation. "I'm sorry things didn't work out."

Maybelle huffed, then turned and stormed out of the café.

With one last dirty look at Hunt, Hank followed her.

"Sorry about that," Gia said.

"It's not your fault," Hunt offered. A look passed between him and Savannah, but no one said anything.

Mark rang the bell to indicate her breakfast order was ready.

Ignoring the uncomfortable silence, Gia went to get the order. After setting Hunt and Sonny's plates on their table, and apologizing one last time for good measure, she dropped onto a stool at the counter beside Savannah. "I'm sorry about that, Savannah."

"Don't worry about it. Maybelle is quick to rush to judgment with absolutely no facts to base her opinions on."

"Sounds like you've dealt with her before?"

She waved off the question. "You look tired. Did you end up getting any sleep at all last night?"

Gia let it drop. Obviously, whatever was between Savannah and Maybelle was going to stay that way. "A little. Thank you for coming out and staying with me last night and getting up with Thor this morning."

"No problem. That pup is a real sweetheart. Better watch out or I'm gonna make off with him one of these days."

"Oh, no you're not." She'd already become attached to the little ball of fur. "How did he do when you dropped him off this morning?"

"He trotted off happy as could be with the other puppies in the room. You have to pick him up by seven, though."

"That's fine. I close at six, and it doesn't look like there'll be much to clean up." At the rate things were going, she'd have everything cleaned up and prepped for the next day by the time she locked the door. She might even make it out early. The only thing saving her from total depression at that thought was knowing Thor was waiting for her. Her excitement about getting home to him lessened some of her anxiety.

"I even managed to unpack a few boxes for you before we left. I got most of your clothes put away, at least."

"That's great, thank you."

Willow placed a cup of coffee in front of each of them along with a plate filled with muffins.

"Thank you, Willow."

"You're very welcome." She rushed to seat two older women who'd just walked in.

The women eyed Gia as they crossed to a table, sat, and thanked Willow for their menus; then they opened the menus, leaned toward each other, and started whispering.

Gia shifted, uncomfortable beneath their not-so-discreet stares. The whole scenario was a little too reminiscent of life in New York after Bradley was arrested. Only this time, she lacked the strength to deal with the controversy. The emotional toll Bradley's trial and the divorce took on her had drained every last ounce of energy. She tossed her half-eaten muffin back onto the plate.

Savannah leaned close and pinched her leg beneath the counter.

"Ouch. What was that for?"

"Don't you dare wither. Now pull up your big girl panties and go say hello," she whispered. She kissed her cheek and gestured toward the women. "I have to run now, but don't you dare let Bradley take this from you."

Savannah slipped her sunglasses on, stopped to say something to Hunt, then strode out the door.

Gia rubbed the sore spot on her leg. Savannah was right. Hiding only made her look guilty. She waved Willow back, took an order pad, stood and crossed the dining room, all too aware of Hunt's stare. When she reached the two busy-bodies, she offered a broad smile. "Good morning, ladies."

They looked at each other before returning the greeting.

"I'm Gia Morelli, owner of the All-Day Breakfast Café. It's a pleasure to meet you both."

"I'm Estelle," one of the women offered, patting her perfectly coiffed blue hair. "And this is my sister, Esmeralda." She gestured toward the other woman who looked remarkably like her. Twins?

"It's nice to meet you." Esmeralda's smile held a little more warmth. "Are you new to the area?"

"Yes. I've been here less than a week."

The sisters shared a knowing look, though what they thought they knew was beyond her. "So, what can I get for you?"

She wrote down their order, then excused herself and practically ran for the kitchen to put the slip up. Willow could serve them once their food was ready. She'd done her part. After she tacked the order slip above the grill, she slumped against the hallway wall. All she wanted now was to go home. But she didn't even know where home was.

"Are you okay, Gia?" Willow laid a gentle hand on her shoulder.

Gia could only manage a weak smile, but she patted Willow's hand. "I'm fine. Thank you."

"I brought the old biddies their breakfast, and they are scarfing it down like they never ate before. Maybe they'll tell all of their friends to come."

"Yeah. Maybe." Of course, if they did come, it would probably just be to stare at the town's new killer.

Willow started to walk away, then stopped and turned back. "I know I'm young, and we don't know each other all that well, but I heard what happened, and I still came back. You know why?"

Gia shook her head.

"Because something about you touched me. You're smart and strong and ambitious and a hard worker. And someone I think I could look up to, admire even, once I know you a little better. Earl came back too. He obviously saw something in you that touched him as well. When I was about to start ninth grade, my mother got a transfer and we had to move, a terrible time to have to start attending a new school. I was sick to my stomach for a week before I started. So worried I wouldn't make friends, wouldn't fit in." She tapped the small gold hoop she wore through her nose.

"I'm lucky my mom and I are very close, and I talked to her about how I was feeling. And you know what she told me?"

"No, what?"

"She told me to be myself. She said not everyone would like me, but that's okay. You don't need to make everyone like you. But the ones who are important will. She also said anything worthwhile is hard work. You've got this, Gia. Just have faith in yourself. I do." She walked away, leaving Gia to think about what she'd said. Smart kid. Full of confidence, even though she was clearly different.

And she was right. Not everyone had to like her. She'd concentrate on getting to know the people who did. Hopefully, there'd be enough to keep her in business.

She headed back toward the dining room. When she passed Willow, she leaned close and whispered, "Thank you."

"That's what friends are for."

The two older women finished eating and left Willow a generous tip. They stopped to let Gia know how much they'd enjoyed their breakfast and said they'd be back again. Maybe things were starting to look up.

A man opened the door and stepped back, smiling and nodding a greeting to the two women as they exited. He looked familiar, but she couldn't quite place him.

A moment of panic gripped her, until recognition hit. How could she have forgotten Mr. Tall, Dark, and Stylishly Disheveled even for a moment? "Caleb. How are you?"

"Hi, Gia. It's good to see you." He greeted her as if they were old friends, gripping her hands and kissing her cheek, even though they'd only met once in the café on her opening day.

She couldn't help a quick glance at Hunt from her peripheral vision when Caleb stepped back. She needn't have wasted her time. He was thoroughly engrossed in whatever conversation he was having with Barbie... or whatever her name was. "It's good to see you too, Caleb. Still have business in Florida?"

"Still looking into a few things."

She seated him at the counter and handed him a menu. "Coffee?"

"Please." He set the menu aside. Though his expression remained aloof, something in his eyes changed, a subtle shift from carefree businessman to…something else. Something predatory. The already deep green darkened to match the color of the ring around his irises. "I heard about what happened. I'm sorry."

With a discreet glance to see that Hunt was still there, she nodded and poured Caleb's coffee.

"Do the police know who killed him?"

"No. Not yet."

"Rumor has it you're a suspect." He caught her gaze and held it captive. She studied him more closely. The distressed jeans and cream-colored tunic top. The brown leather sandals. He almost pulled off the beach bum look. And yet, there was something… "If it's okay, I'd rather not talk about it."

He studied her another moment. Then, just as quickly as his mood had changed the first time, he smiled. "I'm sure they'll straighten it out."

"Yeah. Me too." *At least, I hope they will.* "Can I get you anything to eat?"

"Um… I already had breakfast, but I wanted to stop in for an amazing cup of coffee." He grazed a hand over his scruffy five-o'clock shadow. "And to ask you to have dinner with me tonight."

The request caught Gia off guard. "I uh…" She hadn't given much thought to being with another man. At least, not until Hunt had barged into her life. But trusting another man would come slowly, if at all. Still, that didn't mean she couldn't go out and have a good time. Going to dinner wasn't any kind of commitment. "I'm sorry. I-I'm a bit overwhelmed with getting the café opened and everything else that's happened since I arrived in Florida. Maybe another time?"

"Of course. Perhaps I'll stop back in again before I leave."

"I'd like that. Thank you."

He lifted his mug and sipped his coffee. His eyes brightened back to their normal shade. Then he lowered his mug to the counter, stood, and fished some bills out of his pocket. He started to drop them on the counter.

"No, please. It's on me." She laid a hand over his.

He turned his over and caught her fingers in his. "Thank you. That's very kind of you."

Her hand heated in his. His penetrating gaze sent warmth surging through her. He lifted her hand and pressed his lips against her knuckles.

"Until we meet again, then."

She watched him walk out, fully absorbed in thoughts better left alone. The last thing she needed was involvement with any other man, let alone a stranger from New York. And yet, that was one fine looking, charming man.

"If you can bring yourself back to reality, I'd like the check, please." Hunt stood at the counter, studying Caleb as he stepped outside and the door fell shut behind him.

"Uh..." Her cheeks burned. "Sure, sorry."

"Mind if I ask who that was?" Though he phrased it as a question, she had no doubt it was a demand.

She bristled. "A friend."

"How long have you known him?"

Who was he to question her? Especially after he'd come into her café with another woman. Just because they weren't dating or anything didn't mean he shouldn't show a little respect. "Does it matter?"

"Oh, I don't know, Gia..." He leaned closer, and the breath of his husky whisper tickled her ear. "Your ex was found dead in your dumpster, your house was broken into, and someone quite possibly tried to run you off the road. What do you think?"

If it was possible to die of embarrassment, she would have dropped right there on the spot. She should have realized Hunt's interest was only a logical question from an investigator, and not a bit of jealousy from an admirer. "The garage."

"Excuse me?"

"The garage. Someone broke into the garage, not the house." With that, she dropped his check on the counter, turned, and walked away.

Chapter 14

The lunch rush had consisted of a few tourists, a young couple, and a small group of college students between classes at the local university. Gia sighed and started cleaning up. Might as well get everything prepped for tomorrow. She sorted through what was left from the day, determining what could be salvaged and what had to go in the garbage.

She cracked a couple of eggs onto the grill, then added a small stack of pre-cooked bacon to heat. The sizzle of food cooking made her stomach growl.

"Hungry?" Mark gestured toward the grill.

"Oh, no. It's not for me."

"Have you eaten anything yet today?"

The half a muffin she'd eaten that morning still sat like a lump in her stomach. "Not really."

"Why don't you let me fix you something?"

She waved him off. "I'll eat something when I get home. I'm just going to finish this, clean up, and get out of here."

"All right, then. I guess I'll get going."

"Sure, thanks. I'll see you tomorrow."

He untied the back of his apron and slipped it over his head, then rolled it into a ball. "Sure thing."

"There's a hamper in the bathroom you can toss that in."

"Got it." He offered a two-finger salute and left her alone.

She piled the bacon and eggs onto a roll, topped it with a slice of American cheese, salt and pepper, wrapped the sandwich, and stuffed it into a bag with a container of home fries. Then added a container of grits as well. After she scribbled Harley's name on the bag and poured a large foam cup of sweet tea, she steeled herself and shoved open the back door far enough to put everything on the table.

The bag she'd left for Harley the night before still sat untouched. Oh well. Maybe he hadn't realized she'd opened again. Leaving the new food on the table, she took the old bag and tossed it into the trash. Thankfully, Mark had already emptied all the pails, so she didn't have to go out to the dumpster yet. She wasn't sure she'd ever be able to go back out there.

She made sure everything in back was locked up, then grabbed her purse from her office and started through the café.

A woman sauntered through the front door, oozing diamonds from just about every finger, her wrist, her neck. Even her ears dripped dangling strings of diamonds. Not a local. Gia had yet to see a resident of Boggy Creek who exuded the opulence, or the arrogance, this woman had obviously mastered.

"I'm sorry, I'm just getting ready to close."

The woman eyed her up and down and wrinkled her nose as if she'd smelled something rotten. "That's fine, dear. I'm not interested in food."

"Oh..." She was sorry she hadn't locked the front door when Mark had left. Next time. She slid behind the counter. She'd already cleaned the coffee pots, and she had no intention of starting a fresh pot for this woman. "Then what can I help you with, Ms...?"

"Ainsworth." The woman stopped in front of the counter and slid her clutch beneath her arm. "Bradley left something with you that belongs to me. I'd like it back."

"I don't know what you're talking about. Bradley didn't leave anything with me."

Her smile held more contempt than Gia would have thought possible. "You really do have that innocent routine down pat, don't you? But guess what?" She leaned across the counter.

Gia backed up until she hit the counter behind her. Then, with nowhere else to go, she waited.

"I'm not buying it. I don't know what you did to wrap that weasel around your finger enough that he'd get out of my bed to run home and kill a spider when you called carrying on like an idiot, but I'll never believe you weren't in on his scam. You're just a more practiced liar."

Spider? What was she talking about? There had been more than one time she'd called Bradley upset about finding a spider in the apartment, and if he was close by, he'd usually come home and dispose of it for her, but from another woman's bed? Could that be true?

"I'll give you two days to decide how you want to do this."

"I don't know what you're talking about. Bradley didn't leave me anything." Wait. What had Hunt said? An inheritance? "Are you talking about his life insurance?"

Her laughter held no humor. "Don't play dumb with me. If you want to do this the hard way, that's fine. Two days. Talk to whomever you need to talk to, but the next time I come back, you'd better have answers. Because next time, I won't be so nice."

"B-b-but, I—"

"In case you come to your senses before two days is up, you can reach me here." The woman handed her a folded piece of paper, then turned and slinked away.

Gia stood there, counter top digging into her, and stared after her. True to Bradley's tastes when it came to mistresses, she was a strong, powerful, confident woman. And beautiful. Shockingly so. But only on the outside.

Gia moved away from the counter and rubbed the sore spot near her lower back. She willed her hands to stop shaking. It wasn't the first time she'd been confronted by one of Bradley's lovers. Heck, this one wasn't even all that nasty compared to some. But she'd been used to the constant clashes in New York. This was different, had caught her off guard. Next time she'd be more prepared.

She'd be fine as soon as she picked up Thor and went home. She took a deep breath, struggling for control, and stuffed the paper into her purse, then slung her purse over her shoulder. Before opening the front door, she peeked through the windows, scanning everything within her line of sight. As far as she could tell, the woman was gone. The thought of reporting the incident to the police briefly flickered through her mind, but she'd already been down that road. Numerous times. All it would do is hold her up. In the end, they wouldn't look too hard. If Ms. Ainsworth carried through on her threat to return, she'd give her a warning. Then she'd call the police.

On the bright side, now that she was afraid to merely walk out the door, she wasn't nearly as afraid of being alone in the café where there might be giant spiders. The thought slammed through her. Had that woman planted the spider? It made sense, since the woman obviously had an issue with Gia's phobia. Though if what she'd said was true, Gia couldn't really blame her.

That had been one of the things she'd always loved about Bradley, his need to take care of her, his willingness to accept her as she was. Tears threatened. Anything Bradley had been to her was a lie, a cold, calculated cover for his greed. Killing spiders didn't make him any less of a dirt bag.

She shook off any kind feelings before they could take hold. Thoughts of some jilted lover letting spiders loose in the café propelled her out the door like nothing else could have. Knowing the woman had no way to get in didn't ease her fears. She shoved the key in the lock and turned it, then paused. Maybe she'd have the locks changed anyway. Never could be too careful.

"Hey there," said a male voice as someone laid a hand on her shoulder.

She screamed, whirled around, and slammed her back against the door. Trevor held his hand up in a gesture of surrender, backing slowly away from her. His cheeks flamed red. "I'm sorry. I'm sorry. I didn't mean to scare you."

She shook her head, not yet able to speak, and held up a finger for him to wait a minute.

"Sure. Of course. I really am sorry." He still stood with his hands up. Great. Some passerby would think she was robbing him or something. It wouldn't take long for those rumors to spread. And when they did, she'd have a reputation as a killer and a thief.

Laughter bubbled out. She couldn't help it. And she didn't want to. It felt good to laugh, even at herself. And she was acting a bit foolish. At least it helped get her breathing back under control. "No. I'm sorry. I was lost in thought, and you just startled me."

Mark poked his head around the corner. He looked back and forth between the two of them, his stare lingering on Trevor. "Is everything all right out here? I thought I heard someone scream."

She waved it off. "It's fine. It's fine. Trevor just startled me."

"I didn't mean to. I'm sorry." He frowned. "Seems I have a habit of doing that."

"Trevor?" Gia said.

"Yeah?"

"You can put your hands down now. Please."

"Oh, sorry." He grinned and shoved his hands into the pockets of his khaki shorts.

Gia introduced the two men. "Sorry for scaring both of you. I guess I'm a little jumpy with...well..."

Trevor rushed forward and patted her arm. "Oh, it's perfectly understandable. With what happened and all, I don't blame you. I'd be jumpy too."

Mark shot her a wink. "Well, it was nice meeting you, Trevor. If you two are okay, I'll get back to my unpacking."

After Gia assured him she was fine, he shook Trevor's hand and headed back up to the apartment. She had to admit, it was a little reassuring that he'd heard her scream and come to investigate.

"Anyway. I just stopped by to see if you would you like to, you know, go out to dinner, maybe? With me, I mean." His adorable blush crept all the way to his hairline.

"Oh, Trevor. I can't tonight. I'm sorry, but thank you for asking."

"It doesn't have to be tonight. We could go another night if you want." She'd almost been ready to say yes to Caleb's dinner invitation, but something had stopped her. The hope that she and Hunt might get together? Probably not, since he'd already been sitting in the middle of her café with another woman at the time. "I'd love to go out to dinner with you one of these days, but I just got a new puppy, and I have to pick him up from day care. He's there all day while I'm at work, so I don't feel right leaving him alone to go out afterward. At least, not yet."

An excuse? Maybe, but she didn't think so. She really didn't want to leave Thor alone. Trevor was a sweetheart. And she'd obviously been mistaken about Hunt's interest.

"You know what? I have the perfect idea. How about tomorrow night?" He was nothing if not persistent.

"I already—"

"You don't have to leave Thor at all. I could meet you here after work tomorrow and walk with you to pick him up. Then we could take a nice stroll through the park, maybe get something to eat at one of the food trucks. And after that, we could head back here and get ice cream. I know a place. Right down the road. Outdoor seating. Great service." He shot her a grin. "I hear the owner's a really nice guy too."

"You know what?" If she was going to stay in Florida and make a new life, it was time to move on. She had to at least start making friends. Maybe not close friends. Maybe not anything more than that. But she missed having friends, people to hang out and enjoy an evening with.

His eyes widened.

"It sounds like fun. I'd love to."

"Great. I'll meet you around six?"

"Perfect."

"I'll bring Brandy too."

"Brandy?"

"My German shepherd. She loves to walk in the park. You don't mind, do you?"

"No, of course not. I can't wait."

"Awesome." He started to back up the walkway toward the sidewalk. His foot caught on a cobblestone lining the path, and he went down hard on his backside, legs splayed.

"Oh, my." Gia rushed toward him. "Are you all right?"

"I'm fine." He stood and brushed himself off. "If you spend any time with me at all, you'll find out pretty quick..." He gestured toward the spot on the ground where he'd gone down. "That's normal. Anyway. I'll see you tomorrow."

She waved before he turned around and walked away. The moment of happiness Trevor had managed to bring dwindled quickly once he left. Though she wanted nothing more than to move on and forget about the past, some things still lingered, haunting her. The only way she could truly leave the past behind was to find answers. And she had a good idea where to start.

Chapter 15

Acid churned in Gia's stomach. Hungry or not, she needed to eat something. That being the case, she was going to have to get out of the car and go into the house if she wanted something to eat. She was sure she'd seen a box of cereal somewhere in the mess of boxes waiting to be unpacked.

She looked around the darkening yard. Then, satisfied there was no immediate danger she could see, although snakes would be easily camouflaged, so would bears, probably, and definitely spiders...

Before she could work herself up into a full-blown panic attack, she opened her purse and made sure the bear spray Hunt had given her was on top and easily reachable, then found the key to the front door and held it ready, slung the purse over her shoulder, clutched Thor's leash, got out of the car, and bolted for the house.

Cleaning out the garage shot to the top of her ever-growing to-do list. At least then she could pull in and close the door behind her before she had to get out of the car. With Thor jumping excitedly at her feet, she jammed the key into the lock, flung the door open, then ran in, closed it just as quickly, and leaned her back against it in relief.

This was not going to work out. Either she had to get a grip on herself and get over her fears, or she had to move. Not necessarily back to New York. Maybe she'd look for something in town by the shop. A small flare of regret surfaced. Maybe she shouldn't have rented the apartment to Mark. She could just stay there, sell the house, and look for something else. Of course, the apartment was too small for all the stuff she'd hauled down from New York, but there had to be a storage place nearby.

She sighed and pushed away from the door. No sense circling around the same discussion she'd had with herself a million times since Savannah had sent her the listing for the small house on the edge of the forest. The fact remained she couldn't afford a house in town, or anything else, really. And if business kept up as it had today, she wouldn't even be able to afford that.

"Come on, Thor, let's find something to eat." She unhooked his leash, flipped on the living room light, then skirted a pile of boxes on her way to the kitchen.

Thor dove into the pile of papers she'd been sorting through and rolled onto his back, squirming wildly, all four paws waving in the air, sending papers flying everywhere.

"No, Thor." She picked him up and surveyed the mess. She didn't even remember what she'd been looking at. Now she'd have to redo that pile before she could move on. It was going to be a long night.

Once she fed Thor and got him out, while barely avoiding another panic attack, she found the box of cereal she'd seen earlier and took it with her to the living room. She piled a bunch of Thor's toys next to her and settled down to go through papers and munch dry cereal from the box.

She couldn't shake thoughts of the woman who'd confronted her in the café earlier. She'd been so certain Bradley had left something of hers with Gia. Of course, she'd also been positive Gia had been involved in his schemes. But still.

Four boxes of boring paperwork and half a box of cereal later, she stood and stretched. Her eyes burned from reading so much. At least, she had developed a system to make things move more quickly. She put everything important into one box to sort out later. Everything else went in the garbage. Maybe she could get rid of enough to fit what was left in the apartment. How had she accumulated so much junk over the years? She probably should have taken the time to sort through it all before she'd left New York, but at the time, she'd just been desperate to escape.

She massaged her lower back for a minute and grabbed another box.

Thor lay curled in a ball on his bed beside her, snoring softly.

A surge of love shot through her. She'd never realized how much a puppy could bring to her life, but she knew she wouldn't give him up for the world. Whatever choices she made for her future, they would include Thor.

One more box and she'd take him into her room and go to bed.

She lowered the box carefully, fished a half empty water bottle out of her purse, and settled back down. She opened the box and a musty scent wafted out. She sneezed.

Piles of neatly stacked folders, all labeled in Bradley's precise handwriting, filled the box. She tried to remember where she'd found them, but that whole time was pretty much a blur. Still, she couldn't recall packing them, couldn't recall ever having seen them before. Maybe one of the boxes that had been packed away in the small storage space in the basement? That would explain the smell. And she had no idea if the police had ever searched the storage box. The first folder held a computer printout, page after page of random numbers. At least, they seemed random to Gia. They had obviously meant something to Bradley, or he wouldn't have kept them. She set the folder on the floor next to her. Just because it didn't make sense to her, didn't mean it wouldn't to someone. At worst, she could hand it over to Hunt and let his experts figure it out.

In the next folder, she found handwritten details of the scheme he'd used to cheat his clients out of millions. It seemed to be an earlier draft of what had come out at the trial, much of which Gia didn't understand. She knew it involved taking money from clients and investing it in bogus corporations, then somehow syphoning the money off into his own accounts, but the logistics of it all were lost on her.

She set that aside as well, keeping everything in the exact order she'd found it in. She had no clue if the order was important, but she didn't want to screw anything up. Truthfully, she should probably take the whole box and turn it over to the police as it was, but curiosity got the better of her. This was the first possible lead she'd come across. No way was she giving it up unless she had to.

She took a sip of her water, her throat dry from going through the musty paperwork, then flipped open the next folder. The difference in this paperwork jumped out at her immediately. On these documents, the rows of numbers were preceded by names. She ran her finger down the columns of numbers, searching for anyone she recognized. Six names were on the first page, none of whom were familiar to her. On page three, she stopped her finger over the name, Miranda Ainsworth. The same Ms. Ainsworth who'd come into the café that afternoon?

Seemed too much of a coincidence for it not to be the same woman. She tried to decipher the numbers following her name. Account numbers, maybe? Gia had no idea, but she did recognize the numbers following the dollar signs. She let out a low whistle. If Miranda Ainsworth was the woman who'd come into the café, she had several million reasons to be upset. But was she a victim or a partner? Wasn't that the multi-million dollar question?

And what could Gia do about it? Even if these were account numbers and the accounts still existed, she had no way to know where to find them.

She scanned the remainder of the names contained in the folder. None of them were familiar, and she'd seen a list of the names of Bradley's victims, not that she remembered all of them, but certainly one or two should have stuck in her mind. Now what? If these people were all victims, they deserved to get their money back. Yet, if she turned the information over to the police, what guarantee was there they'd even go through it and try to reimburse the victims? Bradley had already been convicted, and now he was dead. How could she be sure they'd even pursue this? She couldn't be.

Of course, she could turn them over to Hunt. From what she'd seen of him so far, he seemed honest. She tamped down a small niggle of guilt. This had nothing to do with Hunt. Besides, he hadn't been honest about Sonny while he was at Gia's house eating barbeque.

Oh, dang. She'd forgotten about the leftover barbeque. She could have eaten that instead of chowing down a box of dry, half-stale cereal. Oh, well. Next time.

Back to the problem at hand. She could turn the papers over to one of Bradley's attorneys, though she had a feeling they were probably just as shady as he was. If they were able to get their hands on funds Bradley had left, the money would probably disappear long before it could be returned to its proper owners.

That only left one option. She used her phone to take a picture of the document with Miranda Ainsworth's name on it. Even though a lot was lost with the cracks in her phone screen—she was going to have to get that fixed or get a new phone—you could still make out enough to get the gist of what was there.

She fished the paper Miranda had handed her out of her bag and unfolded it. Written on it was a phone number with a New York area code, probably her cell phone, and the name and address of a local hotel. If she called, she couldn't show the woman the picture. Of course, she could text it to her, but then she'd have a copy of it, and Gia didn't want that, at least not until she figured out what was going on.

She stuffed the note into her pocket and settled Thor in his crate in the bedroom. "I'll be back in a little while, Thor. Be good."

She second guessed her decision to leave him home a million times as she traveled the dark roads to Miranda's motel. But she didn't want to leave him alone in the car while she talked to Ms. Ainsworth. At least she knew he was safe where he was.

She checked the address on the paper again, then turned into a motel parking lot filled with pot holes and littered with beer cans, wine bottles, paper, plastic bags, and who knew what else. She had a really hard time believing Ms. Ainsworth was staying in the dump that sat before her, crouched behind a wild tangle of bushes as if hiding from the world. No way that woman strolled through this neighborhood on her four inch stilettos, draped in diamonds, without getting mugged. Or worse. It had to be some sort of hoax. Maybe she figured Gia would show up there and get what she deserved for cheating her out of her fortune.

She checked that her doors were locked for the fifth time since entering the neighborhood and rolled past the line of doors at the back of the parking lot, checking the room numbers against the one Miranda had written down. When she found the room, she pulled in front of the door and sat. Flickering light spilled through the sheer curtains on the window.

It seemed foolish to have come this far and not go to the door. She scanned the parking lot and sidewalk. A small group of men huddled together by the entrance, too far away to reach her before she could make it back to the safety of her car. Other than that, the area seemed deserted. Most of the windows remained dark. Empty? Or had the occupants already gone to bed?

She couldn't sit there all night. That was just asking for trouble. With another quick glance around, she hopped out of the car and hurried to the window. She peeked inside.

At first, she thought the room had been trashed. Clothing lay strewn all over, hanging from chairs, rumpled in corners, draped over a bedside lamp. An open pizza box, half full, sat on the table amid stacks of papers. Beer cans and liquor bottles overflowed from the trash can.

Then something moved on the bed.

Miranda Ainsworth, or someone who looked remarkably like her, minus the classy clothes, gaudy jewelry, and snooty attitude, rolled over on the bed. Her hair stuck up around her head. She wore a ripped T-shirt over a pair of boxer shorts. Her mouth hung open.

Something didn't add up. Gia started to back away.

"Lookin' fer somefin'?"

She barely stifled a scream as she spun around.

A man stood between her and the car, his too-big, filthy sweatshirt reeking of booze. He held up a brown paper bag with a bottle sticking out the top. "Y'all wanna party?"

"Uh, no. Thanks."

He smiled, a huge gap where most of his top teeth should have been, and smoothed his matted mess of long brown hair. "Sure now?"

"I'm sure. I have to go." She inched toward the car without taking her eyes off him.

"Got some friends like to party."

She had no idea what he was talking about, but she had to get out of there. Going to the motel had not been her smartest idea ever. With her gaze glued to the man in front of her, she slammed the side of her knee into the bumper. That was going to leave a bruise if she ever got out of there. Another man stepped out of the shadows a few feet away. "Leave her alone, man."

"Harley?"

"You shouldn't be here," Harley told her.

"No. I mean yes. I mean I know. I was just leaving. Thank you."

He nodded once and waited for Gia to reach her car.

She scrambled in and slammed the lock button down. Thankfully, she'd left it running. She backed up and turned the wheel to angle the car toward the exit, then rolled down the window and called out to Harley. "Do you need a ride?"

He waved and disappeared back into the shadows.

The other man watched him, then ambled down the sidewalk muttering to himself.

First thing in the morning, she'd call Hunt and hand over the box of files and the contact information Miranda Ainsworth had given her. Let him figure out what it all meant.

Chapter 16

Gia poured coffee into an oversized mug.

"Isn't that like your third cup?" Willow nodded toward the pot Gia still held.

"I didn't get much sleep last night."

Willow frowned. "Everything okay? I mean, aside from the usual..."

"Yeah, it just takes me a while to get used to sleeping somewhere new."

"I get that." She took the carafe from Gia and started making a fresh pot. "Seems like business picked up a little this morning."

"I guess." Though there had been a few more customers than yesterday, she would need a lot more to make the mortgage payment come the first of the month.

"It'll get better." Her smile brightened the room, her optimism almost contagious.

"I know. Thanks."

"Any time. Want me to sweep the sidewalk out front?"

"Sure, that'd be great, thanks."

She grabbed the broom and the dustpan and headed outside. On the sidewalk, she paused for a minute and tilted her face up toward the sun, then started sweeping, offering a smile and a greeting to everyone who walked by.

Gia couldn't complain about Willow's work ethic. Despite the lack of customers, she always managed to look busy, finding odds and ends to clean up, rearranging things to make them work more efficiently if they did get a sudden influx of customers.

Gia set her mug on the counter, then went around and sat on one of the stools. Though the breakfast and lunch rush times had past, she would still have expected a straggler or two to be lingering over a second cup of coffee, but the café sat empty.

Savannah stopped to say hello to Willow before joining Gia at the counter. "How y'all doin'?"

Gia just looked at her.

She laughed. "All right, so things are a little slow. They'll pick up."

"And if they don't?"

"Well then, our vacation will last a little longer." She pulled a stack of brochures out of her bag and slapped them on the counter.

"Vacation?"

"Yup. I've decided you need to get away for a little while. You should have taken a break after leaving New York. I understand why you chose not to, Gia, I honestly do, but you need a break. You're pale, your hands are shaky, and you've lost weight. You jump at every little thing. And I've never seen such dark rings around your eyes, not even when you used to fly down on the weekends when everything was going on."

Gia sighed. Trying to hide her feelings from Savannah was useless. And, quite honestly, she lacked the energy to try. "I had a visitor yesterday."

"Okay, I'll bite, but don't think that gets you off the hook about getting away for a few days. But first, have you eaten anything yet today?"

She shook her head and sipped her coffee.

"I'll be right back." She stuck her head through the cutout to the kitchen and asked Mark to make them both omelets, then poured herself a cup of coffee and returned to her seat. "Okay, now, who was your visitor?"

Gia stirred the spoon around and around in her coffee. She needed something to do, but her stomach already burned, and there was no way she could keep down another sip of coffee without eating something. "One of Bradley's mistresses."

"Oh, honey. I'm so sorry."

She shrugged. "What are you gonna do? It's not like I didn't know he had tons of them. I found that out during the trial, along with the rest of the world."

Savannah remained quiet, her gaze pointedly averted.

Gia continued, grateful Savannah was a close enough friend to realize sometimes it was better not to say anything. "Anyway, it was weird. She showed up here dressed to the nines and said Bradley left something of hers with me. I had no idea what she was talking about, so I went home and searched through more boxes."

"Did you find anything?"

"I'm not really sure. I found something, a list of names and numbers, including his mistress's, but I don't know what any of it means. I thought maybe you could call Hunt and give him the box. Maybe he has people who could figure it out."

"Sure, no problem." She pulled out her cell phone and made the call. This is where it got tricky. She'd already planned on turning the box of files over to Hunt, so that was no big deal, but she had a feeling there would be fallout once they heard about her late-night visit. If they heard about it. Maybe she could gloss over some of the scarier details. Or maybe she just wouldn't mention it at all.

"Hunt will swing by and pick it up later."

"Thanks."

Mark slid two plates in front of them with meat lover's omelets, huge piles of home fries, and toasted bagels loaded with melted butter. He then poured a glass of orange juice for Gia and put her half-full coffee cup in a bin of dirty dishes beneath the counter. "Enjoy, and if you need anything else, just give a yell."

"Thank you." Gia eyed her heaping plate, then glared at Savannah. "What are you trying to do, fatten me up?"

She laughed. "Whatever it takes."

Gia put a forkful of sausage, bacon, scrambled egg, and cheese into her mouth and moaned. "Mmm… I didn't even realize how hungry I was."

"Did you ever eat dinner last night?"

"Sort of." If you count dry Cheerios as dinner.

"Did you sleep?"

"Not really, by the time I got home, it was really late."

"I thought you got out of here early yesterday."

"Uh…" Oops. "I did, but then I went out again."

Savannah paused, her fork halfway to her mouth. "Went out where?"

Gia's appetite fled, and she dropped her fork onto the plate. "When I found Miranda Ainsworth's name on the documents, I wanted to know what it meant. So I might have taken a ride by her motel."

"Might have?"

"Uh huh."

"Taken a ride?"

"Yup."

"But not stopped?"

"Weeell… I might have stopped the car and peeked in her window."

Savannah shook her head and shoved in a forkful of potatoes. She chewed and swallowed before responding. "And what might you have seen when you maybe peeked in the window?"

She picked up her fork and started eating again. Now that Savannah knew and hadn't totally freaked out, she was anxious to get her take on Miranda Ainsworth. She would have to be careful not to put her own spin on anything if she wanted to get Savannah's uncorrupted opinion. "The motel was in a really bad neighborhood. And the room was a mess. So was Miranda. She was sleeping on the bed, but no sign of the woman who came into the café was in that room."

"Could it have been a different woman?"

She thought back while she ate. Though Miranda's hair had been up when she'd come into the café, she could tell it was fairly long and bleached blond. And the woman in the bed had hair stuck up all over the place, stiff, as if doused in hair spray. From what Gia could see of the woman's upper body and leg sticking out of the blanket, she was built slim and curvy, but not skinny, the same as the woman who'd come into the café. "I don't think so. I can't say a hundred percent, but I think it was the same woman."

"Do you think the jewelry she was wearing was fake?"

"Hmm… I hadn't thought of that. I guess I just assumed it was real."

"Why?"

Good question. "I think it was her attitude. She just came of as so pretentious and snobby, it never even occurred to me she could be a phony."

"Maybe she wasn't a phony. Maybe she really was a snobby socialite before Bradley robbed her of her fortune."

Gia had thought of that. And her heart ached, not only for Miranda, but for all of Bradley's victims. It was easier to think of them collectively, but every time she came face to face with someone Bradley had robbed, her heart broke a little more.

"Tell Hunt what happened." Savannah used her fork to point at Gia. "Everything that happened."

"Yeah. Okay."

"He'll be able to research Miranda Ainsworth's background."

She threw her napkin onto her empty plate and pushed the plate aside, then pulled out her phone. "I was so tired last night, I didn't even think of typing her name into Google."

"You need to get your screen fixed."

"Yeah, I know." She typed Miranda's name into Google. "Hmm…"

"Something interesting?"

"Actually, nothing. At all. There's a few people with the same name on social media, a pediatrician, and an artist, but from what I can tell, none of them are the woman I saw yesterday."

"You think it's an alias?"

She set her phone aside. "I have no idea what to think."

"Talk to Hunt. Let him worry about it."

"Yeah. I'll tell him when he stops to pick up the folders."

The door opened, and Captain Hayes walked in.

Savannah stiffened.

"Hello, Captain Hayes." Gia stood to greet him and extended a hand. He shook her hand. "Good afternoon, Ms. Morelli."

"Is this a business visit, or would you like something to eat?"

"I just stopped in for a cup of coffee."

"Have a seat."

He settled onto a stool.

She poured a mug of coffee and set it in front of him.

"Thank you." He took a sip. "Delicious. Just like the other night."

"Thank you." She waited, certain Captain Hayes had come in for more than just a cup of coffee and idle chitchat.

He took another sip. "Ahh... It'd be a real shame if it turned out you were guilty."

Savannah crossed one leg over the other and swung her stool to face Hayes. "What's that supposed to mean?"

He studied Savannah over his mug, then took a sip and lowered the mug. "Not supposed to mean anything. But it does seem kind of odd she shows up here and a body she used to be married to winds up in the dumpster out back. Could be she waited until she got down here to do away with him so she wouldn't get caught. The detectives I spoke with in New York certainly seem to think she's guilty."

Experience had taught Gia to keep her mouth shut. Protesting too much only seemed to make those questioning her more suspicious. Let him think what he wanted. He couldn't prove she did something she didn't do. Unless, of course, someone was trying to frame her. Then all bets were off.

Savannah huffed and turned away.

Hayes watched her as he finished his coffee, then left his mug on the counter and stood. "See ya around. Thanks for the coffee."

He stood and started out of the café.

Savannah's voice sweetened. "Don't worry, it's on the house."

Haynes turned long enough to tip his hat and walk out.

"What an ass." Savannah pushed away from the counter and paced back and forth behind the stools. "Can you believe that guy?"

Gia shrugged it off. "No big deal. I'm used to it."

Savannah paused, then slid back onto her stool. "I'm sorry. That was insensitive. I'm letting my own low opinion of that man interfere with being there for you. There's no excuse for that."

"I'm fine, Savannah, really." This wasn't the first time she'd noticed Savannah tense up around Captain Hayes. When he'd entered the café the night Bradley had been found, Savannah and Hunt had both changed, sobered. He was only the second person she'd ever noticed Savannah disliked. The first being Bradley. "What's up with you and Hayes?"

"What do you mean?"

"You are one of those rare people who gets along with pretty much everyone, yet you couldn't stand Bradley, which we can talk about another time, and you practically hate Captain Hayes. I can't help but wonder why?" Oh, and Maybelle. But the situation between Savannah and Maybelle seemed different, as if Maybelle was more of an annoyance. The disdain she showed for the captain bordered on full-blown hatred.

Savannah traced circles with her finger on the counter. "You know my mother passed away when I was young. What you don't know, because I never, ever talk about it, is that she was murdered."

Shock slammed through her. Savannah never talked much about her mother's death, only a mention that she'd passed away when Savannah was young.

"When she was killed, Hayes got it in his head he knew who her killer was. He was a rookie at the time, and he made no bones about sharing his opinion with whoever would listen. To this day, he swears my father got away with murder."

Gia's heart broke. She'd only met Savannah's father a couple of times—he tended to keep to himself—but he'd seemed like a nice man. And Savannah adored him. "Did they ever find out who…"

"No. The investigation wasn't handled properly. Hayes's rush to judgment compromised the whole investigation. That's part of what drove Hunt to become a detective. He's a good man, Gia. A man you can trust to do his job the right way. He will not rest until he finds out who really killed Bradley." She gestured toward the door. "No matter what Hayes thinks."

"Yeah. Thanks, Savannah."

"Any time, my friend."

Chapter 17

"Good night, Gia." Mark interrupted Gia rehearsing her speech about why she couldn't go out with Trevor, the speech she'd recited a million times in her mind and had every intention of delivering as soon as he arrived to pick her up.

She waved, still distracted with thoughts of letting Trevor down easy. "See you tomorrow."

She added a couple of blueberry muffins to Harley's bag and poured a large sweet tea. Then she strode through the back room, cracked the door just enough to set his bag of food and his drink on the table, and pulled it shut. His bag from the night before was gone. She hoped he'd been the one to take it.

Her thoughts went back to the night before. Harley didn't seem the type to hang out in such a drug-infested neighborhood. Despite whatever misfortunes plagued him, the couple of times she'd seen him, his eyes were clear and he'd seemed sober. She'd have to remember to ask Savannah if he used.

"Hello?" Trevor called from the front of the café.

"Coming." She checked the back door was locked and shut the light off, then practically ran for the dining room, not that she was in any hurry to hurt Trevor's feelings, but she couldn't stand the thought of anything crawling in the dark. "How are you doing, Trevor?"

"Great. It's a beautiful night for a walk. I've been looking forward to it all day."

Ugh… How was she supposed to let him down easy when he was standing there with a huge smile and a bouquet of daisies?

He held the flowers out to her. "I hope you like them."

"They're beautiful, Trevor, thank you." She took the flowers around the back of the counter and filled a glass with water. "Didn't you say you were bringing Brandy?"

"Yes. She's outside waiting."

"Is she okay out there?"

"Oh, sure. Everyone knows her, and she's very well trained, but I hooked her leash over the bike rack, just to be on the safe side. We should go, though, if you're ready. I don't like to leave her tied up too long."

"Oh, no. Of course not." Looked like she was not going to be able to back out of their date, after all. She put the flowers in the water and set them on the counter beside the register. "I'm ready. I just have to grab my purse."

"So, you're new to Boggy Creek. How do you like it so far?"

Even though the daytime temperatures still felt like summer, it could get a little nippy at night. Either that, or she just had a permanent chill she couldn't seem to shake. She pulled on her light jacket and slung her bag over her shoulder, then started toward the door. "It seems nice."

He ran ahead of her and held it open.

"Thank you." After he let the door fall shut, she locked it and dropped the keys in her bag, then stuck her hands in her jacket pockets so Trevor wouldn't get any ideas about holding hands while they walked.

He untied a gorgeous, full-grown German shepherd from the bike rack. "This is Brandy."

She petted the big dog's head. "Hello, Brandy. It's nice to meet you."

Brandy barked once.

Trevor kept a loose hold on the leash as they walked, but Brandy remained right at his side regardless.

"She's so well behaved. Did you take her for training classes or train her yourself?"

He kept Brandy on the far side of him and walked close to Gia, but he made no attempt to hold hands or put an arm around her. "I took her to classes. I can give you the trainer's business card if you're interested."

She started to relax a little. "Sure, that'd be great. I want to make sure Thor gets trained well."

"I agree. It's so important, especially with big dogs. You don't want them to hurt someone by accident because they jump up or anything."

She inhaled deeply. He was right about it being a beautiful night. The sun had just begun to sink behind the horizon, painting the sky in bold colors. "How old is Brandy?"

"She'll be six next month."

They walked in silence for a few minutes, not the awkward silence that could often lay between strangers but the kind of comfortable silence that often fell between friends. It seemed a lot of people had decided to take advantage of the clear, warm night. Couples strolled hand in hand, children skipped and ran beside their parents, and young mothers pushed strollers along the sidewalk. It was the first time Gia had walked through town, and she found she was enjoying herself.

"Do you live around here?" Trevor asked.

"Out in Rolling Pines."

"It's gorgeous out there. I take my ATV four-wheelin' through the trails sometimes on the weekends. Maybe you'll join me one of these days."

"Maybe." She needed to get through one night before she committed to anything else, and she didn't want to give him the wrong impression.

"Just don't let the skunk ape stories scare you too much." He laughed.

"Skunk ape?" What in the world was he talking about? Were there some kind of apes running around the forest with the bears?

"You know, skunk ape. The Florida version of Big Foot."

She stopped walking and stared at him.

"Don't worry," he backpedaled. "I doubt the stories are even true."

"Stories?"

"You know, the ones where people swear they ran into the skunk ape out on the roads at the edge of the forest, late at night. Alone. They always seem to be alone. Makes you wonder, right?"

"Uh…"

"Anyway, there's no such creatures running around in Rolling Pines. Probably. But according to local legend, you'll know if they're near because of the awful stench. So I guess, if you smell something horrible, you should…probably…uh… I should probably stop talking now, huh?"

She couldn't help but laugh. "That's okay. I'm scared enough walking to and from my car every day looking for bears and snakes and whatever else might be lurking nearby. I can't imagine skunk ape will make it too high on my list of phobias."

Easy to say while walking down the middle of a crowded sidewalk in a well-lit area, surrounded by open stores and shops. When she drove home later, and the dark forest threatened to swallow her whole, she had a feeling the stories would seem a whole lot more plausible.

They reached the doggie day care center, and she left Trevor and Brandy sitting on a bench out front and picked up Thor. After introductions were made, they headed toward the park. Trevor entertained her with stories of local traditions. She was looking forward to some of the art and craft fairs. Savannah talked about them all the time, but Gia had never been in Florida at the right time to visit one.

"So, tell me a little about New York. I've never been there, not much of a traveler really. Is it very different from here?"

She'd thought a lot about the differences lately. About what she liked better in Florida, like the weather, and what she didn't, like the critters. "There's huge skyscrapers, so high that if you look up, it feels like they're falling over on you."

"Oh. I don't think I'd like that."

"It's not so bad. If you go up to the top of the Empire State Building on a clear day, it feels like you can see the whole city."

Trevor pressed a hand against his chest. "I'm not much for heights. Honestly, the thought of standing on top of a building that tall makes me queasy."

Gia wasn't surprised. He didn't strike her as the adventurous type, more the type to settle down and snuggle on the couch with after a long day. Yikes. Where had that thought come from? "It's beautiful in its way, especially at night, when millions of lights dot the city. But not like here. The forest where I live is so gorgeous, almost…I don't know…primitive. Untouched. It's weird for me."

"Do you miss it? New York, I mean?"

"Sometimes." More than she'd like to admit, even to herself. "And sometimes not."

"I don't think I'd like starting over somewhere new. Some people enjoy new experiences. I'm more of a creature of habit. I admire your courage. It can't be easy to give up everything in search of a new life."

Yeah. Except, she wasn't brave. Not really, because in the end, she wasn't really running toward something as much as she was running away from something. That needed to change. She needed to gain control of her life if she was going to succeed. "You know what?"

"What?"

"I'm really enjoying myself. Thank you."

His cheeks flared red. "You're very welcome."

They walked together with the two dogs trotting happily beside them. Brandy seemed to be a good influence on Thor, and he walked at her side without pulling on the leash or trying to escape.

Trevor led her to a small clearing where several food trucks had set up. "What do you feel like eating?"

After the lunch she'd eaten, she wasn't particularly hungry, but she'd have a little something so as not to disappoint him. "What's good?"

"The tacos are amazing."

"Tacos it is then."

He gestured to a round picnic table in a small gazebo. "Why don't you grab that table, and I'll get the food? We're lucky we got here early. Half an hour from now, there won't be a table free."

"Sure. Why don't you leave Brandy with me, so you can carry the food?"

"Are you sure?"

"Positive."

He walked Brandy to the gazebo and settled her with a bone before heading to the taco truck.

Thor nestled down beside the big dog with a bone of his own.

All in all, she had to admit she was glad she hadn't canceled. Trevor seemed like a nice guy, more than a nice guy really, and she enjoyed the company. It had been a long time since she'd spent a relaxing evening with a friend. Even her nights with Savannah for the past few months had been filled with work on the café.

"Thank you." The man's voice came from directly behind her.

She turned and found Harley standing beside the Gazebo. "Oh, hey, Harley. You startled me."

"Sorry."

"No problem. Did you enjoy the food?"

"Yes. Thank you." He looked down at his hands gripping the gazebo railing.

"Would you like to sit down?"

"No. I… You shouldn't go to that place. It's a bad place."

"The motel?"

"Yes."

"Thank you for saving me."

"You're welcome." He gripped the rail tighter. "You were nice to me."

Her heart broke. Was it so unusual for someone to treat him kindly?

Harley glanced over his shoulder, then leaned farther over the railing and pitched his voice low. "The bad man goes there."

"Bad man? Goes where, to the motel?"

"Yes." He nodded.

"You mean the man who bothered me?"

"No, the other one, from behind your store."

"What?" She shot to her feet.

Harley lurched back.

She held her hands out toward him. "I'm sorry, Harley. I didn't mean to startle you. I was surprised is all."

"I-I-I wasn't looking for anything to eat. I p-p-promise. Newspapers. I was only looking for newspapers in the dumpster, not food. It gets cold at night in the winter and they keep me warm. People don't read them as much anymore, with all these new-fangled computers, so I have to start collecting as soon as it starts getting chilly at night."

"It's okay, Harley. I'm not mad."

"I didn't mean to do anything wrong."

"You didn't." She had to figure out who he was talking about. Could it be Bradley's killer? "Can you tell me about the bad man?"

"No."

"No? Why not?"

"He didn't see me. I don't want him to see me." Harley looked over Gia's shoulder. "I have to go. Thank you. Your food is good."

"You're very welcome. If you tell me what you like, I'll make sure to leave it for you."

"I like everything." He smiled, such an innocent smile, and then he turned and limped off into the shadows. She got the impression Harley was good at going unseen.

"You didn't say what you wanted to drink, so I got you tea. Hope that's okay."

"It's perfect, thank you."

Trevor set two tacos in front of her and a large sweet tea. "Was that Harley?"

"Yes."

"He's a nice guy."

"Yes, he is." She wanted to ask Trevor if he knew much about him, but she wasn't sure how far into the trees he'd gone, and she didn't want him to overhear. But his warning about the bad man haunted her. If not the man who'd approached her at the motel, then who?

Chapter 18

She'd enjoyed spending the evening with Trevor. She had a feeling if she stayed in Florida he could become a friend.

Thor squirmed in the back seat. He still had to be fed, and she wanted to work on his training for a little while before it got too late. He was getting better at sitting on command, plopping down about half the time, but he still needed work. Plus, it would be nice to get some play time together before she passed out. If she could sleep at all.

She hit the turn signal and made a left into her development, leaving the streetlights behind and heading straight into skunk ape territory. Her nervous laughter echoed in the quiet car. Creepy.

Darkness and silence surrounded her, the tall trees nothing more than shadows clawing at the sky. Little moonlight filtered through the canopy of trees and the cloud cover leftover from the afternoon storms. She flipped on the radio, but switched it off just as quickly. It was too loud. Intrusive.

She turned onto her street. Only a few houses lay scattered amid the trees. Soft light spilled from their front windows. Flickering light in one window brought visions of a family gathered in front of the TV. She wondered about these people, her neighbors. What had brought each of them to live on the edge of the wilderness, with bears and snakes and... well, whatever else might lurk in the shadows. Would she ever fit in? Would she ever have a family of her own to snuggle up and watch TV with?

She slowed down as she approached the end of the development. Even with her brights on, it would be easy to go right past the house.

Light pooled at the end of her driveway. She'd left the porch light on, but as far as she knew, there were no lamps close enough to the road to cast the puddle of light.

She slowed even more, creeping toward the driveway that was still blocked by trees. As soon as she passed the tree line, a car came into view. Someone had backed in and parked against the garage. The headlights shone straight at her, keeping her from determining if the vehicle was even familiar. She rolled past the house to the end of the street and turned around. Now what? No way could she call the police and tell them there was a car in her driveway. Yet, with the circumstances surrounding the past week, she couldn't just pull in with a stranger parked there either. She pulled out her cell phone. *Great. No service.*

Resisting the urge to slam the phone onto the seat, she headed toward the front of the development. She moved slowly, keeping her eye on the bars on her phone. Service in the development was spotty at best, but sooner or later she'd get it. Of course, by then the car in her driveway might be gone.

As soon as another bar popped up, she pulled over, locked her doors, and dialed while keeping her eyes on the rearview mirror. Though she couldn't see her driveway from where she sat, she could see the end of the road, so at least she'd know if whoever it was left.

Savannah answered on the first ring. "Hey. What's going on? Want company again?"

"Are you at my house?" She tried to keep her voice neutral, but she couldn't help the slight quiver. Hopefully, Savannah wouldn't notice over the spotty cell connection.

"No, but I can be if you give me about half an hour to shove a few things into my overnight bag. But if this keeps up, you're giving me my own bedroom. Your couch is lumpy and..."

Who else besides Savannah would come to the house? No one she could think of. Other than Savannah, Hunt, and Leo, no one even knew where she lived. She'd only bought the house recently and had just moved in. She had told Trevor what development she lived in, but hadn't given him the address. She really hoped the first nice guy she'd met—well, second if you counted Hunt, but he was apparently taken—wouldn't turn out to be some kind of weirdo stalker.

"Gia? Gia!"

Ah jeez. She'd zoned out, hadn't heard what Savannah was saying, hadn't even paid attention to any cars pulling out from her street. "I'm sorry, Savannah. What were you saying?"

"Are you okay? You sound off."

"Yeah. I'm sorry. I just got distracted. When I got home there was a car in my driveway, and I thought it might be you."

"Where are you?" The slight edge of panic in her voice didn't lessen Gia's fears.

"Down the street from my house. The car backed into the driveway and left the headlights on. It's too dark up here to see anything, so I have no idea who it could be. And with...well...you know, everything that's gone on lately, I was...um...nervous." *Terrified. Chicken. Whatever.* "I thought you might have stopped over, so I figured I'd call and check."

"Stay where you are."

"No, Savannah. I didn't mean for you to come out here. I just wanted to make sure it wasn't you at the house."

"Just stay where you are. Promise me."

She wanted to give in so badly. If she was to be honest with herself, she was scared and she wanted Savannah's company. Even though she didn't want her in danger. "I mean it, Savannah. I don't want you out here. I have no idea what's going on lately, but I want you to stay away from it."

"I'm not leaving you out there by yourself if you're in danger. Promise me you won't go home."

"I won't. I promise. I'm parked down the street. I'll wait until whoever it is gets tired of waiting around and leaves before I go home. For now, I'll just sit here with Thor and wait."

At the mention of his name, Thor poked his head between the seats. She petted his head. "You're a good boy, Thor."

"Hang on a second, and I'll stay on the phone with you until they leave," Savannah said.

"Sure, thanks, Savannah."

Thor tilted his head into her hand.

She weaved her fingers through his soft puppy fur, scratching the spot just behind his ear that he loved having pet.

"Okay, I'm back."

"We'll be fine, Savannah, thank you." She forced a laugh that probably didn't fool her friend for one minute. "It's probably a delivery or something, and I'm just panicking over nothing. Or maybe it's the police. Maybe they came back about the break in at the shop." Or the garage, which Hunt had no so gently reminded her of earlier.

The more she thought about it, the more foolish she started to feel. "I'm sorry, Savannah. I know it's probably dumb, I just—"

"Don't be silly. Of course, it's not dumb. You have every right to be scared. Let's just chat until whoever it is leaves. Okay?"

"Yeah. It's more than okay. Thank you."

"That's what friends are for. Now. What do you want to talk about?"

She didn't want to talk about her night out with Trevor, not yet anyway. Even though he was a nice guy, she didn't really have a romantic interest in him, and she didn't want to have to explain herself to Savannah. She did want to talk about the blonde Hunt had come into the café with, but she couldn't think of a tactful way to ask without pinging Savannah's radar. That was the down side of being so close to someone. They always knew when you were trying to hide stuff. Even from yourself. "You never liked him."

Rustling came through the static-filled cell connection, and she could picture Savannah tucking her legs beneath her on the couch and wrapping a blanket tighter around her as she settled in for what could be a long talk. Exactly as she had so many times when they'd lived together.

"Never liked whom?"

"Bradley."

Silence.

"I've always wondered why?"

"It doesn't matter. I just didn't like him, and I didn't think he was good for you. You deserved better."

"Well, I guess it turned out you were right. He was definitely not good for me."

"Like I said, it doesn't matter now anyway."

Gia wasn't ready to let it go, though. Savannah had told her years ago, before she'd moved in with Bradley, that he wasn't right for her. Gia could tell she didn't like him, but she refused to say why. She hadn't even attended the wedding, had said she couldn't leave her father at the time to go to New York. Gia had been disappointed, but she'd understood. That was Savannah's way, always putting someone else first. "It matters to me. You are my best friend, and you wouldn't have any involvement with Bradley."

"I grew up around boys. Tough boys. I know trouble when I see it, and that man was nothing but trouble."

"But how could you be so sure?"

She sighed. "Are you sure you want to know, Gia? I mean really sure? Because I tried to tell you once before, and you refused to hear it."

She bristled. "What are you talking about?"

"I didn't meet Bradley until you two were getting ready to move in together, which right there, should have been a red flag for you. Every time you wanted to do something with your friends, something came up, and Bradley couldn't make it."

"He was a busy man, didn't have a lot of free time." The excuse sounded lame after all this time, after learning the truth about her ex.

"Yeah, well, he had plenty of time for other women."

The comment stung.

"He was fooling around with one of the other dancers. I saw them together one night. It was after a show, one of the nights I knew he'd canceled out on you because he supposedly had to work. I confronted him." She sobbed softly, then sniffed. "I told him I was going to tell you, and instead of looking ashamed, he laughed at me. Called me naïve. He said if I told you, you wouldn't believe me anyway. Said you'd hate me." Savannah had known he'd been cheating on her and hadn't told her? How could that be true? It couldn't be. She couldn't accept that. "How could you think I'd hate you?"

"Because he said he'd make sure of it. That he would twist it and tell you I was lying, that I was jealous that you were moving in with him. And leaving me. The other woman, a woman I thought was my friend, took his side. She knew about you, but she didn't care. She was content with the arrangement they had. Didn't really care if you were in the picture. She loved the things Bradley bought her, the lifestyle he afforded her, with none of the commitment.

"She said she'd tell you I was lying." Savannah sobbed again, a deep, heart-wrenching sound. "She was supposed to be my friend. I liked that woman. I'd always prided myself on being a good judge of character."

"Savannah—"

"No. I waited too long to tell you all of it. If I don't finish it now, I may never."

Gia waited silently while she gathered her thoughts. Her head spun. Savannah had betrayed her. She knew what Bradley was doing and hadn't told her. Had the situations been reversed, would she have done the same? No. Savannah wasn't a weak woman. Nor was she naïve or gullible. She was strong and decisive. No way she'd have let Bradley's threats sway her convictions, even if his mistress did go along with him.

"I tried to talk to you. I tried to tell you he wasn't what you thought. Do you remember?"

After Gia had learned the truth of what Bradley was, she'd tried to block their years together from her mind. It was too painful to remember the man she'd thought he was.

"And then, even after he was arrested, you still stood by him. It was only after there was absolutely no denying the evidence of his guilt, after he drew you into his trouble, that you even started to come around."

She couldn't manage more than a harsh whisper. "You're right, Savannah."

The memories crashed through her. Sitting on the couch with Savannah while she tried to tell her Bradley wasn't the man she thought he was. She stopped short of telling her the full truth, that she knew for a fact he was cheating on her, but she had tried to warn her about him. And Gia hadn't listened. She'd blown it off. Most likely, if she had told her the whole truth, it would have made no difference. She'd have made excuses for him, listened to the lies he told her, because she wanted so desperately to believe him. She'd hidden her head in the sand for years, because she loved him, and she wanted to believe he was the man she thought he was, the man he pretended to be. No, Savannah wasn't weak and gullible, but Gia had been. Maybe she still was.

"After that, I left and came back home. I was getting ready to leave anyway. My career as a dancer didn't take off the way I'd hoped. But that incident proved to me it never would, because I lacked that cutthroat mentality that launched people to the top. I wasn't that person. I was never going to be that person, and I didn't want to become that person. I'm sorry, Gia. I should have told you the truth."

"No. I'm sorry. I do remember. I remember us sitting on the couch together, like we had so many times. Only that time, you didn't sit on your side and stretch the blanket between us. You moved the blanket away and sat beside me, facing me. I should have realized then you had something important to talk about. I just... I didn't want to know, I guess." Gia dug through her bag for a tissue.

"When you called me and told me that you finally realized what he was, I was so relieved."

"Is that why you helped me so much? Is that why you did so much work on the café, found the house, met the movers? All of it, Savannah. Did you do it because you felt guilty?"

Savannah laughed through her tears. "No, silly. I did it because I'm your friend. I stood by you while you were married to him, because I love you. And sometimes people make mistakes. But a true friend gives you the space to make those mistakes, stands by you while you navigate your way through them, and then helps you pick up the pieces when they blow up in your face."

Gia wiped her tears and laughed too. "You truly are the best friend I've ever had. And I'm sorry I didn't listen to you."

"I know, and it's okay. And now that I'm forgiven, don't forget that, okay?"

"Forget what?"

"That I'm your best friend, and I love you, and you love me, and I would do anything to protect you, and I—"

A knock on Gia's window interrupted Savannah's rambling. She didn't even have to turn her head to know she'd find Hunt standing there. "What did you do?"

"And I am not the least bit sorry I did what any good friend would do. I let you make your own mistakes and learn from them when the time was right, and I called Hunt to come see what was going on at your house when you were being just plain stupid." Savannah's soft laughter came over the line just before she disconnected.

Gia rolled down the window. "Hey."

"Hey. What's going on?"

"Oh, nothing. Just thought I'd hang around on the side of the road for a while and chat with Savannah."

Hunt pursed his lips. "Did you plan on calling me?"

"Uh… no, not really."

He studied her a moment longer, then shook his head. "Do you have any idea who would be at the house?"

"No."

"Lock your doors and wait here. I'll be right back."

She started to roll up the window, but he stopped her. "Make sure it's me before you open the window or door."

She nodded, rolled up the window, and checked the locks were still engaged even though she hadn't opened them. The concern etched in his hard features brought a wave of paranoia. She watched him cross the street, climb into his jeep, and pull out, leaving her alone, surrounded by the darkness of the vast forest.

She stared at the digital clock on her dashboard, wishing it had a second display so it would at least be moving.

Something howled in the distance. Did skunk apes howl?

Thor scrambled between the seats and tried to squirm into her lap.

She pushed the seat back to give him room and hugged him close.

Still, the clock didn't move.

Twenty minutes crawled by before the first police car flew past, lights flashing, though no sirens broke the silence. A second cruiser followed closely behind.

Chapter 19

Gia sat chewing her thumbnail.

Thor had been whimpering for the past few minutes. If she didn't get him out soon, he was going to make a mess in her car.

The last vehicle to pass her had been a police van a little while ago. She debated, as she had since the first cruiser had passed twenty minutes ago, whether or not to go to the house, go back to the café, or wait where she was until Hunt returned. Intense curiosity wouldn't allow her to leave, at least not until she knew what was going on. And yet, some part of her really didn't want to know, wanted instead to pretend all was right with the world, at least her small part of it.

As if not knowing would change whatever tragedy had obviously occurred. Shame on her if she hadn't learned her lesson about ignoring reality, especially when it was staring her in the face.

She clipped Thor's leash onto his collar and looked around before unlocking the doors. "Be quick."

He squirmed in acknowledgment—or maybe because he couldn't hold it any longer.

She opened the door and jumped out of the car, swiveling her head wildly trying to watch every direction at once.

Thor rocketed out of the car and squatted beside the front tire.

Careful to avoid the puddle he left, she coaxed him back into the car, slid in after him, closed and locked the doors, and finally took a breath. Enough was enough. She couldn't sit there all night waiting for Hunt to come back and give her permission to leave. Yeah, right. Like that was happening. In his dreams, maybe.

Besides, what if something had happened to Hunt? What if the other police cars had responded to his call for help? She shifted into gear and pulled away from the shoulder. She put her foot down a little heavier on the accelerator. She'd never forgive herself if something happened to him because of her.

When she turned onto her block, light assailed her. She squinted and gave her eyes a couple of seconds to adjust. Her yard was lit up like Times Square on New Year's Eve. At least it seemed that way in contrast to the surrounding darkness.

Police cars blocked her driveway, so she pulled to the side of the road and parked on the soft shoulder in front of a patch of woods beside her house, then cracked the windows before she eased the door open enough to slide out without letting Thor escape. "Wait here, Thor."

As much as she didn't love the idea of leaving him alone in the car, she couldn't take him with her until she knew what was going on. She slammed the door, locked it, and walked toward the driveway. Radio chatter filled the night, though she couldn't make any of it out.

She approached an officer who stood beside his patrol car and waited for him to get off the phone. "Excuse me."

"Yes?"

"I'm Gia Morelli. I live here. Can you tell me what's going on?"

His phone rang again. "I'm sorry. Just one minute."

He stepped away from her and pitched his voice low but kept a close eye on her.

She resisted the urge to squirm beneath his stare. Barely.

When he hung up, he yelled, "Detective Quinn will be right here."

"Thank you."

He nodded and turned away, leaving her standing alone on the edge of the driveway to contemplate the mess her life had become. And to wonder what on earth had half the Boggy Creek Police Department crawling all over her yard.

Only a few neighbors shared her block, but already a small crowd had gathered by the corner. Apparently, even in the middle of the forest, gossip traveled fast. Pictures of her standing in front of her house looking confused, surrounded by police vehicles, were probably already trending on the Boggy Creek Community pages.

She lowered her face into her hands. What a mess.

"You okay?" Hunt's firm hand on her shoulder grounded her.

"Yeah. Can you tell me what happened?"

"I can, but you're not going to like it. Do you want to go inside and sit down?"

Yes. She wanted desperately to go inside, to get out of the fishbowl, to sit down. To live a normal, quiet, boring life. "Just tell me."

"We found Remington's attorney."

"Horace Rabinowitz?"

"No. the other one. Don Reynolds."

"Did he say why he wanted to talk to me? Or what Bradley left me. Or why he left me anything at all?"

"No. He didn't say anything."

"So what does that have to do with all of this?" She waved her arm to encompass the police presence. Her heart stuttered. "Please tell me he didn't try to say I had any involvement in Bradley's schemes."

"No."

"Then what's going on?"

"We found Mr. Reynolds' body in the backyard."

"Wha—" Everything started to swim in and out of focus. The flashing lights made the entire scene surreal. Nausea threatened, and she bent over and put her hands on her knees, willing the bile back down, burning her throat. She couldn't throw up on the street with Hunt and all her neighbors watching, but chances were good it was going to happen.

"Gia, are you all right?" Hunt rubbed circles on her back, the heat from his hand burning through her shirt.

"I need…" She started to shake her head, then stopped when a new wave of nausea hit. She pressed the heels of her hands against her eyes. She hadn't even known Don Reynolds, had never even heard the name before Hunt had told her about the inheritance, and yet knowing he was dead in her yard burned a hole in her gut. "How? Why?"

Hunt didn't answer. Instead, he held up a clear plastic bag. "Do you know what this is?"

Her head throbbed, and she narrowed her eyes against the bright lights. "A flash drive?"

"Is it yours?"

"No. I use an external hard drive to back up my files. I don't use flash drives at all."

"What about Bradley? Did he use flash drives?"

She tried to remember if she'd ever seen a flash drive lying around Bradley's home office. "I don't know. Bradley always kept his desk locked. I never saw him use one, but I can't say for sure."

Unfortunately, how he backed up his data was the least of the secrets Bradley had kept.

"So, this doesn't look familiar to you at all?"

"I said no," she snapped.

Her curt answer did nothing to deter him.

"What about this?" He held up another evidence bag. That one contained a manila envelope with her name scrawled across the front.

"No."

"Can you tell if it's your ex-husband's handwriting?"

She leaned closer. The sloppy block print slanted downward across the front of the envelope looked nothing like Bradley's precise cursive penmanship. "No. Bradley was meticulous about everything he did. He used to use a ruler to address his letters perfectly."

"All right." Hunt ran a hand over his five o'clock shadow. "I'm going to be here for a while, so why don't you call Savannah to come pick you up."

"Wait. What was in the envelope?"

"Nothing. He was clutching the empty envelope in his hand."

"Where was the flash drive?"

"Tucked into his sock." He ran a hand through his hair. If the way it stuck up around his head was any indication, it wasn't the first time. "Look, Gia. I still have a lot to do. I'm waiting for the ME, I have people talking to your neighbors, and I have to track down where Reynolds was staying and try to figure out what he was doing here. I assume he came to talk to you, but I can't be sure. Now, please, call Savannah and stay with her until I get there. I have to question you, but I have to take care of a few other things first."

Question me? He made that sound an awful lot like he suspected her of something. Of course, it could just be leftover paranoia. "Can't I just go inside?" She wasn't even sure she wanted to, unless it was to get the makings of a "for sale" sign, but he had no right to tell her she couldn't go into her own home.

"Not yet. Maybe later on tonight or tomorrow."

"Did anyone break into the house?"

"Not that we can tell, but I have men searching it anyway."

"You have men searching my house? For what?"

"A man is dead in your backyard, a man I spoke with two days ago who said he had to contact you about an inheritance you supposedly know nothing about. An inheritance, I might add, that came from the last man that was found dead in the dumpster behind your café."

She bristled at his use of *supposedly* with the exact same inflection the detectives in New York had used when they'd come to question her after they first arrested Bradley. Even after she'd cooperated and allowed them to search every inch of their apartment. "So what does that have to do with you and your men invading my privacy?"

His jaw clenched. "Really? Is that how you want to do this?"

"I don't know, Detective." She worked hard to make detective sound like jackass. If his clenched jaw working back and forth was any indication, she'd succeeded. "I guess that depends on just what you're looking for."

"I'm looking for anything to indicate you might be in danger. Does that work for you, Ms. Morelli?"

"Why would I be in danger?" Okay, stupid question, and she knew it the minute it flew off her tongue, but she couldn't take it back, and she wasn't about to admit it. She folded her arms across her chest and stood her ground.

"Savannah called earlier. She said you found a box of folders Bradley left. Is that the box on the counter in the kitchen?"

"Yes."

"All right. Call Savannah to pick you up. I don't want you alone until I figure out what's going on." He started to walk away.

"Who died and left you in charge?" she yelled after him.

He turned back slowly and met her gaze. "Bradley Remington and Don Reynolds. So far."

At least this time she resisted the urge to stick her tongue out at his retreating back, leaving herself with some small shred of dignity. She got back into the car, slammed the door harder than necessary, and gave in and dialed Savannah's number.

She picked up on the first ring. "Are you okay? What's going on? I've been calling you for the past ten minutes. You didn't answer, so I tried Hunt, and he didn't answer, and I was—"

"Savannah."

"What?"

"Stop rambling, so I can tell you what happened."

"Sorry. Is everything okay?"

"No. Hunt found Bradley's attorney in my yard."

"What was he doing there?"

"I have no idea."

"Well, did you ask him?"

"No."

"What did Hunt say? He would have asked him."

"I'm sure he would have, if Reynolds was still alive to ask."

Savannah gasped.

"Hunt won't let me go into the house. He suggested I call you to pick me up, but could we just meet somewhere?" An idea was beginning to take form, an idea Hunt would be furious about if he knew, and even more furious she was involving Savannah. "How many hotels and motels are in the area?"

"One hotel, two small motels, and a couple of bed and breakfasts. But you are not staying at a hotel. You can stay with me. I'll be right there to get you."

"That's okay. I'm not planning to stay at the hotels, I'm just looking for someone. Could you do me a favor, though, and make a list of any lodgings you can find and their addresses? I'm leaving now, so I'll be there in about twenty minutes."

"Didn't Hunt say I should come pick you up?"

"Yup." She disconnected before Savannah could argue. Hopefully, she'd do what she'd asked. She had a feeling there was little to no chance Hunt was going to share whatever was on that flash drive any time soon. And there was absolutely no chance Gia was going to sit by while a bunch of detectives smeared her name and cast suspicion on her. Again.

If Don Reynolds was in town for any longer than one day, he'd need a place to stay. If she could find where he was staying and get into his room, she might be able to find out what he was doing there.

She petted Thor, sent him into the back seat, and started the car.

Police vehicles now lined both sides of the street, and portable lights had been set up on her front and back lawn. Half the police force milled around her yard. She searched for Hunt among them. She spotted him by the front walkway, pointing toward the garage.

She shifted into gear and started to pull away.

Hunt looked over at her.

She waved as she pulled out. She'd trusted the police the last time, and by the time they reluctantly cleared her, it had been too late to save her reputation. She wouldn't let that happen again. Time to take matters into her own hands.

Chapter 20

Gia reached across the passenger seat and held her hand out for the paper Savannah held. "Is that the list of hotels?"

Savannah leaned into the passenger side window and clutched the list tighter. "Are you out of your mind? You can't go to that attorney's hotel. Hunt will kill you. Then he'll kill me for helping you."

"I don't want you to help me any more than you already have. All I need from you is the list, and if you wouldn't mind watching Thor for a little while, that would be a big help."

Savannah contemplated her for a moment.

She should have just looked them up herself. If she hadn't said anything to Savannah, there'd be no witnesses to her lack of judgment. She'd just figured it would be easier for Savannah to do it since she knew the area.

"Fine. I'll let you have the list, but I'm coming with you."

"For the last time, I can't take you with me, Savannah."

"Then you don't get the list." She crumpled the paper and stood up.

"Oh, fine." She held out a hand. It was a fight she wasn't going to win. When Savannah dug in her heels, she could be stubborn as they come.

"Fine, what?" Savannah offered her sweetest smile, the one that meant you were treading on dangerous territory.

"Oh, just get in." She shoved open the passenger door.

Savannah hopped in, dialed, and pressed her phone to her ear. "Hey, Joey. Can you do me a favor?"

Joey's tinny laughter echoed through the car.

"Ha, ha. It's not really a favor for me. It's for Gia. Can you watch Thor for a little while?" She paused for a second. "Thanks. We're out front."

She hung up and smirked at Gia. "Not that I don't trust you to wait for me, but my brother will be right out to get him."

"Give me the list."

She smoothed the crumpled paper on the dashboard. "I wrote down the phone numbers too. I'll take the bigger ones, and you take the bed and breakfasts. I don't want to take a chance of getting someone I know on the phone and having Hunt find out I called."

"We definitely do not want that to happen." Gia started on her half of the list.

A knock on the window stopped her mid-dial. She rolled down the window. "Hey, Joey. Thank you for keeping him for me."

"No problem. Savannah told me you got a dog." He opened the back door and scooped Thor into his arms. "Oh, wow. He's gorgeous."

Thor wiggled wildly and licked Joey's cheek.

He laughed. "Better not be gone too long, or you might not get this big fella back."

Gia petted Thor's head. "You be good, Thor, and I'll be back in a little while."

He licked her hand.

"See ya in a few." Joey waved over his shoulder as he trotted off with Thor.

Savannah hung up her cell and crossed the second name off her list, then dialed the next number.

Gia struck out at the first bed and breakfast, then dialed the second on the list. She waited for the clerk to pick up.

Savannah hung up and shook her head.

"Boggy Creek Bed and Breakfast. How can I help you?"

"Hi. I'm trying to reach a friend of mine who's staying with you."

"What is your friend's name?"

"Don Reynolds."

"Umm..." The sound of keys tapping came over the line. "Yup, he's staying with us. Would you like me to put you through to his room?"

"Oh, uh..." She hadn't given any thought to what she'd do if she found him. Leaving a voice mail didn't seem like a good idea. She had to figure Hunt would eventually get around to listening to it, and that would be rough to explain. "You know what? I'll think I'll surprise him and stop by and say hello."

"Are you sure?" A slight note of suspicion had crept into the clerk's tone. She probably thought Gia was Mrs. Reynolds trying to catch her husband cheating. Well...better that than knowing the truth.

"Positive. Thank you for your help." She disconnected before the woman could ask any more questions.

"Where'd you find him?"

"Boggy Creek Bed and Breakfast. Do you know where it is?"

"Yes, actually. It's on the outskirts of town, not far from your development and surrounded by woods."

Gia shifted the car into gear and backed out of the driveway.

"Where are you going?"

"To see if I can find anything out at the B&B."

"You do know this is crazy, right?"

"Yup."

"Hunt will eventually go out there and search his room."

"I know. That's why I have to hurry. Hunt's probably closer than we are." She hit the accelerator. "If we don't get there first, I'll lose my chance. Do you want me to let you out?"

"No. I'm in, but..." She bit her lower lip. "Do you think it's dangerous?"

"He's already dead, so I figure whoever killed him probably took off. Why hang around after the police are already all over the crime scene?"

"I guess that makes sense."

They drove in silence. Despite her assurances to Savannah, she couldn't help having misgivings. This could be a really bad idea. But what else could she do? Trust the police again? Not after what happened the last time. She didn't have the strength to go through another trial, cameras flashing in her face every time she turned around. Besides, even though she wasn't sure she wanted to stay in Boggy Creek, it should be her choice. She didn't want to be forced to flee another home because of circumstances beyond her control.

Savannah pointed to a dirt road on the right. "It's up there."

Gia slowed. "If you want, I'll park down the road and you can wait in the car."

"Heck no."

She was going to owe Savannah big time when all of this was said and done. She might even have to give in and head to the Keys with her for a weekend of rest and relaxation.

Gia followed the dirt road as it wound through the forest, then opened up into a large clearing. An old southern mansion stood amid lush gardens. Large trees draped in moss lined the small circular parking lot. "Is this it?"

"Yes."

"No police cars. I guess, that's a good sign." She backed into a spot in the darkest corner of the parking lot—just in case she had to make a quick getaway—and parked. "Ready?"

"Do you have any sort of a plan?"

"Like what?"

Savannah rolled her eyes. "I don't know, but they're not going to just let you waltz up to his room and have a look around."

"Hmm...true."

"Do you have a piece of paper lying around?"

Gia dug through her purse for her notepad. "What are you going to do?"

"This is crazy, you know that, right?"

"You might have mentioned it."

"Yeah, well, I just want to make sure you realize it, so I can say I told you so when things don't work out."

"Ha ha." Gia handed her the notepad and a pen.

Savannah scribbled, *Just stopped by to say hello,* then signed it with an *L* surrounded by a fancy heart and ripped the page off the pad.

"What's the L stand for? Lover?"

"No. Lunatic," she huffed and folded the note in half. "Let's go, before I change my mind."

Gia hopped out of the car and they strode toward the front entrance.

Lanterns on arched poles lined the cobblestone walkway. Paddle fans turned lazily on both the wraparound porch and balcony ceilings. Rocking chairs and checkerboard tables sat sporadically across the porch. "This is beautiful."

"Yes, it is."

"Have you stayed here before?"

"Once, when I first returned to Florida and needed peace and quiet for a little while."

Forget the Keys. She could easily be talked into spending a weekend at the old mansion.

Savannah held the big front door open for Gia to precede her. She leaned close and pitched her voice low. "Let me do the talking."

No problem, since Gia had no idea what to say. She scanned the lobby. Ornate moldings, white columns, traditional furnishings. A curved stairway separated halfway up, each side leading to its own wing. No crime scene tape. Hopefully, that meant they'd beaten Hunt.

Savannah strode across the lobby to a small desk in the far corner.

An older woman turned her book over and propped her glasses on top of her gray hair. "Can I help you, ladies?"

Savannah turned on her most charming smile. "I sure hope so. I'm looking for a friend who's staying here. Don Reynolds?"

"Oh, are you the young woman I spoke with earlier?" She frowned. "I could have sworn you had a New York accent."

Gia started to open her mouth.

Savannah stepped on her toes. "Nope. I didn't call. I thought I'd just pop over and visit."

"Hmm…popular man, your Mr. Reynolds."

"Sure is." She shot the woman an exaggerated wink.

A blush crept up her cheeks. "Yes, well. Let me just ring him and see if he's in."

Savannah waited patiently for the woman to hang up, as if she didn't already know he wouldn't answer.

"I'm sorry. He's not answering."

"No worries. I didn't really expect to get him, just figured it was worth a shot. Would you mind giving him this?" She held the note out.

"Of course, dear." The woman took the note from Savannah and stuck it into a small box labeled *204.*

Bingo. Gia followed Savannah back across the lobby and out the front door. "Now what?"

"Now we get into room two-oh-four before Hunt does."

"How are we going to do that with her sitting smack in the middle of the lobby?"

"Oh, please." She shot Gia a wicked smile. "Don't even tell me you never snuck in a friend's window after everyone went to bed when you were a teenager?"

Gia just stared at her. "I grew up in Manhattan. We lived on the ninth floor. Think about that for a minute."

"Come on, then. I'll show you how it's done." She laughed as she hooked her arm through Gia's, looked over her shoulder to be sure no one was watching, and detoured off the path and around the side of the house.

Gia kept glancing behind her, but the night remained serene. Bugs chirped, something croaked loudly… She pushed away any thoughts of what might be hiding in the darkness, told herself her sweaty palms had nothing to do with whatever critters might be lurking in the dark and everything to do with the fact she was seriously considering breaking and entering. Despite what a lot of people believed, this would be her first ever illegal act. "Are you sure about this, Savannah?"

She stopped and turned to Gia, studying her in the moonlight. "It's your call. If you don't want to get in there, we'll leave right now. Just say the word, and we'll go get half a gallon of ice cream and a couple of spoons and sit on the couch and watch old movies. It'll be just like old times."

Gia studied the back of the building. Dim lighting lined the porch and balcony that ran all the way around the house. "How are we even going to get up there?"

Savannah toed off her sandals, took something out of her bag and stuffed it into her back pocket, then dropped her bag on top of her shoes. She climbed onto the porch railing, then reached over her head and gripped the second story balcony railings.

"You have got to be kidding me," Gia mumbled under her breath.

"It's this or strut through the lobby. Take your choice." She walked her feet up the pillar, inching her hands up the railings a little at a time, until she could hook her elbow over the top of the railing and hoist herself onto the balcony.

Gia slid her shoes off and tried to follow the exact path Savannah had taken. Her hands slid off the pillar, and she balanced herself atop the porch railing and wiped them on her jeans. There had to be a better way.

"Hurry."

Gia took a deep breath and tried again.

Savannah leaned over the railing and grabbed her wrists, then helped her climb over.

When she finally had her feet firmly planted on the balcony floor, she looked over the side. "Should I ask how we're going to get down?"

"Probably not."

Savannah had already turned away and was counting the windows and doors from the corner of the building. "The layout is really easy. Rooms one through ten are along the back of the house, starting at that end." She pointed toward the closest corner. "There's two double windows and a door leading onto the balcony in each room. So this one should be 204."

She slid a nail file from her pocket and slipped it between the double windows.

"Seriously? That's it?"

"Old-fashioned locks. Should pop right open." She stepped back as one window swung wide. "Voila."

"You're sure it's the right room?"

"Only one way to find out." She climbed into the window and held the lace curtains aside for Gia to follow.

Once they were inside, she closed the window and flipped the hook over to lock it, then pulled the big privacy curtains closed and turned on her phone's flashlight.

"Do you think it's safe to turn on the lights?"

"Probably better not to. No sense drawing attention if the clerk walks by for anything."

Gia turned on her own light. "Do you see a suitcase?"

"No. Try the closet." Savannah slid the dresser drawers open, then slowly closed them, careful not to make any noise. "Nothing. They're empty."

Gia opened a set of louver doors. A small suitcase and a briefcase sat in the middle of the closet floor. "I wonder why he didn't take the briefcase with him."

"I don't know."

She set the bags on the bed and opened the briefcase. She rifled through the papers as fast as she could while juggling the phone to keep the flashlight beam aimed at what she was reading. Nothing caught her attention. What appeared to be case files, but none of them had Bradley's name on them. She pointed at the letter head with Don Reynolds's name embossed in gold script. "At least we know it's the right room."

Savannah nodded absently while she dug through his suitcase. "Something seems...wait."

Gia put everything back into the briefcase the way she'd found it and set it back in the closet. "Did you find something?"

"Here, help me." She scooped out armfuls of clothes and set them aside on the bed.

Gia grabbed a pile and set them aside in a neat stack. "Seems like an awful lot of clothing for a quick trip to drop off a flash drive."

"And there's no business clothes. It's all khaki pants and flowered shirts. Either he was planning on doing some vacationing while he was down here, or he wanted someone to think he was." Savannah used her nail file to pry open the lining of the suitcase.

"Are you crazy?"

"Look." She smoothed her hand over the lining, and a rectangle appeared. "Feels like an envelope. I can feel the clasp."

Muffled voices echoed down the hallway. A man and a woman.

"Hurry," Gia whispered.

Savannah's hands shook as she peeled back the lining and grabbed a white envelope with Bradley Remington's name printed on the front. She shoved it at Gia and started cramming the clothes back into the suitcase.

The voices moved closer. Another woman's voice joined them.

Gia jammed the envelope into her waistband, yanked her shirt over it, and stuffed the last stack of clothes into the bag.

Savannah zipped it, stuck it in the closet, and closed the doors, then whirled toward Gia. "Go."

"...told you Mr. Remington is out. I called just a little while ago, and he didn't answer. I would have seen him if he came in." The doorknob jiggled.

Savannah yanked the window open and climbed out onto the balcony. Gia practically dove after her, pushing the window shut behind her. It bounced back open a crack. "We can't lock it."

The door opened from the hallway, spilling light into the room. Gia dropped flat onto her stomach beneath the window. "Get down."

Savannah crouched beside the window with her back to the wall. "Oh, man. We're gonna die," she whispered between gasps.

Okay, that was probably a little dramatic. Arrested maybe, but dead? She doubted it. Unless... "You think it's the killer?"

"No. Worse." She swallowed hard. "Hunt."

Ah jeez. Savannah was right. He was going to kill them.

Chapter 21

"When was the last time you saw Mr. Reynolds?" The man's voice drifted from the barely open window. Definitely not Hunt.

"When he checked in this afternoon. He checked in, put his bags in his room, and left again. He hasn't come back." Gia recognized the voice as the clerk they'd spoken to earlier.

Heels clacked against the wood floor. The closet door swooshed open.

"Hey. What are you doing?" the clerk demanded.

"Just taking a look," a woman answered.

"I said you could look in the room. I didn't say you could touch anything."

"Would this help?" the man asked.

There was a short pause, then the voice Gia recognized as the clerk spoke again. "No. Taking a few hundred dollars to let you take a peek in a room is one thing. I can't let you go through a guest's bags for any amount."

"We could—"

"That's fine. We understand, thank you." The second woman in the room put an end to the argument. "We're done here anyway. Thank you for your cooperation. I'm sorry we didn't believe you about Don not being here. He's a good friend, and he was supposed to meet up with us more than an hour ago. We were just concerned."

"Of course. I'm sorry I couldn't be more help, but I'm sure you understand I can't allow you to go through his things."

Footsteps retreated, followed by the room door clicking shut.

Savannah gestured wildly from the corner of the balcony.

Gia pushed off the floor and bolted toward her. The man and woman had paid a few hundred dollars just to get the clerk to open the door. Odds were, they'd be back to have a look for themselves as soon as they got the chance. She scrambled over the railing after Savannah, inched her way down to the porch railing, then launched herself onto the lawn.

By the time they grabbed their shoes and bags, made it to the car, and locked the doors, she was huffing and puffing like she'd just run a marathon. Savannah grabbed Gia's arm and slid down onto the floor.

Gia lay across the seats and whispered, "What?"

"The front door just opened."

"Did you notice where their car was?"

Savannah shot her a dirty look. "If you think I noticed anything out there, you're nuttier than a five-pound fruitcake."

A car door closed, and a car started. Tires rolled over the cobblestone. Gia and Savannah stared at each other.

Savannah held up one finger.

Gia nodded. Only one person had gotten into the car. "Maybe it wasn't them."

Shifting to contort herself farther beneath the dashboard, Savannah moaned. "I'm getting a cramp in my leg."

Gia tried to think. They had to get out of there, but she couldn't very well sit up without knowing if a killer lurked in the shadows. "All right. If it was them leaving, only one of them got into the car. If not, they're still lurking around somewhere. What do you want to do?"

"Can you peek out and see if anyone's out there?"

She was afraid Savannah would suggest that. She rolled over a little and elbowed Savannah in the head.

"Ouch."

"Sorry." She slid up just enough to peek out the passenger side window. Nothing. She sat up farther. Everything seemed quiet. "Let's get out of here."

"Whoop de freakin' doo," Savannah mumbled and unfolded herself from the floor.

Gia started the car, shifted into gear, and scanned the parking lot one last time.

"Wait." Savannah gripped her arm and slid lower in the seat. "Someone just came out."

A man strode down the porch steps and across the parking lot, duffle bag slung over his shoulder. Caleb Williams unlocked his car and slid behind the wheel. A guest who just happened to be headed out? Or was he the man who'd been in the room? She tried to remember if the man had any kind of accent, but she couldn't bring his voice to mind. She'd been so terrified of getting caught at the time, she hadn't noticed. Nothing had stood out to her, but then again, she was new enough to Florida that a southern accent would have drawn her attention more.

She waited for him to leave, then hightailed it out of there before anyone else came out. She considered following him, but with nothing else around for miles, there was no way he'd miss her on his tail. She checked her rearview mirror every two seconds as they wound down the dark driveway. When they hit the road, she looked around, then turned and headed toward home.

"Where are you going?"

"I just want to swing by the house for a minute and see if the police are still there."

Savannah flipped down the sun visor, looked in the mirror, and smoothed her hair. She wiped the mascara that had smeared beneath her eyes, leaving her looking like a raccoon. When she was done, she flipped up the visor and turned to Gia. She grinned. "Can't say I want to do that again."

Gia laughed. "Me neither."

Savannah rubbed her chest. "I thought my heart was going to explode."

"I know, right. All I could picture was Hunt poking his head out that window and seeing us there." Gia laughed harder, an image of Hunt's shocked expression etched firmly in her mind.

"Can you imagine? He would have killed us for sure." Savannah held her side and laughed harder.

Holding the wheel with one hand, Gia wrestled the envelope out from her waistband and handed it to Savannah. "I just hope this was worth risking Hunt's wrath for."

Savannah wiped the tears from her eyes and switched on the interior light, then opened the envelope. "It looks like his will."

"Are you sure?"

She flipped through page after page. "Most of it is legal mumbo jumbo I can't decipher, but it says here Mr. Reynolds was supposed to give you a flash drive and a one hundred forty-eight page document. He was supposed to hand deliver it to you in the event of Bradley's murder."

Gia's gaze shot to Savannah. "It says murder?"

"Yes. If he died in an accident or of natural causes, he was supposed to do something else with the document and flash drive."

"What?"

Savannah flipped the last page and turned the document over. "It doesn't say, just that he should follow an alternate arrangement in that case."

"He knew."

"Knew what? That someone was trying to kill him?"

"Yeah."

"Gia..." Savannah rubbed her hand up and down Gia's arm. "What he did to people, swindling them out of their life's savings, lying to them, hurting them, with no regard for anyone but himself, not even his own wife, who he vowed to love and cherish... You just can't treat people like that without expecting karma to come around and bite you in the ass."

"You're right."

"I know." She smirked. "I wouldn't have said it if I wasn't."

That coaxed a small chuckle from Gia. "It's just hard to believe he could be that deceptive. Even now, I still have a hard time wrapping my head around it. How could I have been so blind?"

"Because you're a good person with a big heart. You can't imagine someone you loved would treat people that way, because you never could. The fact that his behavior appalls you says a lot about your character." She pointed up ahead to the right. "Slow down, or you're going to miss the turn."

She let off the accelerator. "Thanks, Savannah. Not just for that, but for coming with me tonight."

"Heck, girl, I haven't had that much fun since I was sixteen, and I broke into old man Hardy's stable with Lorraine Helms and took his prize stallion out for a joy ride."

"You're kidding?"

"Nope. And the best part was Hunt and one of his buddies got blamed for it. But you know what?"

"What?"

"Hunt knew darn well it was me, but he didn't rat me out. Never even said a word, just took his punishment. Poor guy spent the whole summer shoveling horse poop."

Gia could imagine the young Hunt taking his baby cousin's punishment without complaining. "Why do I get the feeling there's a point in there somewhere?"

"My point is, you can trust him." She lifted the stack of papers still clutched in her hand. "Tell him. Let him figure it out."

"Tell him what? That I broke into a hotel room and stole documents from a secret compartment in a dead man's suitcase."

"All right, I can see where that might seem like a bit of a problem, but I'm telling you, after he gets all huffy and yells a little, he'll help you." She squeezed Gia's hand, then turned and looked out the window at the dark forest.

They drove in silence past Gia's house. It was still lit up like Grand Central Station, so she didn't bother stopping. Hunt would just chase her anyway. Besides, she wasn't ready to face him yet. First she had to figure out what to do with the documents now in her possession. "Is that legal?"

"Is what legal?"

"Having two separate wills depending on the circumstances surrounding your death."

Savanah pursed her lips and flipped to the last page of the packet. "I don't know. It's signed by Reynolds and Bradley, but I don't see a witness's signature or any kind of official stamp from the state or anything. Maybe it was just an arrangement between the two of them. If he wasn't murdered, Reynolds could just destroy this version and be done with it. Who'd know?"

"I guess." It still seemed off to Gia.

"Especially since all it said, for the most part, was to give you a flash drive and papers. If they were in his possession already, all he had to do was swing by and drop them off."

"And now, it's possible whoever killed Reynolds has the document."

"And if the document mentions the flash drive..."

"The killer will be looking for it," Gia finished for her.

Savannah looked at her, the dull light from the dashboard instruments illuminating the concern in her eyes. "Let's just hope whoever it is doesn't think you have it."

"Yeah."

By the time they reached Savannah's house, Gia could barely keep her eyes open. "I feel like I could sleep for a week."

"Yeah, well, you'll be lucky to get a few hours at this point."

"I know."

"You can park in the driveway. No one else will be leaving before you."

She parked and started to get out. "When this is over, we'll go away for a couple of days, if you want."

"Oh, I definitely want." She pointed at Gia. "And I'm holding you to it."

"All right, all right." It would be nice to get away, even just for a couple of days. She probably should have taken a break before she threw herself into the café. Who knew? Maybe if she had, none of this would have happened.

The minute Savannah opened the front door, Thor pounced, jumping up and down on his back legs while his front paws scrambled frantically against Gia's legs.

She picked him up and hugged him. "Yes, I missed you too."

He nuzzled her cheek.

Joey walked into the foyer. "He's awesome."

"Thank you. Did he behave?"

"Yeah. We played for a while, then he settled down on the floor at my feet and took a nap. A long one."

Gia looked around the small foyer. She'd never been to Savannah's house before. Savannah lived with Joey and her father, and although they'd invited her for dinner a few times when she'd been down, there just hadn't been time. Savannah had said she had four dogs, but Gia didn't see any sign of them. "Where are your dogs?"

"Pa took them upstairs with him when he went to bed. It was the only way to calm them all down." Joey grinned. "They sure did love having a puppy around."

Savannah punched his arm on her way past as she headed toward the kitchen. "Don't get any ideas."

He followed her. "Oh, stop. Once you have four, what's one more?"

"If you come home with another dog, you are taking over vacuuming duties."

"No way. That's women's work."

"Oh, you did not just say that."

He laughed.

"I'm just going to walk Thor and I'll be right in," Gia called after them.

She hooked Thor's leash to his collar, grabbed a plastic bag from a basket in the foyer, and headed out toward the road. As much as she enjoyed the interaction between Savannah and her family, it sometimes made her feel lonely. She'd lost everyone she loved…well…almost everyone, and sometimes the loss weighed more heavily than others. And the betrayal. Bradley's betrayal had been devastating, but the fact that many of her friends turned on her had left its mark as well.

She cleaned up after Thor, dropped the bag in the garbage pail beside the garage, and headed in. Standing there wallowing in self-pity all night would accomplish nothing.

The scent of coffee hit her as soon as she walked into the kitchen. "Mmm… That smells delicious."

"Sit." Savannah gestured toward the table. "I would have preferred ice cream, but I'm out, and there's nowhere to get it this late."

Gia washed her hands, then flopped onto a chair at the table, and Thor settled at her feet with a chew toy he found somewhere. "Do you ever miss New York? Being able to run out at any time to get anything you wanted?"

Savannah set out two mugs, spoons, and a creamer. "Not really. It was never right for me. The crowds, the pace, the tall buildings everywhere you looked. The gray sky all winter. It just never felt like home."

"I know what you mean." She'd hoped a new start in Florida would be the solution to all her problems, that she would love it, that the small community would embrace her and she'd find her place. But no matter how much she wanted it to be, Florida just wasn't home. Maybe it never would be.

The front door opened and closed.

Gia looked toward the sound. "Is that Joey?"

"No. He went up to play video games." Savannah glanced at the will sitting on the table. She tossed a dishtowel over it just as Hunt walked in.

"Hey there." He kissed Savannah's cheek, petted Thor, and sat across the table from Gia. "So, what did you two do all night?"

"Uh…" Gia couldn't tell if he was just being curious or if he knew full well exactly what they'd done all night.

He fished a paper out of his pocket and held it out to her between two fingers. "Look familiar?"

"Why would it?" She glanced at Savannah before taking the note and unfolding it.

"Oh, I don't know. Maybe because your fingerprints are all over it."

"My…"

"Were you ever fingerprinted for any reason in New York?"

Dang. She'd forgotten about that. "For comparison when they searched the apartment after Bradley was arrested."

"Mmm…hmmm. It took about two seconds for your prints to come back. Which really wasn't necessary, since the clerk was able to give such a vivid description of you and your sidekick." He shot Savannah a pointed glare. "Now, someone better start explaining something, or we're all going to take a ride down to the station and chat there."

Savannah propped her hands on her hips and huffed. "You wouldn't dare."

"Wanna bet?"

She pulled out a chair and sat, her best pout firmly in place.

"It wasn't her fault, it was mine." Gia sat up straighter. She wasn't about to let Savannah take the blame for something she did. Not that she believed for one minute that Hunt would drag Savannah down to the police station, but he was her cousin, and they were close. She couldn't come between them.

"I don't understand. You already knew Reynolds was dead. What did you hope to gain by going to the hotel?"

"I was hoping to take a look around and see if there was any indication why he was at my house."

"And how did you expect to do that? Did you think the clerk was going to open the door to his room and let you have a look see?"

"No." She sulked. She knew it was childish, but she couldn't help it. "Not exactly."

"Then what exactly were you thinking?"

"I thought if I could get into his room, I might be able to find something." She caught her lower lip between her teeth and looked up at him from beneath her lashes, hoping he'd be willing to let it go at that.

No such luck.

"That innocent look doesn't work on me. Just ask Savannah."

Savannah shook her head.

Great.

"So, when the clerk told you he wasn't there, you thanked her politely and went home, right?"

"Um…about that."

"Stop right there." He held up his hands as if to ward off the truth. "Let's just pretend the two of you left when the clerk said good night, went straight home together, and Joey saw you come in and hung out with you for a few hours. Let's also pretend I arrived at a crime scene that hadn't already been tampered with."

"Crime scene? What are you talking about?"

"The man staying in that room was found dead. In your yard. That means I get to search his room before anyone else does."

"Then you'll be thankful I didn't go in and get any papers or anything before someone else did."

"Someone else?"

"Well, hypothetically, of course…"

"Of course."

"Hypothetically, a man and a woman could have arrived at the bed and breakfast soon after us…I mean me…"

Savannah winced.

"And they might have paid the clerk a few hundred dollars to let them take a peek in the room to see if Reynolds was there. When he wasn't, they thanked the clerk politely and left. At least, one of them did. The other never got in the car. Hypothetically."

Unless Caleb Williams had been the man in the room. Then he had gotten into a car and left. But she knew all too well what it felt like to be innocent and in the crosshairs of an investigation, to be suspected when you had no involvement in anything illegal. She'd keep her mouth shut about Caleb. For now.

Hunt propped his elbows on the table, shoved his fingers into his shaggy hair, and sat that way for quite a while.

Gia kind of felt bad for him. He wasn't in a good spot. Thanks to her. After a few minutes, he held out his hand.

Without a word, she set aside the dishtowel and handed him the will.

"Get your stuff," he said.

"Excuse me?"

"Get your things. I'm taking you home."

"You mean, it's safe for me to go home now?"

"Yup. As long as I'm with you. Which I will be for the foreseeable future."

"Will be what?"

"With you. Now let's go. It's getting late and I still have to swing by my house and pick up a few things."

"You mean, you're staying with me? At my house?"

"Yes."

"What will Sonny think of that?" All right, petty, but she couldn't help it. Who did he think he was issuing orders and expecting her to just jump up and obey?

"She will not be the least bit amused, but right at the moment, I really don't care." He stood and pushed his chair in, then leaned over her with one hand on the table and one on the back of her chair, caging her in. "You will learn to trust me one of these days, Gia."

She slid her chair back and stood toe to toe with him. "Somehow, I doubt that."

"We'll see." He turned and walked out the door without so much as a good-bye.

"I'm really sorry, Savannah. It's my fault he's angry with you."

"Angry?" She laughed. "Trust me, honey, that was not angry. That's just a little miffed. He'll get over it."

He stuck his head back in the kitchen. "Uh-uh. You two don't get to be alone together anymore, since you obviously can't be trusted."

Savannah lowered her head and let her hair fall into her face to hide her smirk.

Hunt ignored her and pinned Gia with a stare. "Coming?"

She sighed, said good-bye to Savannah, and turned up her nose as she strode past him into the hallway.

Thor got excited and dodged between her feet.

She tripped and would have gone down if not for Hunt catching her arm. So much for her grand exit.

Chapter 22

Gia headed straight for the kitchen. Joey had fed Thor, so all she had to do was let him out and she could go to bed. Thankfully, Hunt had followed her home in his own car, after a brief detour to his house where she waited in the car, so she'd been spared his wrath during the half hour trip home. The front door closed before she made it out the back door with Thor. She cringed as she listened to his footsteps coming toward the kitchen. He pulled a chair out and set his duffle bag on it, then turned to her.

She braced herself for the lecture she fully deserved for involving Savannah in her problems.

"Is there still any barbeque leftover from the other night in the fridge?"

She stared at him for a moment, unsure what exactly he was up to. "There wouldn't be if I'd thought of it before I ate half a box of Cheerios for dinner last night."

"Good, I'm starved." He started taking food out and piling it on the counter. "Did you eat dinner?"

"Actually, I had a couple of tacos in the park earlier."

"Are you hungry?"

He opened the bag of chicken and the scent of barbeque sauce wafted out. "I could eat."

"Do you have plates around here somewhere?"

She opened the cabinet where she'd managed to get the plates put away, took two out, then pointed toward a drawer. "The silverware is in there. I don't have much to drink, though. A couple of bottles of water."

"That works." He took two bottles of water out of the refrigerator. "Do you have a microwave somewhere, or should I stick it in the oven to heat?"

"Actually, I'm pretty sure I was using the box with the microwave in it as a table in the living room."

He laughed and shook his head, then disappeared into the living room. He returned a few minutes later with the microwave in his arms. He lowered it into one corner on the counter and plugged it in. "Okay if I put it here?"

"That's fine."

She put the plates on the table while Hunt warmed the foam containers with the potatoes and gravy, then heated the chicken.

Finally, she couldn't take it anymore. "Why are you being so nice to me?"

He grinned, that cocky grin that made her want to slap him upside the head. Or maybe throw her arms around his neck and kiss him or something. "Would you prefer I be nasty?"

"You know what I mean." She huffed out a breath. In all fairness, it wasn't anything he did that had her so irritated. It was the fact that she was drowning in her own guilt. "I'm sorry."

His puzzled expression seemed genuine. "Sorry for what?"

"For making Savannah go to the bed and breakfast with me."

"Gia." He moved closer, until he stood face to face with her, then slid his fingers through her hair and tucked the loose strands behind her ear, but he didn't let go.

A shiver rushed through her.

"No one makes Savannah do anything. She's her own person. She makes her own choices. And if she chose to go with you to that bed and breakfast, I trust she had a damn good reason for doing so."

"I...uh..."

"I only wish you'd trusted me enough to talk to me."

"I...um..."

The microwave dinged, saving her from having to answer. Except, he made no move to get the food.

"I want to help you, Gia." His husky voice lowered, and he leaned closer. "I am going to help you, whether you let me in or not, but it will be a lot easier if you do."

She looked into his eyes, such a deep brown they seemed bottomless. "I'm sorry. It's hard for me."

"I know. I understand how hard this must be on you. And the fact that you had to go through so much of it alone breaks my heart. But you're not alone now, Gia."

She wanted so badly to lean a little closer, to wrap her arms around him, to lose herself in him.

"You have family now."

Family. Right. She took a step back, trying not to look too disappointed. "Thank you, Hunt."

He yanked her hair. "Any time. Now, let's take our food out back and eat on the deck and let Thor run around the yard and tire himself out."

She smiled, though her insides were a jumbled mess of confusion. "Sounds like a plan."

They each filled a plate and took them out onto the deck.

Thor took off as soon as they opened the door. Luckily, he didn't wander far, especially after dark.

Hunt sat on the wide top step, leaned his back against the railing, and took a bite. "Not quite as good leftover, but still delicious."

Gia settled down opposite him on the step. She popped a piece of potato into her mouth. "Mmm... I didn't even realize how hungry I was."

"So, tell me, do you think you'll stay in Florida once this is all over?"

Gia stared up at about a gazillion stars, more than she'd ever seen at one time. She didn't want to lie to him, but she honestly didn't have a clue where her life was headed. "I haven't figured out what I'm doing yet. Right now, I just want to get through each day." True enough. Until Bradley's killer was caught, she couldn't leave anyway. "Captain Hayes stopped by the café earlier."

"Oh?"

"Yeah. Seems he's not convinced of my innocence." She tried to keep the comment flippant, but Hayes's accusations still stung. She forked some shredded chicken into her mouth and chewed, but it suddenly seemed too dry.

"Don't worry about him. He's an ass."

She covered her mouth to keep anything from flying out when she laughed, then forced the bite of chicken down. "Savannah seems to think so too."

"Savannah is the kindest soul I know. She wouldn't hurt a fly, wouldn't wish harm on anyone, and she detests that man."

"So I saw." She moved the food around the plate with her fork, suddenly not as hungry as she'd been, then put the plate down. "I didn't know."

"Didn't know what?"

"About Savannah's mother. She never told me."

Hunt dropped his fork onto his plate and set the plate aside, then got up and held out his hand to Gia.

She studied him for a moment before putting her hand in his and letting him pull her up.

He weaved his fingers through hers and descended the remaining steps to the yard. He picked up a ball and tossed it to Thor, then strolled along the perimeter of the yard with Gia. "Savannah was young when her mother was killed, and she almost never talks about her. I never really knew if she didn't remember much about it or if she just kept it inside." "I always considered us very close. I thought I knew everything about her. She told me all about growing up in a family full of boys." The memory of some of the escapades Savannah shared over the years brought a smile. "She talked about her dad, her brothers, her cousins, her friends. But not her mother. All I knew was that she passed away when Savannah was young."

"Savannah found her."

A vice squeezed Gia's chest, making it hard to take a breath. She stopped walking and faced Hunt. Tears leaked out before she could stop them. "She came home from school and found her in the kitchen. They never found who did it." Hunt caught one of her tears on his finger. "Savannah… She's strong. But she keeps a lot inside. I worry about her."

"I know." And Gia had put her in danger. Now she felt like an even bigger jerk. She lowered her gaze, turned away, and resumed walking.

Hunt accepted the change and walked beside her. "Did she tell you Leo asked her to marry him?"

"What? No." Maybe Savannah didn't share as much as Gia thought.

"He's asked every year since she came back to Florida, and every year she says no. It's obvious she has feelings for him, but she won't even date him seriously. As far as I know, she's never had a serious boyfriend."

"Come to think of it, she never really dated in New York either. Occasionally, she'd go out with a male friend, or in a co-ed group, but not a real date. I always kind of assumed there was someone back home she cared for."

"Leo loved her even then. He bought a ring before she left, but he never proposed." Hunt laughed out loud. "Not even when I caught him and jacked him up against a wall and threatened him."

"Why did you do that?"

"Because I thought if he asked her she'd stay."

"So why didn't he ask her?"

"That's what I asked him. And he told me he couldn't ask her for that exact reason. He loved her too much to ask her to give up her dreams. So, instead, he waited for her to come back. And he's been waiting ever since."

Gia tried to digest everything he'd told her. She had to admit, she felt a little hurt Savannah hadn't shared so much with her, but her friend obviously had her reasons for remaining quiet. Just like Hunt had his reasons for sharing. Gia knew him well enough to realize he would never gossip about Savannah. "Why are you telling me now?"

"Savannah has been happy since she found out you were moving here, happy in a way I haven't seen her in a long time. She withdrew after her mother's death. She was still the same happy kid she'd always been, friendly to everyone, but she changed too, became distant. She held everyone at arm's length. She never got very close with anyone, never trusted anyone enough to let them in. Until you."

They finished their circuit of the backyard, and he stopped before climbing the steps to the deck. "It's obvious you and my cousin are close. I honestly believe she'd have told you about her past if she could have. I just..." He raked a hand through his hair. "I guess, I just wanted you to keep her in mind while you're deciding what to do. Not that I want you to do something that's not right for you, but I think you and Savannah are good for each other. Need each other. Family is important."

Gia nodded.

"Anyway, that's all I really wanted to say." His cell phone rang, and he pulled it out and checked the screen. "I'm sorry, I have to get this."

"Sure."

He pressed the phone against his ear. "Yeah?"

"Where are you?" A woman's voice came across the line clear as could be, breaking the serenity of the night. And whoever it was, was not happy.

"I'm at Gia's."

A long, awkward pause followed.

"Did you need something, Sonny?"

"Yeah, but don't think we're not going to discuss this later."

"Yup. What's up?"

As much as she wanted to stand there and listen to the rest of his conversation with Sonny, Gia forced herself to walk away. No way was she getting in the middle of a lover's spat. As far as she was concerned, Hunt was just a friend. Though she was starting to regret that just a little. The more she got to know Hunter Quinn, the more she thought he might be a man she could learn to trust, a man deserving of her trust.

She opened the back door and called Thor from his favorite digging spot beneath the big tree in the middle of the yard. After cleaning the sandy dirt from his paws, she took him with her to the bedroom to hunt for some sheets for the couch. If Hunt was really staying with her tonight, he'd need something to sleep on. She hit the jackpot in the fifth box she opened and pulled out a clean sheet and a light blanket. He'd have to settle for using the arm of the couch as a pillow, since she couldn't seem to find any.

When she returned to the living room, he was still outside on the deck by the back door, phone pressed to his ear, so she left the bedding on the couch, settled Thor in his crate, put on shorts and a T-shirt, and lay down in bed.

She picked up the novel she'd started, but had only read a couple of pages when her eyes started to close. For the first time since she'd moved in, she started to doze off feeling safe and unafraid. Half asleep, at the total mercy of her subconscious, she fell asleep thinking she could get used to having Hunt around.

"Gia." A man shook her shoulder.

Was she dreaming?

"Gia. Wake up."

She shot up to sit in the bed and yanked the blanket up to her chest. "Hunt?"

"Yeah. Sorry, I didn't mean to scare you. I need you to look at something for me."

"What?" She scooted up farther, until her back hit the headboard, then pulled her knees up to her chest. "What time is it? Is something wrong?"

"You've only been asleep for a couple of hours, and I wouldn't wake you if it wasn't important." He sat on the edge of her bed and scrolled through something on his phone. "I heard from one of the detectives in New York. They've been following up on anyone who made threats against Remington in the past, and they found one man, a victim. He boarded a flight for Orlando the day after your ex flew down, the morning of the murder, then disappeared. No one's seen him since." He settled on an image, enlarged the picture, and held out his phone. "Do you know this man?"

She squinted to get a better look, her eyes still blurry from exhaustion. "Oh my..."

"You recognize him?"

"Yes."

"From New York, or have you seen him down here?"

"I saw him in the café. He's been in a couple of times since...well...you know. He said his name was Caleb Williams." She'd read over the names of the people involved in the civil suits against Bradley and her numerous times. "I don't remember seeing his name anywhere, though."

"Because his name isn't Caleb Williams, it's Caleb Fontaine."

"Oh. Oh no." She recognized the name immediately. He'd been one of the many to call and harass her during the trial. He'd never believed she was innocent, even after she was exonerated. And he'd vowed to get even.

"When was the last time you saw him?"

"Um…" She tried to remember, but everything seemed foggy. He'd asked her out to dinner the same night Trevor had. And she'd almost said yes. Had she almost gone out with Bradley's killer? Had he intended to kill her? "Gia?"

"Oh, uh…sorry. He came into the café… I think it was the day before yesterday. The day you were there with Sonny."

"Is that the man you were talking to at the counter? He had his back to me, so I never got a look at his face."

"Yes. And then I saw him again tonight when we were at the bed and breakfast. He came out and got in his car when we were leaving. He had a duffle bag with him, but I didn't leave until after he'd gone, so I don't even know which way he went."

Hunt nodded. "Do you remember if you saw him at all before Bradley was killed?"

"No. I can't remember. I can't think straight yet."

"It's all right. If you think of anything else call me and let me know."

"Call you? Aren't you staying?"

"I can't. Leo is going to be here in a few minutes. He'll park out front and keep an eye on the house until morning, then he'll bring you to the café. I'll pick you up when you close and drive you home." He stood and dropped a quick kiss on the top of her head. "Hopefully, we'll have him in custody by then, now that we know he's probably still hanging around."

He didn't have to tell her he was probably still hanging around to kill her. She'd pretty much figured that one out on her own.

Chapter 23

Gia recounted the money from the register drawer. She had to have made a mistake. Her mind had been everywhere but on business all day. She hadn't heard a word from Hunt since he'd left in search of Caleb the night before. He was supposed to pick her up after they closed, which, technically, wouldn't be for another hour, but they hadn't had a single customer since lunch time, so she'd closed early. At least, they'd had a fairly steady, but slow, breakfast and lunch.

All she wanted to do was clean up, get Thor from daycare, and go home. She couldn't help but wonder if Hunt still planned on staying with her. She'd be lying if she didn't admit some small part of her hoped they didn't find Caleb Fontaine.

As much as she'd enjoyed her walk in the park with Trevor, that spark of attraction just wasn't there. But with Hunt…well…what could she say?

She threw the pile of bills she was holding onto the counter after losing track again. No wonder she kept coming up short. She had to clear her mind. She'd be better off if Hunt found Caleb and went back home to Sonny. The last complication Gia needed in her life was a man.

"Okay, let's try this again." She rubbed her eyes and tried to concentrate. She sorted all the bills into piles separated by denomination, then grabbed an order pad and pen. At least then if she got sidetracked and lost count, she wouldn't have to recount all of it. Not that there was more than a couple thousand dollars.

Mark stopped at the counter before she made it through the first pile. "Do you want me to wait while you lock up?"

"Is everything done? The garbage out?" She still avoided going out back, except for cracking the door open to leave Harley's dinner, which she'd almost forgotten to do. She'd have to take care of it as soon as she finished with the register.

"Yup, and the back is all locked up, but I could hang around if you want, just so you don't have to leave alone."

She waved him off. "I'll be all right. Detective Quinn is picking me up. Thank you, though."

He frowned. "Detective Quinn? Is something wrong?"

Unsure if Hunt wanted anyone else to know they had a suspect, she dodged the question. "No. Everything's fine. I just didn't drive in this morning, and he offered to pick me up and drive me home."

"All right then. I'll see you tomorrow." He started toward the door but turned back. "Make sure you lock up behind me."

Distracted by the fact that the day's receipts didn't match the amount of money in the register, she followed him to the door, waved, and locked the door when he left. Then she returned to the register and counted the drawer again. Still three hundred dollars short. "This doesn't make sense."

But there was no arguing her findings this time. She'd counted one pile at a time and written her results on the pad, then added them up. And she came up with the exact same total she'd come up with every other time she'd counted.

She racked her brain for where the money could have gone but still came up empty. She hadn't gotten any deliveries, hadn't run out for anything, hadn't given Mark or Willow money to run errands. There was simply no other excuse. Someone had stolen from the register.

Willow was the most likely suspect, since she was the only person, other than Gia, to regularly ring up customers, but the thought broke Gia's heart. She liked Willow. A lot. The girl was a hard worker. She was good with the customers. Gia couldn't believe she'd steal from her.

Perhaps the money had slid down the back. She pulled out the drawer and searched underneath. Nothing. She replaced the drawer and slid it shut. No way could she confront Willow without being a 110 percent sure the money was missing.

She emptied the shelves beneath the register and looked at all the shelving. If the money had fallen into the bins she kept underneath for dirty dishes, she or Mark would have found it when they'd emptied the bins and loaded the dishwasher.

Hmm…Mark? She couldn't remember Mark having used the register that day, but he certainly knew how it worked. She'd trained him herself.

Maybe she should just suck up the loss this time and give everyone their own code to access the register. At least if it happened again she might be able to narrow down when the discrepancy occurred. As it was, there wasn't much she could do.

With a sigh, she pulled out the drawer and started counting again. Whatever the amount this time, it was going in the deposit bag. She'd hoped to get out early, but by the time she finished making Harley's dinner and cleaning up, she'd be lucky if she finished before Hunt got there.

She started counting again, but a knock on the door interrupted her. She glanced up, expecting to find Hunt standing there, but instead, she found Miranda Ainsworth.

Giving up on counting, she jotted the amount she'd kept getting on the deposit slip, stuffed that and the money into the deposit bag, and shoved the bag into her purse on the counter.

Fading sunlight glinted off Miranda's ring when she gestured for Gia to unlock the door.

Gia stuck her purse on the shelf beneath the counter and went to open the door. May as well get this over with. She probably should have called her after she'd fled the hotel and let her know she'd turned everything over to the police. Hopefully, they'd be able to help her get her money back. And if not, well maybe she'd be more careful who she got involved with in the future. Though Gia felt bad about the uncharitable thought, she couldn't help it. The woman had obviously known Bradley was married to her when she'd gotten involved with him. Not that it served her right—no one deserved to lose everything—it just wasn't Gia's problem.

She unlocked the door and stepped back. "Come on in, Ms. Ainsworth."

She strutted through the door like she owned the place. "Did you find it?"

"Find what, exactly?"

"Don't play with me. Did you find anything that belonged to me?" She pointed a dagger sharp, blood-red nail at her. "Or did you come to your senses and decide to give me what's mine?"

"Look, I don't know exactly what you're looking for, but I did find paperwork with your name on it." She could at least give her that much, though it probably wouldn't help. She rounded the counter, retrieved her purse from the shelf, and dug through for her cell phone. She pulled up the picture she'd taken of the paperwork and held the phone out. "That's all I found."

Miranda yanked the phone from her and stared at the picture through the cracked screen. She played with it until her name showed between cracks, then ran her finger along the line her name was on. "This'll do for now. Where is it?"

Uh oh. This was the part where she wasn't going to be happy. "The police have it."

"What!" She slammed the phone onto the floor.

"Hey!"

"Are you crazy?" Smoke practically poured from her ears. "Why would you give it to the cops?"

"It was in a box with a bunch of folders. The police confiscated it all." Confiscated, she handed it over, same difference.

"Why would they take the folders?"

"I-I-I don't know. They took them when they found the lawyer."

"What lawyer?"

A noise came from the back room. It sounded like the door clicking shut, but Mark had locked it before he left, so it was probably wishful thinking. "Don Reynolds."

"Did that snake tell them anything?"

"N-no. He wasn't able to."

"You mean, he's dead?"

"Yes." Maybe she shouldn't have said that. Oh, well. Not like she could take it back. And right now, she'd say just about anything to get this woman out of her shop. "So, you'll need to get the papers from the police. Sorry, I can't help you further, but I really have to get done. My ride will be here any minute."

Miranda paced back and forth in front of the counter, tapping a fingernail against her chin. "No."

Gia slung her purse over her shoulder. "Excuse me?"

"I said, no." She pulled a gun out of her purse and pointed it at Gia, her hand shaking wildly. "You're not going anywhere."

Gia froze. She focused on the back room, desperate to hear a repeat of the sound she'd heard indicating that someone had come in to save her. She couldn't hear a thing over the blood rushing in her ears and her ragged breathing. She was going to have to get out of this herself. "What do you think you're doing?"

"You are going to get the papers back from the cops. Call them and tell them you need the paperwork back. And where's the flash drive?"

"Flash drive?"

"Reynolds should have had a flash drive with him when he died. Where is it?"

"The police found it."

"What!" The scream she let out sent shivers running through Gia. The woman was completely and totally unbalanced.

"I don't know what you're—"

"You don't know anything, right? Innocent little Gia. Wasn't involved in anything her big, bad husband was doing. Didn't even suspect anything. Just another victim." She lifted the gun toward Gia. Her hand steadied. "Well, I'm not buying it."

"I—"

"What's going on?" Mark strode through the door from the back room. She'd never been so relieved to see anyone. "Call 911. Hurry."

Miranda kept the gun trained on Gia. "Oh, nothing much. Gia here was just telling me how the police found the flash drive on the dead lawyer."

"Hmm…" He stuck hands in the pockets of his khakis and rocked back on his heels.

"Don't stand there and hmmm me." Her cheeks flushed purple, and strands of hair came loose from her up-do and tumbled into her face. "You weren't supposed to kill him until you had the flash drive, you moron."

"I got interrupted."

"What?" Gia's head spun, then realization dawned. "Oh. Oh, no."

"Is that all you have to say for yourself?" Spittle sprayed from her mouth. Miranda Ainsworth was definitely losing it.

And if Gia didn't find a way out of there soon, she probably wasn't going to get out.

"Give me the gun, Miranda, before you hurt yourself." Mark held out a hand and inched toward her. Maybe he was on Gia's side after all.

"You know how important that paperwork is. I have to have those names." She shoved the loose strands of hair back into her bun.

"I know."

"I already lost everything, and we can't continue Bradley's work without that information."

"It's okay. We'll get what we need," Mark told her calmly.

"How?"

"Hand me the gun, and I'll show you."

She raked her gaze over Gia, then relented and handed him the gun. Her shoulders slumped.

A breath of air whooshed out of Gia's lungs in a painful burst. "Oh, thank you."

"Don't thank me yet." Mark held the gun out in front of him, aimed right at Gia's chest. "You are going to get that information from your new friend, Detective Quinn."

"But I—"

"But nothing. I have no intention of leaving here poor. Remington's entire scheme is outlined in those papers and on the drive. Names, account numbers, contacts, everything. As soon as we get it, we can get out of here and start over."

"Start over? You mean swindling people?"

"That's exactly what I mean. Three hundred dollars is not going to get me very far."

Gia gasped, and despite the desperateness of her situation, anger surged. "You stole the money out of the register."

He laughed. "Not like you'll be needing it where you're going. Now come around the counter and pick up your phone."

She glanced at the clock. Hunt should be coming soon to pick her up. If she could just stall...

"Don't bother. He won't make it in time."

She bit back an angry retort before it could slip out. The last thing she needed to do was antagonize a man holding a gun on her. She rounded the counter, bent, and retrieved the phone. One look at the screen sank any hopes of calling for help. She held up the shattered screen for him to see. "Your friend had a temper tantrum."

He shrugged it off and moved behind her. "No problem. Use the phone in the back."

If she could call Hunt, maybe she could find a way to let him know she was in trouble. Or maybe she could call Savannah. Savannah knew her well enough to read between the lines. Hunt, not so much.

Miranda shoved her toward the back room. "Move faster."

Gia stopped and glared at her. Once she made it into the back, the chances of anyone looking in the front window and noticing what was going on dropped to about zero. "I don't know what Bradley ever saw in you."

Miranda looked down her nose at Gia. "Do you know what got Bradley killed, Gia?"

"No. What?"

She stared directly into Gia's eyes and lowered her voice to a conspiratorial whisper. "He didn't move fast enough."

"What are you talking about?"

"He was supposed to contact you and get the box you took out of the storage area, but he kept making one excuse after another, avoiding me. Had he moved just a little faster, Mark wouldn't have had to put a bullet in his head. Now..." She shoved her again. "Start moving, or you will be joining him soon."

Gia had no intention of joining Bradley in the afterlife. As she started toward the back room, she slid the cracked phone into her purse.

Mark followed her.

She could feel the gun aimed at her back. If she lived through this, she'd have—

Her fingers brushed something cool and hard in her purse. Hope soared. She'd only have one chance, and if she screwed it up, she'd be dead. Heck, she was probably already dead. She yanked the bear spray from her purse and depressed the button as she whirled on him.

Mark screamed, pressed his hands against his eyes, and started choking.

Miranda waved a hand wildly in front of her face, choking and crying.

Gia bolted. With Mark and Miranda between her and the front door, she ran through the back. There was nowhere to go but out the door into the parking lot where Bradley had been found. She hit the door at a dead run, and slammed her face and shoulder into it. Locked.

She fumbled the keys out of her bag, found the right one, and shoved it into the lock.

Footsteps pounded behind her. Mark was almost on her. "You're dead now."

Finally opening the lock, she shoved through the back door into the parking lot.

The door didn't even fall all the way shut before an irate Mark shouldered through and stopped in the doorway, holding the door open with his foot. "Stop right there."

She did as he said. Even though there were several cars and a new dumpster in the lot, she'd never make it to any of them before he could pull the trigger.

"Hands up."

She slowly raised her hands.

"We can do this the easy way or the hard way."

She turned toward him, keeping her hands in sight. "Does the easy way involve you not killing me?"

"Nope. But it can be a lot less painful if you give us what we want." He sniffed and swiped at the tears tracking down his face. Unfortunately, she hadn't managed a direct hit.

She nodded. She had no clue how she'd get the information they wanted, but she had no intention of dying in the parking lot behind her café, a mere twenty feet from where Bradley had been found.

"Let's go." He waved her toward him with the gun.

She started forward. Movement from the side of the building caught her attention. She tried to see what it was from the corner of her eye, without alerting Mark. From where he stood in the doorway, the door he still held open blocked his view of the corner of the building.

She inched forward slowly, allowing tears to flow. Her anger would have allowed her to hold them back—at least, for the moment—but she wanted to appear weak, vulnerable. Maybe he'd make a mistake.

Hunt poked his head around the corner.

She sucked in a breath, then cried harder. This time she couldn't have held it back if she'd tried.

"Hurry up. I don't have all night."

Hunt crept around the corner and edged closer to the door, gun trained firmly on the open door.

Gia kept her gaze locked on Mark. "You don't have to do this, you know."

"Yeah, I know. But I have no intention of spending the rest of my life living in some ramshackle motel. Or a one bedroom apartment over your café."

Hunt silently held up a finger.

"You're a great cook. I'm sure you could get a job in a restaurant that pays better." She didn't really care what he did. If she could keep him talking another few seconds, Hunt might be close enough to help her. Then maybe Mark could spend his days cooking for the other inmates.

He laughed. "No thanks. Now get in here."

Mark let go of the door and lunged for her.

She dove to the side, slammed into the concrete, and rolled.

"Freeze, Cooper." Hunt held the gun steady. "Lower your weapon."

Ignoring Hunt's order, he spun back toward the door, but it had already fallen shut. He punched the side of the building, then laid the gun on the ground and held his hands out to the sides.

"On your knees." Hunt crept closer, gun still pointed at Mark. "Hands behind your head."

Sonny rounded the other corner of the building, gun in hand, attention fully focused on Mark. "Go ahead. I've got him."

Hunt finally holstered his gun and handcuffed Mark, then hauled him to his feet.

"Take care of her." Sonny grabbed his other arm then nodded toward Gia and led Mark away. "Mark Cooper, you have the right to remain silent..."

Hunt held out a hand. "Are you all right?"

She nodded and took his hand. "Miranda Ainsworth is—"

He pulled her to her feet and looked her over. "We already have her."

"But how?"

"She was running out the front door when we arrived. Sonny arrested her. We knew Mark had gone in, but we couldn't see him or you. I was just coming around the back of the building when you burst out and nearly gave me a heart attack."

She forced a little laugh. "I mean how did you know I was in trouble?"

"Harley."

"Harley? I don't understand."

"Harley saw you at the park with Trevor, so he knew the two of you were friends. A little while ago he ran into the ice cream shop demanding Trevor call the police. Said you were in trouble. Trevor has known Harley for a long time, and he said he'd never seen him inside a building. Figured if he came inside, especially as agitated as he was, you needed help."

"But how did Harley know?"

"He stopped by to pick up his dinner, but it wasn't out yet. He sat down just over there." He pointed to a wooded area at the far edge of the lot. "There's a clearing a few feet into the trees, with an old stump Harley likes to sit on, that allows a perfect view of the back of the shop. And the dumpster. He was hanging out there the night Remington was killed, saw Cooper dump him."

"Why didn't he tell anyone?"

Hunt shrugged. "Harley is a nice guy, a really nice guy, and he saved your life, but he has...issues too. When it mattered, he called. He said he just saw the bad man he told you about going into the café."

Oops. She was probably going to have to explain why she hadn't mentioned that.

Hunt pulled her into his arms and rested his chin on her head. "Are you sure you're okay?"

"I am." It surprised her to realize that was true. She wrapped her arms around Hunt's waist and laid her cheek against his chest. The strong, steady rhythm of his heart soothed her. And she indulged in the comfort he offered. She needed it, even if just for a moment.

He set her back too soon and took her hand. "Come on. Savannah's waiting out front, and she'll kill me if I take too much longer."

"Savannah? What's she doing here?"

"She came as soon as she heard."

"You called her?"

"Of course not." Mischief danced in his eyes. "This is Boggy Creek, Gia. Half the town knew the instant Harley stepped through the ice cream shop door."

This time her laughter was heartfelt.

Chapter 24

Gia stood on the sidewalk, staring up at the All-Day Breakfast Café sign above her front window. With Bradley gone and the mystery of who killed him solved, she could return to New York and try to begin putting her life back together. But did she really want to?

"Are you going to stand here all day, or are you going to open?" Savannah's voice held a note of worry.

"Sorry, just thinking."

"Yeah, well don't think too much."

Gia laughed and headed toward the door. Even if she planned to return to New York, she'd still have to open the café today. "Thank you, again, for staying with me last night. I really didn't want to be alone."

"No problem, as I told you the last hundred or so times you thanked me."

She fitted the key into the lock and opened the door, then flipped the lights on before turning and locking the door behind her. She wouldn't open for another hour. "You're sure you don't mind driving all the way back out to the house to pick Thor up for daycare?"

"Of course, I'm sure."

Having Thor, who would probably weigh in at over a hundred pounds full grown, might be an issue in an apartment in New York. Especially the size apartment she'd be able to afford. Plus he wouldn't have a yard to explore.

"I wanted to get here early this morning, so I'd have time to prep everything. With Mark gone, I'll have to do all the cooking myself."

"You'll be fine. You love to cook, and I'm confident you'll find a replacement. Besides, if you ask me, Mark made the eggs a little too well done."

Gia laughed. She couldn't help it. As far as Savannah was concerned, you couldn't make eggs too well done. "You're a good friend."

"Yes, I am." She tilted her head and smirked. "And you can check that in the plus column of the reasons to stay in Florida list you've been silently compiling in your head since last night."

"How—"

"Oh, please. I know you better than you know yourself." Savannah sat on a stool at the counter.

"I haven't decided to leave." Gia started filling the coffee pots. Not that she expected any big rush, but she still had to have coffee going. Besides, after sitting up most of the night talking with Savannah, if she didn't fuel up, she wasn't going to make it through the day.

Savannah looked around the empty dining room, then leaned across the counter and lowered her voice. "I'm not supposed to tell you this."

Her interest piqued, Gia stopped what she was doing and moved closer. "Tell me what?"

"I'm supposed to add another name to the list of reasons to stay. Discreetly, of course." She winked.

"Oh, and who's name would that be?"

"Seriously?"

She honestly couldn't think of who she meant.

"Hunt."

Gia's heart skipped a beat, but then reality hit. "He thinks I'm good for you."

"Oh, please. You mean to tell me you didn't see the way he looked at you last night? The way he hovered over you?"

"He considers me a good friend of yours, Savannah, maybe even family. That's all." She couldn't hide the disappointment that thought brought. Not from Savannah. She knew her too well.

"Girl, you have been out of the game too long if you can't spot a man who's interested in more than just friendship."

"Stop." She held up a hand. The last thing she needed was Savannah playing matchmaker. "He's not interested in me that way. Besides, I don't poach."

"Poach? What are you talking about? Who would you be poaching from? Hunt hasn't had a serious relationship since...hmmm...ever."

"What about Sonny?"

"Sonny?"

"Yeah, you know, the blonde?"

She shook her head. "I don't know her."

A knock on the front door interrupted the bit of hope that had started to surface. Earl peeked in and gestured toward the lock, then held up two shopping bags.

"What the heck?" She unlocked the door and let him in. "Hey, Earl."

"Hey there. How y'all doing?" He set the bags on a table and tipped his hat.

"Hi, Earl." Savannah waved.

Earl pulled off his fisherman's cap and dropped it on the stool where he usually sat. "Heard you had a bit of trouble yesterday and lost your cook."

"How did you hear that already?"

Earl laughed, a deep, contagious belly laugh. "Boy, you really do have a lot to learn about Boggy Creek, don't you?"

"I guess I do." She wasn't sure whether the rumor mill went into the plus or minus column, so she'd just keep it in mind, for now.

"Anyway. I figured with losing your cook after closing yesterday, and opening as early as you do, you wouldn't have had time to get grits."

Gia's cheeks heated. "I'm sorry, Earl, I—"

He held up a hand to stop her and gestured toward the bags he'd put on the table. "No worries. I wasn't sure if the boy even taught you how to make them."

"Actually, he didn't."

"Well then, you're lucky to have me." He picked up the bags and headed toward the kitchen. "I picked up everything I needed as soon as I heard, so I was able to soak them overnight. I'll make them this morning while you do everything else you have to do, but tomorrow, I'll be here bright and early for your first lesson."

She choked up. "I don't know what to say, Earl. Thank you."

"Nah. That's what friends do," he threw over his shoulder as he pushed through the door to the kitchen.

"Earl goes in the plus column." Savannah made a check mark in the air with her finger.

"Yeah, yeah." But the rumor mill moved a little toward the plus column as well. "Can you do me a favor and start cutting up the vegetables for the omelets?"

"Sure. Where are you going?"

"There's something I have to do." She left Savannah in the kitchen with Earl and pushed open the back door. She paused in the doorway a minute, remembering how Hunt had snuck up on Mark from the corner of the building, then peeked behind the door before walking out.

She kept her gaze straight ahead as she hurried past the new dumpster that now sat in place of the one Bradley's body had been found in. Now that Mark was gone, she'd have to put her own garbage out, so she'd have to be able to look at a dumpster in the parking lot again at some point. But not today.

She checked the ground for snakes and spiders before stepping into the woods at the edge of the lot. Luckily, the clearing was only a few feet in. Otherwise she would probably have chickened out and run.

Harley sat on a stump in the middle of the small clearing, eyes closed. He opened his eyes when he sensed her. "What are you doing here?"

"I came to say thank you."

He nodded once. "You're welcome."

She'd racked her brain all night for some way to repay Harley, something he would accept from her, something more than just a meal. "I was thinking about something."

He tilted his head and studied her but didn't respond.

"When I worked in the deli in New York, the owner ordered newspapers every day. I thought it would be nice to offer the same thing at my café. Customers could buy them or just sit and read them while they waited for their food. The thing is, if the papers don't all sell, you have to rip the cover off those that are left and return them to the company. But that leaves the rest of the paper, and I hate to let anything go to waste, so I was thinking. I could leave a stack of papers on the table out back for you with your dinner every night. Would you be interested?"

"I sure would."

"All right then." She wanted to offer him more. "Also, I know you don't like to be inside much, but I've decided to leave the apartment over the café empty for now. I'll leave a key in a fake rock by the door. If you ever need a place to sleep or want to take your food upstairs to eat, you're more than welcome."

The early morning sunlight reflected off the tears in his eyes. "Thank you, ma'am."

"You're very welcome, Harley. You're a good friend. Thank you for everything you did for me. I know it wasn't easy for you, but you saved my life." She crossed the clearing and leaned down to give him a quick hug, then left, not wanting to make him uncomfortable. But Harley definitely went in the plus column.

As she stepped out of the woods, a snake slithered from beneath the leafy underbrush. She screeched a little, then started to hyperventilate. Okay. Snakes went in the minus column. Along with spiders. And alligators. And bears. And skunk apes. Of course, she could just lump them all together as critters. Then she'd only have to put one check in the minus column.

She ran across the parking lot, yanked open the back door, and plunged into the shop.

"What happened?" Hunt grabbed her arms and studied her.

"S-s-snake."

"Did it bite you?" He looked down at her ankles sticking out of her capris.

She shook her head.

Humor filled his eyes. "Did it do anything to you?"

"Not exactly."

"So you are simply offended by its existence?"

"I wouldn't say offended exactly...more like terrified."

"So, I suppose snakes went in the minus column."

She poked him in the chest. "Hey. Don't you make fun."

"I would never make fun of you." He pulled her into his arms.

"Yeah right," she mumbled against his hard chest, surrounded by the woodsy scent of his aftershave. "Okay. Maybe a little."

She breathed in his scent one last time, then stepped away. Even if he wasn't seriously involved with Sonny, she didn't feel right getting too close to him while he was seeing her.

"Did you get to talk to Mark?"

"Yeah. Come on out front. I need a cup of coffee."

When Gia walked into the dining room and saw Sonny sitting at the counter, she stopped short, but recovered quickly. "Good morning, Sonny."

"Good morning, Ms. Morelli." She stood and extended a hand, which Gia shook. "My full name and title is actually Agent Sondra Keller."

"Agent?" Fear gripped her. "I don't understand."

Hunt laid a hand on her lower back and guided her to a table, then pulled out a chair for her to sit, and lowered himself into the seat next to hers.

Sonny sat across the table from them and pulled out an ID card. She offered it to Gia, waited while Gia looked at it with no clue if it was real, then put it back into her pocket when Gia handed it back.

"I don't understand. What would an FBI agent want with me?"

"I'm with the Cyber Division."

"Cyber?"

"Yes, we were in the middle of an investigation involving your ex-husband when he was killed."

"What kind of investigation?"

"Cyber fraud. He was allegedly stealing credit card information online."

"Credit cards?" Gia hadn't thought he could get any greedier, or steal any more than he already had. Yet, even out on bail, he was looking to score another hit. He was obviously confident he would beat the charges. Typical of him.

"Yes. I was already here, trying to determine if you had any involvement with Mr. Remington's activities, when he was found dead. Detective Quinn was kind enough to turn over the boxes of evidence you found, and we were able to track all the transactions back to Mr. Remington. You've been cleared of all charges." She stood and slipped her thin purse strap over her shoulder.

Gia stood. "Thank you, Agent Keller."

"Sonny."

Gia smiled. "Would you like a cup of coffee or something to eat before you go?"

"No, thank you. I have a flight to catch. But I did enjoy my breakfast the other day, so whenever I'm in the area, I'll be sure to stop in."

"Thank you. It was nice meeting you."

"Nice meeting you too." She turned and said good-bye to Hunt.

He walked her to the door and unlocked it for her, then locked up again before returning to Gia. At the rate people were stopping in this morning, she'd have more visitors before she even got the café open than she'd had in the past two days.

"Why didn't you tell me she was an FBI agent?"

"I couldn't, Gia. Besides, it was better for you that you didn't know. I wouldn't have let anything happen to you, but I knew you weren't guilty, so I figured she'd clear you and that would be the end of it."

"And what if I was guilty?"

"Then I guess I'd have had to help you get out of trouble, but I never doubted you. Not even for a minute."

Heat flared in her cheeks. "Thank you."

He wrapped an arm around her shoulders and squeezed. "Any time."

"What ended up happening with Mark and Miranda?"

Hunt pulled a chair out from the table where Savannah was sitting and gestured for Gia to sit. As soon as she did, he pushed her chair in and sat next to her. "They turned on each other almost immediately. You don't have to worry about them ever getting out. Turns out, the gun Mark was holding on you is the same one that was used to kill your ex."

Gia shivered at the thought of how close she'd come to joining him. "Oh, did you ever find Caleb Fontaine?"

"Yes. I questioned him for hours, but it seems he had no involvement in Remington's murder. Everyone knew Remington couldn't pull off his schemes by himself, so Fontaine had been keeping an eye on him, watching to see who he met up with. When he started hanging around the café and Fontaine realized it belonged to his ex, he wanted to meet you for himself, see if he thought you had any involvement. Apparently, he was pretty hellbent on bringing everyone involved to justice."

Understandable, considering the enormous amounts of money Bradley stole from people. "I can't really blame him."

"Still, he had no business stalking you."

"So, what's going to happen to him?"

"Nothing right now. He's headed back to New York with a stern warning to stay away from you."

Warmth rushed through her. "Thank you."

"Any time."

Willow carried a tray of coffee cups to the table and set five of them out with a tray of muffins, then squeezed Gia's shoulder and leaned close. "I hope I'm a plus too." She laughed as she sat down alongside Hunt, Gia, and Savannah.

Heat flared in Gia's cheeks. Apparently, Savannah had shared her mental to-do list with everyone. "You are definitely a plus."

Earl joined them a moment later.

"So…" Savannah blew on her coffee and took a sip. "Have you got more checks on the plus side yet?"

"I suppose maybe I do."

"So, what now? You still going home?"

Gia studied her four friends. Though she hadn't known three of them for long, they'd already proved more loyal and supportive than people she'd known most of her life. Maybe Boggy Creek wasn't such a bad place to start over after all. "Like you said the day I got here…" She smiled. "I'm home now."

If you enjoyed *Scone Cold Killer*, be sure not to miss the next book in Lena Gregory's All-Day Breakfast Café Mystery series,

MURDER MADE TO ORDER

To save her cozy Florida diner, Gia Morelli must choke down a heaping helping of murder . . .

New York native Gia Morelli is just getting used to life in Florida when she gets word that the town government wants to shut down her pride and joy: the charming little diner known as the All-Day Breakfast Café. A forgotten zoning regulation means that the café was opened illegally, and hardboiled council president Marcia Steers refuses to budge. Gia is considering hanging up her apron and going back to New York, but before she gives up on her dream, she discovers something shocking in the local swamp: Marcia Steers, dead in the water. There's a secret buried in the books at town hall, and someone killed to keep it hidden. To save her café and bring a killer to justice, Gia and her friends will have to figure out a killer's recipe for murder . . .

A Lyrical Underground e-book on sale June 2018!

Meet the Author

Lena Gregory lives in a small town on the south shore of eastern Long Island with her husband and three children. When she was growing up, she spent many lazy afternoons on the beach, in the yard, anywhere she could find to curl up with a good book. She loves reading as much now as she did then, but she now enjoys the added pleasure of creating her own stories. She is also the author of the Bay Island Psychic Mystery series, published by Berkley. Please visit her website at www.lenagregory.com.

Printed in the United States
by Baker & Taylor Publisher Services